W9-BOM-971

TALL POPPIES

Recent Titles by Janet Woods from Severn House

AMARANTH MOON
BROKEN JOURNEY
CINNAMON SKY
THE COAL GATHERER
EDGE OF REGRET
HEARTS OF GOLD
LADY LIGHTFINGERS
MORE THAN A PROMISE
PAPER DOLL
SALTING THE WOUND
THE STONECUTTER'S DAUGHTER
STRAW IN THE WIND
TALL POPPIES
WITHOUT REPROACH

TALL POPPIES

Janet Woods

This first world edition published 2012
in Great Britain and in the USA by
SEVERN HOUSE PUBLISHERS LTD of
9–15 High Street, Sutton, Surrey, England, SM1 1DF.

British Library Cataloguing in Publication Data

Woods, Janet, 1939–
Tall poppies.
1. Dorset (England) – Social conditions – 20th century – Fiction. 2. Illegitimate children – Fiction. 3. Love stories.
I. Title
823.9′2-dc23

ISBN-13: 978-0-7278-8136-6 (cased)

All Severn House titles are printed on acid-free paper.

Severn House Publishers support The Forest Stewardship Council [FSC], the leading international forest certification organisation. All our titles that are printed on Greenpeace-approved FSC-certified paper carry the FSC logo.

Typeset by Palimpsest Book Production Ltd.,
Falkirk, Stirlingshire, Scotland.
Printed and bound in Great Britain by
MPG Books Ltd., Bodmin, Cornwall.

Dedicated to my dearest friend
Sheila Sullivan
For fifty years of friendship
And lots of laughs along the way.
Bin there, dun that!

One

Dorset, February 1918

Livia Carr's head jerked up when she heard the distant bell. At that particular moment her imagination was whirling her around the floor in a ballgown of ivory lace over lavender satin, with silver beads on the bodice – exactly like the one she'd admired in her mistress's wardrobe. Handsome and dashing in his evening suit, her equally imaginary and impossibly handsome dancing partner evaporated into the shadows of the hall.

'What now?' she muttered, throwing her scrubbing brush into the bucket of dirty water that was nearly as cold as her hands. Didn't the housekeeper realize there was only one maid-of-all-work left at Foxglove House – and that was herself.

Of the rest of the staff, there was Connie Starling, the cook, and an ancient gardener called Bugg, who, despite his name, managed to keep them supplied with vegetables in this time of shortage.

Livia supposed the housekeeper should be counted as staff, though she did very little. Rosemary Mortimer had appeared a year ago and did nothing but order the rest of them about. Cook had told Livia that the woman was Major Henry's mistress, but it was such a scandalous thought that now she'd reached an age to understand what it meant, Livia didn't know whether to believe it or not – especially with the major's invalid wife living in the house.

The sound of footsteps tapped across the floor and Mrs Mortimer frowned at her. 'Livia, do stop your daydreaming. Didn't you hear Mrs Sangster's bell? Go up to her before she wets her bed, or something equally disgusting.'

'Where's Nurse Gifford?'

'It's her day off.'

'You usually see to her when the nurse isn't here, and I haven't had any nursing experience.'

'Mrs Sangster said she'd prefer you, so now you'll get some experience, won't you? You're a maid-of-all-work, and will do as I tell you. You came from an orphanage I'm given to understand. I could soon send you back there again.'

That had been four years ago, and Mrs Mortimer had had nothing to do with hiring her. Besides, the orphanage wouldn't offer her shelter now she was an adult. Livia had turned twenty the previous September, and nobody but she had known it, or cared. But she couldn't afford to lose her job. She didn't know what else she'd do, since it had been arranged that most of her wage went to the orphanage to help support her sister and brother.

For the past three months Livia had been doing the work of two. The other housemaid had joined the Women's Royal Naval Service, and the last Livia had heard from her she was undergoing training at a place called Whale Island. Fanny had left a suitably nautical recruitment poster on the wall . . . a woman in a smart uniform standing on a cliff top, looking into the distance with her arm outstretched. It seemed to promise a life of freedom and adventure.

Livia had to admit she'd been tempted to sign up herself, if it hadn't been for Chad and Esmé. When they were a bit older, one way or another she hoped to be able to provide her sister and brother with a home. But that goal didn't seem to be any closer than when she'd first started out.

Not that she resented the money, since she didn't need much for herself. Her uniform and meals were provided, and she had a roof over her head and a comfortable bed . . . except for the lumpy bit in the middle that no amount of pounding had managed to flatten.

Mrs Mortimer took hold of her earlobe and Livia had no choice but to follow its painful tug until she was standing upright. A pair of eyes, as cold and grey as a winter sky, gazed into hers. 'What are you waiting for? Off with you, then. You know Mrs Sangster likes you better than anyone else here.'

And Livia liked Mrs Sangster. She was easy to talk to and didn't complain much, though she had cause to. 'What about the mop and bucket?'

'You can empty it when you come down.'

Mrs Mortimer could quite easily have taken it with her and

emptied it, and Livia glared at the housekeeper's retreating back. Then she remembered she'd been promised a day off, so she could take the train up to London to visit her brother and sister.

'You haven't forgotten about tomorrow, have you, Mrs Mortimer?' she called after her.

The woman turned to frown at her. 'What about tomorrow?'

'It's my day off and I'm going up to London. I'll need to get off early to catch the train. It's almost a year since I last saw my sister and brother, and it's their eighth birthday.'

'Oh that's too bad, and a teensy bit selfish of you, just when we're so short-handed.' Mrs Mortimer thought for a minute, then sighed in exasperation. 'It's inconvenient, but if you must have time off, you must, I suppose, though I don't care much for your attitude. Make sure the ironing is done first . . .' She drifted off, leaving the suggestion behind in a cloud of perfumed irritation.

Damn the woman, Livia thought. She'd have to stay up until midnight to get that done.

She managed to get Mrs Sangster on to the commode without mishap, and then stoked up the fire, which had burned down almost to ashes. The scuttle hadn't been filled with its daily ration of coal.

Her mistress had been crippled by arthritis after a fall from a horse at the beginning of the war, which had damaged her spine. She'd also crushed several bones. The accident had left her frail, though on a good day she could shuffle for short distances, if someone supported her.

Livia gazed at the tray. 'You haven't eaten your breakfast, Mrs Sangster.'

'I wasn't hungry, dear. Besides, the nurse rushed off without cutting it up for me.'

Livia tut-tutted when she picked up the teapot. It was still full, and barely lukewarm. The woman couldn't even get a grip around the handle, let alone lift it.

'The doctor said you should eat nourishing foods if you want to get better.'

'My specialist tells me there's no cure for the damage I suffered, or the arthritis. You've got no idea what it's like lying here day after day, dependent on others. My hands are really bad today. I think we're in for some rain.'

'You should have rung for help sooner.'

'I don't like to be a bother to anyone.'

Livia felt sorry for her. 'It's no bother to me, though I don't think I have the skills to match those of Nurse Gifford.'

'Thank goodness for that. She's a shrew, as well as having cold hands. I think that's one of the requisites for taking up nursing.'

Livia giggled at that. 'Would you like to sit in front of the window for a while? I can wrap a blanket round you and you can watch the birds. There are still a few around, even if it is February. The blackbirds and robins look for worms where Mr Bugg has turned over the soil in garden beds, and the cook usually throws crumbs and pieces of fat out for them about now. Did the nurse wash you?'

'No . . . she was in a hurry, and had an appointment in town. She said Rosemary Mortimer would see to me, but I'd rather stay dirty than have that woman touch me.'

Livia stifled her sigh. 'I'll take this down while you're doing what you have to do. I'll tell cook to bring up some fresh tea, and a boiled egg and toast . . . I'm sure the hens would have laid their eggs by now.' It was just another task to add to her busy day. 'I'll bring a jug of warm water up, too, and help you wash. Your hair is knotted. You have such lovely hair . . . do you think you'd be able to bear it if I brushed it? I'll try and be gentle, Mrs Sangster . . . perhaps I could braid it for you, as well.'

'Thank you, Livia dear, that's kind of you.'

Livia soon had the cook organized. Of Mrs Mortimer there was no sign.

'She got a telephone call earlier,' Connie Starling told her. 'It was from the master, I expect. She'll be going off to London for the weekend, you mark my words. She'll take a bath and primp herself up before she goes, so she smells nice. As far as I'm concerned, anything as vile as that woman will never smell nice, since she's out for all she can get.'

Livia's eyes rounded. 'Shush . . . she might hear you.'

'Serve her right. Henry Sangster should be horsewhipped.

He kept her in a flat in London. Then brought her down here when the last housekeeper left. A pity he didn't leave her there.'

'Do you think his wife knows?'

'Mrs Sangster would have to be deaf and blind as well as disabled if she didn't suspect something was going on between the pair. Not that she'd care much. Husband and wife never did get on, on account of the Sinclair legacy.'

'Sinclair legacy?'

The cook huffed laughter through her smile. 'How long have you been here, four years? You must walk around with your head in the clouds, or else those pretty brown eyes of yours see only what they want to. But then, you're a nice girl who rarely sees bad in people.' Her smile was replaced by a fierce expression. 'Most of the money in this household comes from the mistress's side of the family, and is controlled by the legal establishment her father used.

'The major married Mrs Sangster for her money, and expected to gain control. But all he got for his trouble was an allowance. The Sinclair family didn't consider him to be good enough for Margaret Sinclair. She was engaged to a titled gentleman, you see. But then along came big bad Henry, with his charm and his wicked ways.' She lowered her voice to a hush. 'The wedding had to be a hurried affair.'

'Why was that?' Livia asked.

'On account of Master Richard, of course.'

'You mean . . .?' Livia clapped a hand over her mouth.

Connie nodded. 'They reckoned he arrived early. Anyway, that's water under the bridge. When Mrs Sangster dies everything will become the property of their son. And if Richard dies without issue, which is quite possible with the war going on and him away fighting, and all, it will go to some remote Sinclair cousin in Scotland.'

'How do you know all this, Connie?'

'Henry confided in the chauffeur, who told me. 'Sides, I keep my ears open.' Connie Starling's plump arms wobbled as she kneaded the bread dough angrily. Setting it aside to rise, she muttered, 'I'll see to Mrs Sangster's tray.'

Livia went back up, heavy brass scuttle in one hand and jug of water in the other. She was still shocked by what she'd learned. She'd thought Major Sangster was such a nice gentleman, too. To hide her disquiet she chatted as she got on with the job of making Mrs Sangster comfortable. 'I'm going to see my little sister and brother tomorrow.'

'That's nice. You must miss them.'

'Yes, I do. I can't help thinking I've become a stranger to them. They were very young when they went to the orphanage, and it's a year since they last saw me.'

'You should go more often.'

Easy to say, when you had time and money to spare. All the men had gone about the business of war, and the house was short-staffed. Even women didn't want to work in the big houses; they could get much more exciting and better paid jobs doing the work that men used to do before they went off to fight.

They'd heard that the former gardener had died on a beach without firing a shot at the enemy. The chauffeur had become an ambulance driver and had gone off to war, leaving his pride and joy, the gleaming Rolls Royce that belonged to the family, to gather dust in the garage.

Major Henry Sangster was in London doing something important in the war office. He got home sometimes, but rarely used the car.

The son of the household was at the front. At least, she thought he was. Livia glanced at his photograph. Richard Sinclair Sangster was handsome, with eyes as blue as his mother's and a devil-may-care smile like his father. She remembered him as being tall, strong and full of fun, and he'd made her giggle with his silly jokes. When she'd first come here she'd fallen in love with him a little, though it was more hero worship. But he was several years older than her, and had hardly known she'd existed, which was just as well considering her age then. She missed him now he'd gone overseas. The house no longer rang with his laughter, and seemed to have settled back into a staid middle age without his presence.

With Mrs Sangster settled comfortably in front of the window, Livia helped the woman eat her breakfast and drink her tea. Afterwards, she placed the bell in her lap. 'I've got to get on with my work now, but I'll drop back in later, in case you need anything. Don't forget, you can ring the bell if you need something in the meantime.'

'Thank you, dear. You're very kind.'

Livia inwardly sighed. She didn't feel kind. She felt harassed and run off her feet, and to tell the truth, trapped. But she'd felt that way for a long time now. Only God knew how Mrs Sangster felt, being almost bedridden. At least she had her own health and strength, so she couldn't really complain.

'Livia,' Mrs Sangster said when she turned to walk away, 'there's a bar of Cadbury's milk chocolate in my bedside table; the reverend brought it for me. Take it to share with your sister and brother.'

Now who was being kind? Tears pricked her eyes as she slid the chocolate into her pocket. 'Thank you, I'm sure they'll love it, because I doubt if they get any treats in the orphanage.' Impulsively, she kissed the woman on the cheek.

She had a thousand tasks to do before she went to bed, and she'd better get on with them if she wanted to visit her sister and brother tomorrow. She wouldn't put it past Mrs Mortimer to cancel her day off if she didn't get everything done.

As it was, Connie found time to do the ironing for her. 'I've made some gingerbread men for your sister and brother . . . a little treat for them.'

'How can you, when everything is rationed?'

'I have my ways. I skim a little bit off here and there, and hide it for special occasions. I'll pack you some lunch to take with you. Don't tell Mrs Mortimer, though . . . and come down early, before she gets up . . . though the nurse might be up then.'

The next morning Livia threw a long jacket over her grey, ankle-length skirt, which had been purchased from a used clothing shop. She'd learned which fabrics were durable at her mother's knee, for she'd been a designer as well as a dressmaker. Livia knew the outfit would last her for some time when she bought it. The collar was trimmed with a narrow strip of fur, and had a hat with a turned-up brim, which she'd decorated with two pretty striped pheasant feathers she'd found in the garden.

As she hooked up her boots she noticed how shabby they

looked, even though she polished them with beeswax each time she put a shine on the long dining room table. The sole of the left one was worn through, so she hoped it wouldn't rain as she pressed a piece of cardboard over the worn patch – though it looked as if it was going to be a cold, dry day. They would have to do, because they were all she had, but she must ask the gardener to repair them for her when he had time. He was good at doing things like that.

Connie had packed the lunch in a square tin, along with the gingerbread men for the children. She must carry it carefully. Slinging her bag over her shoulder she set out, feeling glad to be alive on such a day.

Though cold, the sun was just peeping over the horizon. Mist rose from the hedges and hovered in a head-height cloud before it curled off into the air and evaporated. It was as if the earth was breathing as it began to wake. The hedges were brown and peppered with orange hips of rambling roses. Daisies dotted the fields, waiting for the touch of the sun to open their petals. Catkin flowers drooped from winter-bare branches and blue-tits had already begun to quarrel with the great-tits over territorial rights. It seemed that everything in nature went to war at one time or another.

Livia reached Creekmore Halt station and bought a ticket to London. She was the only passenger waiting for the train, and she stood on a platform of wooden railway sleepers until it came steaming into the station. The last carriage was empty, and she took a corner seat facing the engine.

The whistle had just sounded when she heard a shout, and footsteps pounding. It was a soldier, almost level with her window. She managed to throw open the door as the train lurched forward. His kit bag came in first and she staggered backwards with it clutched against her body. Her reverse momentum was interrupted by the edge of the seat, which effectively tipped her over backwards. The door slammed, the train gave another couple of jerks and picked up speed.

The bag was hauled off her and a pair of brown-flecked, dark-green eyes gazed down at her. Amusement fought with concern in his expression. 'I'm awfully sorry . . . are you all right? I cut that a bit close.'

'I'm just a bit winded, so you can laugh if you wish,' she said, scrambling upright.

The chuckle he offered her was a pleasant, low rumble. 'I'm relieved to see I didn't squash you completely.'

'How on earth did you manage to run carrying that bag? It's so heavy.'

He tossed it into the rack with a certain amount of pânache, as though it weighed nothing. 'Necessity. If I'd missed this train, my superiors would have stood me against a wall and shot me.'

The colour drained from her face at the thought of such a horrible fate for this handsome young man, and her eyes widened. 'How frightful.'

'Hey, you look quite pale . . . you're not taking me seriously, I hope. They won't shoot me, I promise.'

Now she blushed a little. 'You must think I'm silly.'

'I think you're rather sweet for caring. I'm actually a very good liar, and on the strength of it was offered the leading role in the pantomime in my last year at Cambridge. I turned it down, of course.'

'Why, of course?'

'It was Cinderella.'

When she laughed he leaned forward and held out his hand. 'I'm Captain Denton Elliot . . . you may call me Denton if you wish.'

'I'm Olivia Carr, though most people call me Livia.' An imp of mischief lodged in her mind. 'You may call me Miss Carr if you wish, Captain Elliot.'

'Your wish is my command, Miss Carr.' His glance went to her hat. 'One of your feathers is bent.'

They both laughed as she took the hat from her head to examine the damage.

'I found them in the garden and sewed them on. Vanity, I suppose.'

'It's natural to want a feather in your hat. It always amazes me that a bird can fly on such fragile supports.'

'I read somewhere that their bones are hollow, which makes them light. Why did you say it was natural to want a feather in your hat?'

'To see what your answer would be, of course.'

His eyes came up to hers and they gazed at each other for a moment. A slow, beautiful smile lit up his face. 'So, you're intelligent as well as everything else. The shaft of this is broken so you'll just have to fly on one feather. You have pretty hair, you know. I like the shiny golden reddish bits amongst the brown colour.' He pulled the broken feather from her hat, snapped off the end and stuck it into the band of his army cap, which he'd placed on the seat next to her tin of food. 'I'll take this one with me if you don't mind. It will remind me of home . . . and of a girl called Livia.'

He'd probably forget her the moment the train reached his destination. 'Home? Do you live far from the station?'

'A couple of miles. My father has a medical practice . . . I'll be joining him after the war, I expect. You?'

'Foxglove House.'

'I know the Sangster family. I was at Cambridge with Richard, and we joined up together. We were sent in different directions though, and I haven't seen him since. How is he?'

'I don't know . . . he's away you see,' and she shrugged. 'France, I think.'

For a moment his eyes held an expression of such suffering that she caught her breath. 'Ah . . . yes, I suppose he would be there, considering. I don't envy Richard that. And the rest of the Sangster family, how are they holding up?'

'Mrs Sangster is still an invalid after an accident.'

'I remember it . . . such a sad thing to have happened. Margaret was such a lovely woman and didn't deserve that.'

'Does anyone? The major does something at the war office.'

Denton Elliot nodded. 'Give Mrs Sangster my best wishes, if you would be so kind. Tell her I'll call in on her next time I'm down this way. I should have done so this time, but you know how it is . . . the war has changed everything. Now I'll have you to visit as an extra incentive.'

He would have a shock when she served him tea, she thought wryly, and wondered if she should tell him she was the maid. But no . . . she wasn't a maid today. She was Livia Carr, on the way to London to visit her sister and brother.

Gradually they picked up people at every station. The

carriages quickly filled so they were packed end to end, mostly with soldiers and sailors.

She watched with curiosity as they stood in a fug of pipe and cigarette smoke, exchanging badinage and talking of this and that; avoiding the war; giving occasional hearty bursts of laughter, and mindful of their language and manners. But it was all in a self-conscious manner that drew attention to the fact that they were on their best behaviour in the company of a female.

Most were tall, young men, some just of an age to fight for their country. The veterans could be recognized by their gaunt cheeks, and by hollow eyes that had seen too much. They carried with them all the despair, and all that was brave in the world. But they didn't mention the war that was going on barely more than twenty miles across the English Channel. Some of them just stared out of the window, watching the countryside go past, lost in a world of their own making. What were they thinking . . . of what had gone past, or of what lay ahead? Of loved ones they might never see again? How courageous they all were. How sad they made her feel.

Most of them disembarked at Southampton, including Denton Elliot. They were probably destined for the drab grey troop ship, of which she could glimpse the upper structure with its sinister smoking funnels.

A little shiver ran through her and she reached out and touched his face, saying gently, 'Goodbye, Denton Elliot, it was nice to meet you, and good luck.'

He took her hand in his. 'Let's make that *au revoir,* because I enjoyed meeting you and intend to do so again, Livia. In the meanwhile I have my lucky feather to keep me safe.' He leaned forward to lightly kiss her mouth, laughing when she blushed and called him a rogue . . . but she couldn't be cross with him.

The next time she saw him was when the train pulled out. He was speaking to another officer on the platform, but he turned and his eyes sought hers and he blew her a kiss, smiling when she blew one back.

The encounter left her feeling strangely happy.

Two

It was obvious that the orphanage suffered from the same food shortages as the rest of England. From where she stood she saw that the twins were dirty, thin and wore ill-fitting clothes. Chad's wrists protruded from his jacket sleeves like bones and he had bruises; Esmé's light brown hair was matted. And their eyes were dull. Both of them had runny noses.

Livia went to see the harassed-looking matron, and said, 'Most of my wages go into the support of my sister and brother, yet they look neglected.'

The woman shrugged. 'We're overcrowded, so we don't have time to give the children individual attention, whatever their circumstance. We're also under-staffed, what with the war casualties – and there's an influenza outbreak.'

'Flu . . . that's the first I've heard of it.'

'Well, you mightn't have, living in the country, and all. But you will, because they expect it to spread quickly once it takes a real hold. There's only a few cases as yet, but the death rate is high amongst those who are infected, and the soldiers are beginning to bring it back from the front. They're calling it Spanish flu. It's going to be a bad one.'

A chill of fear ran through Livia as she thought of Mrs Sangster. 'Is there anything to help guard against it?'

The woman shook her head. 'Otherwise perfectly healthy people are dying. If you can stay out of crowded areas it might help. Take your sister and brother to the country if you can. You must understand, that with so many children orphaned we can't give them the individual attention they need.'

The many empty rooms in Foxglove House came into her mind, and she wondered if she'd be allowed to take her brother and sister there. But no . . . that's what orphanages were for . . . and Foxglove House wasn't an orphanage.

'Of course. I'm sorry I complained.'

'They're good kids on the whole, though the boy is getting a bit sullen. He hasn't been well lately,' the woman told her. 'They've both had colds on their chests. He's got a good brain, but he's not doing at all well at school.'

'How did Chad get those bruises?'

The woman shrugged. 'He's a boy . . . they all get bruises. He's small for his age, and he's probably being picked on by the older boys. They tend to form into packs.'

Livia sighed. 'I'll see if I can make other arrangements for them . . . until I can, they'll have to stay here.'

The twins hadn't been expecting her and hadn't looked up when she approached them.

'Esmé . . . Chad . . .? It's me . . . Livia.'

Chad stared at her. Recognition flickered in his eyes, replaced by anger. 'You've been gone a long time,' he accused. 'We thought you'd died.'

Esmé gave a shuddering sniff then burst into tears. 'I don't want to stay here any more, Livia. Have you come to take us away?'

Livia gathered them both into her arms. Esmé clung, but Chad's body was tense and resistant to her.

'Let go else they'll think I'm a sissy,' he said. He relaxed a little when she did, but it nearly broke her heart. If only he knew how much she loved them.

Feeling wretched, she said, 'My darlings, I can't at the moment . . . I have nowhere for us to go. But I'll do my best to find somewhere where we can be closer to each other.' They were empty words, to give them hope. She made an attempt to cheer them both up by opening the tin. 'I've brought you a birthday treat.'

The cook had been generous. There was three of everything.

A couple of boys who'd noticed what was going on sidled up like thin greyhounds and gazed through hungry eyes at the contents of the tin. Chad lashed out when one of them made a grab for the gingerbread, snarling, 'Get away, you're not having any. It's ours.'

'That's not very nice, Chad,' she remonstrated.

'He spilled Esmé's porridge yesterday and she was hungry all day. I hate him! I hate them all!' He turned his head against her chest and burst into scalding tears.

'I didn't do it on purpose; my sleeve caught on it and knocked it from the table,' the boy who'd tried to steal from them called out. 'Stop being a cry-baby-bunting. Just you wait and see. When you're asleep I'm going to put a spider in your mouth and it will eat all your insides.'

'No you won't.' Esmé jumped to her feet and kicked him in the shin. 'If you don't go away I'll tell on you and you'll get the strap, Billy Bastard!'

Shocked, Livia stared at her. '*Esmé!* It's naughty to call people names like that.'

'No it's not, because it's the truth. He is a bastard, so is his brother . . . they haven't got a father and their mother's a jam tart.'

'It's not my fault, and your mother and father are mouldy bones, so there,' the boy said, a dribble of saliva appearing at the corner of his mouth as his eyes went to the food again.

She sighed. He wasn't going to go away. In fact he seemed the type of lad who would fall on the floor and lick up the crumbs, just to make her feel guilty. All the same she felt sorry for him. 'Come here, Billy.' He slid towards her like a beaten dog, and if he'd had a tail she knew it would have been tucked firmly between his legs.

'I suppose you're going to tell me off, Miss?'

'No, though some better manners from all of you wouldn't go astray. I was having a celebration with Chad and Esmé for their eighth birthday. It's not much use having a party without guests, but I don't want you to ruin it for them. Here, you and your brother sit with us. You can share it if you wish, but don't snatch anything.'

She divided the repast into four, ignoring her own hunger, as well as the glares Esmé and Chad were exchanging with the boys. They'd get over it. As for herself, cook would keep her dinner warm for when she got back.

The four of them forgot their angst at the sight of the boiled eggs, cheese, and some ham and bread. They pushed the food into their mouths, eating quickly, and barely chewing it before swallowing. By the time they got to the gingerbread men they had slowed down and were smiling at each other.

Their parents would have been ashamed of the twins, behaving like this, she thought. But then, if they hadn't died, the twins wouldn't be in here. They'd be at home.

Livia knew she couldn't act as an example to them, either. The children were surviving as best they could, in an environment, which, although not the best, had become a familiar one to them over the years. It *was* their home. They'd adapted to it, and knew how it worked better than she did. It was she who was the outsider – she who didn't understand.

'Thank you, Miss,' Billy said afterwards, and grinned at her surprise.

'I really will try to arrange something better, even if it's only to get here to see you more often. Give me a hug now, the pair of you.' And she whispered in Chad's ear when they did, 'Chad, slide your hand into my bag. There's a bar of chocolate on top for you to share with Esmé when you're on your own. The lady I work for gave it to me to give to you. Put it in your own pocket, and don't eat it all at once in case it makes you sick.'

She kissed his cheek while the exchange was taking place. 'Promise me you'll try and do better at school. The matron said you're clever and only need to put your mind to it. Your future depends on getting the best education you can, you know, so don't waste what's on offer.'

'I promise.'

Esmé clung tightly to her as Livia told her, 'I want you to stop saying dreadful things to other people. Mummy and Daddy would have wanted you to grow up being polite, and they would have been ashamed to hear you sounding so . . . *rough*.'

'Were they a nice mummy and daddy?'

'They were the best in the whole world. Our mother was like a princess, and you look very much like her, Es. Daddy was so handsome. He was very clever, and was a parliamentary secretary.'

'What's that?' Chad asked.

Livia wasn't sure. All she knew was that when her parents died in a boating accident they were in so much debt that there was nothing left to support their children. 'It means he was an important man and worked for the government. They loved us all, and I love you both. Always remember that.'

'I love you too, Livia,' Esmé said. 'I'll be good, I promise.'

Livia sighed as her gaze went to her brother. 'You as well, Chad.'

He rolled his eyes. 'I promise.'

It was a promise they'd probably forget as soon as she was out of sight, and an impractical one under the circumstances. But she was doing her best to keep the thread between them intact.

She was surprised when Billy's brother crept up to gaze at her through large dog-like eyes.

Billy laughed. 'Tom's a sissy. He wants a hug too. He hasn't said a word to nobody since we've been in here. He misses our mum, I reckon.'

She slid her arm about the boy's waist and pulled him close. He was a thin little thing. 'Do you miss your mum, Tom?'

When he nodded she gave him a big hug and kissed his cheek.

Billy tousled the grinning boy's head. 'That will have to do you till the next time she visits.'

'What about you, Billy?'

Alarm filled his eyes. 'I'm not much for hugging.'

In any case, Chad pushed between them, making it obvious that, although he'd been forced to share the food, he didn't intend that his elder sister should share her affection with anyone except his twin.

It was hard tearing herself away, since the children clung to her. Livia was as upset as her siblings seemed to be at the parting.

The train was crowded, but once again she managed to get a seat in a corner. The smell of bodies mingled with the tobacco smoke, and the sniffs and coughs from the travellers reminded her of what the matron had said about the coming flu epidemic. She placed her handkerchief against her nose. It had a faint smell of lavender to it, for Mrs Sangster had given her a lavender bag to place in her top drawer. 'It will keep the moths away,' she'd said.

It was dark when she alighted at Creekmore Halt, bitterly

cold, and drizzling with rain. She set off at a fast pace, hoping the rain wouldn't get heavier, and that she wouldn't step on a hedgehog or fall into a pothole on the two-mile walk.

The cardboard in her shoe had worn through and a couple of small, sharp pebbles found their way inside her boot. One lodged in the gap next to her big toe. Damn! That meant her stockings would need darning. The second worked its way under her heel and pricked with each step. Soon her heel was slippery with blood.

She sat on a log, emptied the pebbles out and removed her stockings. Without the button hooks she wouldn't be able to get her boots on again, so she tucked them under her arm.

There was a sudden cloudburst and the icy rain pelted her. Soon she was soaked through, her feet numbed by cold. But that was marginally better than the pebbles. Mrs Sangster's arthritis had been telling the truth about the rain that morning, she thought, her teeth beginning to chatter.

Rounding the bend, with a sigh of relief she saw the lights of Foxglove House ahead on the next hill. Her stomach rattled emptily, and the thought of having a warm dinner inside her spurred her on.

Behind her she heard the engine of a car. It came at speed around the bend, its horn blasting to clear anyone in its path, so she was forced to jump backwards into the hedge. It went through a large puddle barely a foot away, and she was splattered with muddy water.

Livia called the driver a name, then laughed, because she'd told her sister off for using the same word . . . besides, she couldn't get any wetter if she tried.

It was another ten minutes before she got to the house. Light spilled from the front door, illuminating the car. It belonged to the doctor's practice.

She went in through the kitchen, surprising the cook, whose hand flew to her chest. 'Oh my God, it's you, Livia. Thank heavens you're back. You gave me such a fright. Come in and shut the door. Look how wet you are!'

'What's wrong . . . why is the doctor's car here?'

'Mrs Sangster had a fall. She got out of bed to use the commode.'

'Where was Nurse Gifford?'

'About an hour after you left this morning she telephoned to say she wouldn't be coming back, since she'd joined the Queen Alexandra's nursing service, and we should pack her things up and send them on. Mrs Mortimer told her that we weren't going to put ourselves out for her and if she wanted her things she could come collect them herself. A good nurse she turned out to be, leaving her patient in the lurch.'

'How did Mrs Sangster manage to fall?'

'Rosemary Mortimer was furious when she found out you'd gone. She was in a foul mood all day, and told Mrs Sangster she'd have to stay in bed because there was nobody to look after her.'

'Poor Mrs Sangster.'

'I saw to her at lunchtime, when I took her soup up. And again when I took her up some tea. She was all right then. Mrs Mortimer answered when she rang the bell next time. I could hear her shouting from where I stood at the bottom of the stairs. She was sharp with Mrs Sangster. She said she wasn't hired to be her nurse, and if she kept ringing the bell she'd confiscate it.'

Connie was twisting her apron in her hands, the tears brimming over.

'I never heard the bell ring again until about an hour ago, and it kept on ringing. I was about to go when I heard Mrs Mortimer stomp off up the stairs. The ringing stopped and I thought nothing more of it. I saw Mrs Mortimer go into the bathroom a few minutes later. The wireless was on really loud, and she had Mrs Sangster's bell in her hand. I did wonder if she'd put Mrs Sangster on the commode, like Nurse Gifford does, and forgot to go back to help her into bed.'

'Then what happened?'

'About half-an-hour later there was a thud. I didn't know what to do so I banged on the bathroom door and told Mrs Mortimer what had happened. She shouted out that she couldn't hear me over the wireless, and told me to deal with whatever it was and she'd be out when she'd finished bathing.

'I went back to the kitchen. Then I heard a moan. I went upstairs to investigate, and I found Mrs Sangster lying on the floor.' She applied the crumpled skirt of her apron to her eyes.

'Mrs Sangster had a cut on her head and was unconscious, though she was groaning a bit.'

Tears filled her eyes again. 'It was a right shock seeing her like that . . . and I wished I'd gone up earlier, that I do.'

'Hush, Connie. It wasn't your fault, and even if you had gone up it wouldn't have made much difference.'

'I reckon she tried to get off the commode, because it was tipped over and the contents were everywhere. I think she might have slipped in it. I knew she wouldn't want to be seen by anyone like that, so I fetched the mop and bucket and cleaned up the mess as best as I could. She looked right poorly. Her eyes were rolled up in her head. She was trembling and had blood on her face and in her hair. I wrapped a blanket around her and rang for the doctor to come out. Only her usual doctor wasn't there so I called his partner.'

'You did the right thing.'

'You wouldn't have thought so when I told Mrs Mortimer. She was furious I did that without her permission, even though she told me to deal with it myself. She said she'd not long been up there and made Mrs Sangster comfortable, and she must have got out of bed by herself and fallen on to the commode and pushed it over. That was a lie, since she'd been in the bath with the radio on loud for nearly an hour. When I pointed that out she got real nasty and told me to keep my mouth shut, else I'd find myself looking for another job.'

Standing in front of the warm stove, Livia's clothes had begun to steam.

'Go and change into something dry, love,' Connie said. 'I've kept you some dinner, and you might as well get it into yourself because I think it's going to be a long night. Bring what you're wearing back down and we'll sponge the mud off and hang it somewhere to dry. We might as well be doing something useful, as not.'

Dressed in her uniform, her damp hair pulled into her cap, Livia was grateful for the dinner, despite her worry over Mrs Sangster. The lump of pudding studded with minute brown chunks of sticky date was a small, tasty island in a sea of thin yellow custard. Connie knew how to economize with the rations and still dish up a delicious meal.

Livia wondered what her sister and brother were eating . . . very little by the look of them, but at least they had the chocolate for tonight. She reminded herself that she must try and get them out of the orphanage . . . but how? She could barely manage to look after herself.

She and Connie sat in the kitchen, talking, and after a while they heard footsteps on the stairs. They went into the hall, gazing expectantly upwards as the doctor came down escorted by Mrs Mortimer.

'Ah, there you are, Carr. I suppose Mrs Starling has informed you of what's happened. Next time you decide to gallivant off to London, check with me first.'

'But Mrs Mortimer—'

'I'd never have allowed you to go if I'd known the nurse was absent. It was too bad of her to leave without giving notice.' She turned to the distinguished man standing next to her, giving him a simpering smile. 'Perhaps you'd like to be the one to put their minds at rest, Doctor Elliot.'

Livia remembered Denton Elliot saying his father was a doctor, and wondered if this was him. Yes . . . he had the same greenish eyes, the same height and build.

'Is Mrs Sangster going to be all right?' Livia asked him.

'She's concussed, but is now conscious, and although she's quite bruised, the cut on her head doesn't need any sutures.' He also had the same type of voice, soft and clear, but with a growly undertone. 'Mrs Sangster will need someone to stay awake with her all night, in case her condition deteriorates.'

Mrs Mortimer nodded. 'That will be you, Carr, since you've had the day off while the rest of us have been doing the work of six.'

Connie Starling found the courage to give an unbelieving snort, though she quickly turned it into a cough.

'I'd be pleased to look after her.'

'I'll see if I can find someone older to nurse her tomorrow, though the person I have in mind won't be qualified, she's strong. I'll call in to see Mrs Sangster in the morning.' The doctor took Livia aside. 'Now, young lady, I must tell you what to look out for. Nausea and, or, vomiting, slurred speech, confusion . . .' He ticked off the symptoms on his fingers and made her repeat them back before he handed her his card. 'Good girl. Telephone me if you need to, or if there's anything you're worried about.'

'Doctor . . . I should like to look after Mrs Sangster, if I may? I know I haven't had any experience, but we get on well together.'

'Won't that leave you with a housekeeper short?'

Livia nodded. 'I suppose it will.'

'Perhaps Florence can do the maid's work instead. She's very practical. Let's leave it up to Mrs Sangster.' He stared at her for a moment. 'Were you the person I puddled on the road?'

She nodded. 'I was already wet, though . . . I'd come off the train from London.'

His smile had also been passed on to his son. 'They say that mud is good for the complexion, but your complexion already looks perfect. I'm sorry.'

'Your apology is accepted.'

'It's sweet of you to let me off lightly. I should have taken more care.'

He was just as nice as the younger Elliot on the train. 'Doctor, do you have a son called Denton?'

He looked surprised. 'Are you acquainted with him?'

'We took the same train this morning, though he got off at Southampton. He only just managed to catch it because the whistle had gone and the train had begun to move. He practically bowled me over with his kit bag as he threw himself through the door.'

'I hope he had the grace to apologize, too.'

'Yes, he did, and very nicely.' If she were to overlook the stolen kiss . . . or even if she didn't, she amended.

The man laughed. 'That's Denton for you . . . always in a hurry. He takes after his mother.'

'The way you were driving, I rather think he takes after you, Doctor Elliot.'

He laughed, and pulled on a pair of brown leather gloves. 'I'll take more care on the corners from now on, I promise. There are enough casualties caused by the war, without creating some of my own at home. Denton has been on leave. He's going back to one of the field hospitals. He was going to join the practice when this damned war is over, though the way things are going I've a feeling that he may become a surgeon.'

'You must be very proud of him.'

'I am.'

Mrs Mortimer coughed. 'You're keeping the doctor from his duties, and it's about time you got on with yours, I think, Carr. Poor Mrs Sangster shouldn't be left alone for all this time.'

Doctor Elliot winked at her. 'It was nice to talk to you, Miss Carr. Don't be afraid to call me if I'm needed.'

'I will, Sir.'

He was gone, his head butting into the pouring rain as he made a dash for the car. So, Denton was a doctor as well, she thought, as she closed the door with a final wave.

'Don't you ever do that again, Carr,' Mrs Mortimer snarled.

'Do what?'

'Show yourself up by flirting with a visitor to this house, especially a man invited here in a professional capacity.'

'Show myself up? We had a normal conversation; in fact, he was a very friendly and pleasant man.'

'Sometimes you forget that you're nothing but a servant.'

'Hark who's talking,' Connie said, and sniffing as she walked back towards the kitchen, she threw over her shoulder as a last word, 'You'll be expecting us to call you Madam one of these days.'

Three

Richard Sangster dreamed he was asleep and safely snuggled in his own bed at Foxglove House. Wind-driven rain lashed against the window, the firelight threw dancing shadows upon the walls, and the flames spit and crackled. Cozy and safe in his warm flannel pyjamas and nest of blankets, he toasted his feet on the stone hot-water bottle. He was reluctant to abandon the bed, and the boy he used to be, but he badly needed to take a piss.

Someone gently shook him. 'Are you awake, Sir. I've brought you a mug of tea.'

'Tea? My mother doesn't allow me to drink it.'

For a moment his dream seemed real, then he thought: How silly to be standing outside your own dream looking in on it. Still, he stole another moment of comfort until the damp and cold intruded.

'Give me a few seconds, would you, Sergeant Beamish.' He turned his back, unbuttoned his trousers and urinated into the mud. A wisp of steam escaped from his body with the trickling stream. His kidneys ached. Everything damned well ached. He twitched and juddered as well. He should go to the field hospital and get something to help calm him. His shaking hands fumbled with the buttons, and he turned back when he was done.

'Here you are, Sir. Don't let it get cold.'

'Thank you, Sergeant.' His palms closed around the tin mug to warm them, but inside Richard's smile his teeth began to chatter, so he felt like a mechanical clown being jerked around. Funny how you could feel warm in a dream, but as soon as you woke from it and moved, you were cold to the core. No wonder people died from hypothermia, when sleeping was such a pleasant state of oblivion to indulge in.

'Are you all right, Sir?'

'Are any of us all right? I'll be glad when this damnable war is over.' When it was over he was going to stay snuggled in his bed, until he grew cobwebs and died. 'Do you ever dream that you're back home sleeping in your own bed, Sergeant?'

'I wouldn't mind having my woman here to snuggle up to sometimes.'

'What's your wife like?'

'Doreen? She's not what you'd call a beauty, but she's a good cook and is comfortable where she should be, so she gives a man a good ride. Don't tell her I said that, though. Not that it matters here. The same urges don't seem to trouble me, thank goodness.'

There were rumours about bromide, and Richard wondered now if they were true. It was so long ago that he couldn't remember the last woman he'd been with . . . or even experienced the last urge. The sergeant was correct. They had other bodily irritants to contend with, most of which had no easy relief: body lice, crabs, lack of sleep, and fungal infections that drove a man mad with itching.

Richard was hardly likely to meet the sergeant's wife, anyway. 'Do you have children?'

'None . . . and we've been married for fifteen years, so I don't suppose we'll have any now. A pity, since we'd have liked some. You, Sir?'

'I'm not married.' Richard couldn't imagine being married, though he supposed he'd have to take a suitable wife to bed sooner or later, if the Sinclair legacy was to stay in the family. He'd been displayed with pride by his father and spoiled by his mother, so he'd probably make some unfortunate woman a lousy husband, since he'd expect her to be at his beck and call.

'What's the time?'

'We have five minutes before dawn, when we go over the top. We'll have the sun behind us so they'll be looking into it.'

'Break out the rum, then, Sergeant.' Richard took in a deep breath and checked his equipment. The Mills bombs were ripe lethal plums tucked into his webbing. He was a walking ammunition dump, and if a bullet hit him in the right place he'd explode, and they'd never find the scattered fragments of his body in all this mud.

He stared into the shit brown horizon. It reminded him that he'd been in a bit of a funk these past few months. Not that he was scared of dying. He'd lost that fear in the first gung-ho weeks of the war, when his body had been fully nourished and he'd been pumped up with the bullshit of propaganda, convinced that if he died for his country it would be a hero's death.

Now he felt like an old man with the ague, and the courage and conviction, along with the youthful venom, seemed to have been sucked out of him by the everlasting mud. Men died all around him. They didn't look like heroes, but victims of some lethal game of cricket, as they lobbed chunks of hot metal back and forth, trying to score points with the number of people killed.

Those who didn't catch a bullet often died of the flu. It was unstoppable. It felled the healthy, striking them down. It was said it could kill you in three days, and that if the lips turned blue the patient wouldn't survive. It had only just begun to make real inroads into the ranks, and soldiers were dropping like flies. Others got over it.

Richard had heard that the opposing forces were just as ill, just as hungry, just as dispirited – and just as low on ammunition. There were rumours that peace was being negotiated. Now he was scared because he could see an end to this war, and although he'd survived the disease he had an irrational fear that he might survive the conflict, but emerge from the war without honour in the process. When all was said and done, most people would prefer a dead hero than a live coward in the family. It was less embarrassing.

The golden-haired youth who'd marched bravely off to war, carrying the pride of his friends and parents on his shoulders, would return to Foxglove House changed. He had killed – he'd smelled death. It had sickened him even while he did what was expected of him. And those left behind would expect him to be the same as he'd been before, if he survived – the remainder of his life would have to be an act.

He didn't want to kill any more of the enemy . . . in fact, he no longer thought of them as the enemy, but as men like himself, with families waiting for them to come home. He wanted to turn and run, not fight . . . and that made him feel like a coward.

'It's almost time, Sir,' the sergeant said.

Richard nodded, trying to look nonchalant to give courage to his men. His army-issue Lee Enfield had been cleaned the best he could, and his ammunition and bayonet were at the ready. He hoped they didn't run into any machine guns. If they did, he hoped none of his men would suffer. He fingered the cross he wore around his neck, a gift from his mother. 'God be on my side today,' he whispered, tossing back his ration of rum, which would give his legs the courage and fuel to keep moving onwards instead of backwards.

A tremor of extreme fear ran through him as the Verey Light ignited and began to float across the sky in a beautiful halo of white mist that looked as though it had been sent directly from heaven. He had a strong urge to cower into the mud with the grisly, maggoty remains of those who'd tried to escape from the trench they'd occupied before he'd arrived. The war was over for them.

Instead, he scrambled out of the trench almost recklessly, urging his men forward. The sun came flaming up to warm his back and send its glory to shine over the glistening sea of mud and gore. He was up to his neck in death and destruction. His comrades-in-arms were falling, eyes glazing over, or crying out with the agony of their wounds as the hot metal lodged in their guts.

Yet he mustn't show any weakness in the face of the enemy. *Don't think! Don't think!* His sphincter muscle tensed.

The sergeant landed next to him. His hand went to his buttock and came out covered with blood. 'The bastards have shot me in the soddin' backside.'

'Drop your trousers, Sergeant, let me look.' There was no sign of the bullet. 'It's just a crease. I've seen better wounds, so I'm afraid it won't get you home. If it did we'd all be shooting each other in the arse.'

Beamish swore with such feeling that Richard began to laugh.

The man grinned at him. 'It's better than getting the bits blown off, I suppose.'

They made the next trench, falling over the edge with guns at the ready.

They ignored the corpses. The burial detail followed behind, and would find the dead or injured, and either assign them to stretcher-bearers or dispose of them. If they didn't, then the tank tracks would roll over them and mince them into the mud, where they'd become part of the soil.

His gaze went to his men. Half of his regiment had been cut down. The survivors leaned wearily against the wall of the trench. All this for a few yards of mud, he thought. A machine gun chattered, but it was too far away to raise any alarm in them. A light wind blew across the battlefield, bringing various smells to their nostrils. A wisp of smoke caught in the current and drifted towards them.

'Gas!' somebody yelled.

There was a scramble for respirators. Richard had lost his. Quickly he peed onto his handkerchief and held the damp square to his nose, even knowing it wouldn't be good enough. The sergeant ripped a mask from a body and pulled it over Richard's face. It stank of decomposition . . . of the last living breath of a man.

Bile roiled in his stomach. He threw the mask aside and began to gag. His body jerked uncontrollably. The sergeant wrestled him to the stinking mud, and when he tried to struggle he pushed the mask against his face, saying calmly, 'Easy now, Sir . . . let's get this on and you'll be all right in a minute.'

As if he were a fractious horse being soothed. Of course he'd be all right in a minute. He just needed a good night's sleep. If he stood on the edge of the trench, somebody would shoot him and he could sleep forever.

Even knowing such thinking was dangerous, he found the concept to be almost irresistible and began to scramble up a ladder. The sergeant closed a hand round his ankle and jerked him back down.

'I can't seem to control myself, Beamish,' Richard muttered, his words muffled by the stinking mask, and he burst into tears.

'Don't worry. It's nerves, Sir . . . just nerves. You've been at the front too long and need a good night's sleep. Don't worry about anything . . . I'll look after you and make sure you get back to base safely.'

The smoke thickened. Tapping him on the shoulder the sergeant pointed along the trench. They began to run, hoping the wind would change and the gas would kill somebody else.

Half an hour later, and a few yards away to the left, a young man in a shallow hole gazed down the sight of his rifle. Both his legs were broken, and half his intestines were now outside his body. He'd been left for dead, but he wasn't dead yet – not quite.

The man had two bullets left. He'd been the best shot in the gunnery class, and he took careful aim at the spot where he'd last seen movement.

His finger caressed the trigger as a head was raised. The

Britisher was careless and took his hat from his head, as if inviting the caress of a bullet. He ran his fingers through his mud-streaked golden curls and they ruffled in the breeze, reminding the marksman of the baby daughter he'd left behind in Germany.

Their eyes met. Both of them had eyes the same colour, startling blue. The Britisher smiled. They could have been brothers.

The marksman understood why a man would invite death in this stink-hole. He hesitated, wondering if he should oblige him. After all, it wasn't as if he was going to survive himself. He would never live to see his wife, or hold her and his daughter in his arms again. He wondered . . . did the British soldier have someone to mourn for him? Did it matter? He was here to kill or be killed.

He sighed regretfully. Gently, almost lovingly, he lifted the gun slightly, took careful aim and stroked the trigger. The man received the gift he sent him, and dropped out of sight before he had time to hear the sound of death.

'That will teach you to keep your bloody English head down,' he muttered.

The marksman had only one bullet left. He didn't intend to squander that one on a Britisher, but would use it more wisely. After all, he wouldn't hesitate to relieve a horse of its misery, had it been suffering.

Two days later, Richard Sangster opened his eyes. He couldn't see much, just blurred shapes. He was puzzled. His body hurt all over and there was a sharp smell of carbolic soap about him. A pain in his head pounded and he found it hard to breathe.

There was movement around him. A light shone in his eyes. He whimpered and cringed away from it.

'Good . . . he's come round,' a voice said, and a shadow moved across. 'Try not to worry, old chap.'

Richard stared in the direction of the voice and he began to jerk and shake uncontrollably. Pain filled him and he wanted to shriek. Rather he'd died on the battlefield than this.

'Morphine,' the man whispered to someone, and he leaned over him. Though Richard couldn't make out his features, he seemed familiar. 'Your name is Richard Sangster. Try not to worry about anything. The war is over for you, my friend. We're sending you back to England, to the hospital.'

Richard screamed silently as the needle pierced his skin. A little while later he sank back into a soothing black vapour of oblivion.

Tears in his eyes, Denton Elliot gazed down at his friend. Richard would recover to a certain extent, though the bullet in his back had damaged nerves, and only time would tell if he'd be able to walk again, though he might regain some use of his legs. He'd probably regain most of his faculties now the bullet had been removed from his skull. But he was also suffering from shell shock, a nervous condition brought on by fatigue, and the result would be depression. His lungs were on an irreversible journey to ruination from the gas he'd inhaled.

Denton didn't know how long, or how well Richard would survive, but he did know that his friend wouldn't live to be an old man. His fingers went to his top pocket and he touched against the pheasant's feather as his glance went to the other soldiers awaiting attention . . . so many of them.

'There but for the grace of God go I,' he whispered.

Margaret Sangster was delighted to have Livia to look after her.

Three days after her fall she was feeling a little better, though there was still a lump on her forehead, and it was very tender.

Florence Hutchins, the woman the doctor had sent over, had been happy to take over the maid's position. In the absence of the housekeeper, who'd scurried off to London to spend a couple of days with Henry, or so it was said, and without thought for anybody but herself, Margaret had hired Hutchins, so Livia would be free to look after her.

Florence was about twenty-five, angular, with dark hair and eyes. She was outspoken in her manner, and had lost her last job because she'd been rude to the person who'd hired her.

'The parson's wife over in Sudbury called me a dirty slattern because I wasn't quick enough to pick up after her. Who's the slattern if you made the mess and need someone to clean up after you? I asked her.

'You have no respect for your betters, she says, and she sacked me on the spot. Uppity madam. If people wants respect they should respect others.'

'Quite right, Florence,' Margaret Sangster had said, for she'd met the wife of the Sudbury incumbent, and she certainly was an untidy creature.

Rosemary Mortimer would be cross when she found out, but Margaret didn't care. She'd had enough of the woman's rudeness and intended to send her packing. Who cared what Henry said? His mistress could go back to London and live with him. She didn't care if she never saw either of them again. This house belonged to the Sinclair family. She had grown up here, and was still its mistress. It would be passed on to her son when she died.

Even though there was a sense of purpose about Livia, she was gentle in her ways. Not like Nurse Gifford who had been a bit of a martinet, and who did everything by the clock. She'd had no sense of humour.

Livia, on the other hand, was so sensible and cheerful, and was such a dear. She made Margaret laugh, and as a result, she felt livelier.

'Cook has made you something special for lunch,' Livia said this particular morning.

'What is it, Livia?'

'I won't tell you until you've finished your oatmeal. There's only a couple of spoonfuls left. Open up.'

Margaret made a show of shuddering as she swallowed it. 'It reminds me of boarding school.'

Livia laughed. 'We called it goatmeal at the school I attended.'

'You attended boarding school? I thought you were employed from an orphanage in London.'

'Yes . . . I was.' She shrugged. 'My parents lived beyond their means, I'm afraid, and they tended to entertain a lot. Daddy was a secretary to a government minister and my mother designed ladies fashion. When they died there were debts to pay, and after that there was no money left so the three of us ended up in an orphanage.'

'Oh . . . my dear . . . how perfectly awful. Didn't you have any relatives to take you in? No, of course you didn't, else they would have. What did you say your parents' names were?'

'George and Eloise Carr.'

'Eloise Carr? I do believe I have a gown in my wardrobe designed by your mother. Was she part of Cuthbert and Associates?' She remembered that the girl had siblings to support. The cottage was going to be without a tenant soon, so she might be able to do something for her . . . she would think about it.

'I'm not quite sure, it was so long ago now . . . I think she may have designed for Cuthbert.'

'Then you should be really proud, for she designed a gown for Lady Asquith, amongst other notables. If you climb on to the chair you should be able to reach the gown. It's in a box at the top of the cupboard. I was going to wear it to the hunt ball . . . that was a while ago . . . but I didn't manage to get there.' She made a face as the girl stretched upwards, showing the hem of a drab flannel petticoat. Livia was neatly made, and if she were her own daughter, she'd be wearing silk and lace.

'Be careful you don't fall, my dear.'

'It's you who should be careful. You gave cook and me quite a fright, you know.' The box was slid carefully out.

'Throw it on to the bed, dear. There are shoes and an evening bag in the other box.'

The gown was so delicate, a blush of pink silk with a three-quarter gossamer chiffon overdress. A wide band of gold lace with embroidered dark red rosebuds on the skirt matched the bodice with its scoop neckline and loose short sleeves.

'How exquisite it is,' Livia said, looking for the label, and Margaret could almost see the tears spring into her eyes when she said, 'Yes, it's my mother's design.'

'Then you must try it on.'

'I couldn't, Mrs Sangster.'

'Of course you could. Off with that uniform now . . . go on, dear,' she urged, when Livia hesitated. 'I'll close my eyes.'

The girl was petite, and the gown fitted her perfectly, as did the shoes.

'No . . . don't look in the mirror yet. Brush out that plait and put that little garland of silk roses round your head.' When the deed was done and Livia's hair was a fall of foxy ripples, she said, 'Now you can look.'

Livia gasped. 'I look like a different person.'

'The outfit is yours, my dear.'

'No . . . I can't take it. It's too expensive. Besides, I never go to balls.'

Margaret snorted. 'Neither do I now. I want you to have the gown as a memory of your mother. She was a very talented woman.'

There was a knock at the door, and Cook called out, 'Doctor Elliot is here.'

'Tell him to come in, Cook. You come in as well.'

'I haven't got my uniform on,' Livia said, panicking a little as the door opened.

Connie Starling's mouth dropped open at the sight of Livia.

Doctor Elliot smiled. 'Am I to take it that the fairy godmother has visited this establishment?'

'Isn't she lovely?' Margaret said.

'Absolutely breathtaking.'

'In case any accusations are made, I want you both to witness what I'm about to say. I'm giving this ensemble to Livia in memory of her mother, who designed it. She doesn't want to take it because she thinks it is too expensive a gift.'

The doctor nodded. 'You'd better accept it, young lady, because I don't want my patient to get upset.'

Connie smiled. 'Is there anything else, Mrs Sangster? I've just remembered that I've got some chicken broth on the stove.'

'Go then, Connie. You know how much I love your chicken broth.'

The doctor examined her before drawing Livia aside.

'Whatever you have to say, I want to hear it,' Margaret told him quietly.

He nodded. 'Then you shall. Your pulse is fast, and your heart is a little on the erratic side. I want you to stay in bed and rest. No excitement. I'll leave you a couple of sedatives. Are you sure you haven't got a headache?'

'Only a small one where the lump is.'

'The cut seems to be healing nicely. I'll come back tomorrow and see if you've settled down.'

Mrs Sangster nodded. 'Will you leave us now please, Livia. I want to talk to the doctor in private.'

The same afternoon, Mrs Sangster's lawyer arrived with his clerk. Connie was called up, and came down bursting with importance. 'They wanted me to witness Mrs Sangster's signature on some papers.'

Two days later the housekeeper returned. Mrs Sangster called the woman to her quarters and terminated her employment.

'Henry might have something to say about that.'

'Be out of my house by the end of the week.'

In the early hours of the morning, Margaret woke with a severe pain in her head. She couldn't find the words and they all slurred together, but she managed to knock the bell from the bedside cabinet.

Almost straight away Livia appeared at her side. 'Try not to panic, Mrs Sangster . . . I'll go downstairs and telephone for the doctor.'

Rosemary Mortimer came in to gaze down at her, a strange little smile on her face. Cold grey eyes narrowed in. 'Are you dying at long last, Margaret? Henry will be so pleased.'

The woman had come to gloat. 'I want Livia,' she whispered.

'I told the girl to watch out for the doctor. It's just you and me . . . alone.' The housekeeper picked up a pillow and gazed down at her. 'I could do you a favour and put you out of your misery.'

Livia appeared at the door and crossed swiftly to Mrs Sangster's side, saying crisply, 'I don't think that would be wise, Mrs Mortimer.'

The pillow was thrown aside. 'It was only a joke.'

'One in poor taste. You can see that Mrs Sangster is suffering.'

'Of course I can, Carr. Poor Mrs Sangster. I'm here to comfort her, and you're supposed to be keeping a watch out for the doctor.'

'I've roused Connie, and she's watching out for him in my place. Would you leave us please? Mrs Sangster needs to rest and you're upsetting her.'

'If you're not very careful, Carr, you'll lose your job without reference, then you and your precious brother and sister can starve on the street.'

'Not while there's breath left in my body,' Margaret forced out. 'I'll report what you said to me, to the doctor.'

The girl seemed unafraid by the thought of the loss of her job when she told the housekeeper, 'And I'll back it up. Now . . . would you please leave?'

'Who are you to tell me—?'

'Get out,' the girl hissed at her. 'Mrs Sangster is agitated enough without you adding to it.'

The housekeeper turned to go, saying quietly, 'Don't think I'll forget this, Carr.'

'I'm sure you won't, and to be frank, at this moment I don't care whether you forget it or not.'

'The door closed rather loudly behind the departing housekeeper, and smoke puffed down the chimney.

As Margaret felt Livia's hand close gently around hers in comfort, peace stole over her. She'd done the right thing yesterday . . . she knew it. The girl was loyal and caring, and had the strength to stand up to Henry's tart. 'Thank you, dear . . .' Margaret wanted to tell her what she'd done, but she couldn't quite get the words out.

'Shush, don't try and talk,' the girl soothed. 'I can hear the doctor's car coming. You'll soon have some help.'

Mrs Sangster was almost incoherent when the doctor came in. Livia hovered while he carried out his examination, wanting to reassure Mrs Sangster, while keeping out of the doctor's way.

He said in a quiet aside, 'Her brain is swelling, and there is the possibility a clot is blocking the flow of blood. If I can get her into hospital in time, a surgeon might be able to drain the fluid off. Can we telephone her husband? I'll need his permission, and I expect he'll want to be with her.'

Livia could see by his grave manner that he didn't expect his patient to survive, and she could barely keep her tears at bay. 'The housekeeper probably has his address.'

'I imagine she does,' Dr Elliot said, not quite able to keep his distaste at bay.

'No . . . not . . . Henry.' The words issued from Margaret Sangster's mouth in a slurred fashion, but were quite firm. 'Die . . . own . . . bed.'

They were Mrs Sangster's final words before she was gripped by a seizure. When it subsided her lips were blue-tinged and her breath came in rattling gasps. Ten minutes later she relaxed completely.

Livia smiled through her tears at the doctor, who was already busy with his stethoscope. Hopefully, she asked, 'Has she gone to sleep?'

'I'm afraid not, my dear. Mrs Sangster has died.' He glanced at his watch. 'She'd never have lasted long enough to get to hospital. I'll issue a death certificate, then I'll ring her husband and inform him.'

'Is there anything I can do?'

He nodded. 'Perhaps you'd like to lay her out.'

'I've never done that before.'

'Wash the body, tidy her hair and dress her in a clean nightgown so she looks clean and cared for. She will need fresh bedding, I imagine. You'll require someone to help you.'

Livia felt relief at the thought. 'Florence will help, I expect.'

'Good, because despite her lack of refinement, Florence is a sensible young woman who has done it before.'

'I'll go down and tell her what's happened,' Livia said.

'Good girl. Would you send in the housekeeper? I'll get that phone number from her and make out the death certificate.'

'Mrs Sangster was a nice woman. I liked her a lot. She looks so relaxed now, and younger.'

'It's because she's no longer in pain. She liked you too, young lady.'

There was a knock at the door and Rosemary Mortimer came in. Her glance went to the bed and her hand fluttered to her heart. 'Oh . . . my goodness. I didn't realize she was quite so ill. Is she . . . is she . . .?'

It was apparent she'd been listening through the keyhole, and the doctor and Livia exchanged a glance. Dr Elliot told her 'Mrs Sangster has passed away. I understand you have Major Sangster's telephone number.'

'I've already contacted him, Doctor. The major will soon be on his way down.'

The physician looked displeased. 'I'm surprised you took it upon yourself to do that, considering you were unaware of her condition.'

'The major asked me to keep him informed of any developments.'

'And now must be contacted again to be told his wife has passed away. The protocol in such situations is for the attending physician to inform the next of kin.'

She nodded. 'I was only trying to help, and you should have told me earlier. Did Mrs Sangster say anything?'

He raised an eyebrow. 'Specifically?'

She became vague. 'Oh nothing. Sometimes people tend to offer little confidences to their doctors when they die.'

'Do they . . . do they indeed? I must admit I've never met a doctor who was unprofessional enough to pass any little confidences on to the housekeeper. I would suggest you keep your curiosity under control, Mrs Mortimer. Now, would you be good enough to give me the major's telephone number.'

'He'll already be on his way, I expect.'

'The number?'

'In the index next to the telephone in the hall,' she said sulkily.

'Are you staying to help Miss Carr lay out Mrs Sangster's body?'

Mrs Mortimer shuddered. 'Me . . . good gracious . . . the very idea turns my stomach. Besides, I heard you say that Florence can do that.'

'Then your presence isn't needed. Perhaps you could ask Florence to come up and help Miss Carr. It will save her having to go down.'

Thus dismissed, Mrs Mortimer said, 'Report to me when you've finished, Carr.' She gave the doctor a haughty look and walked off.

The doctor turned to Livia. 'I'm going downstairs to use the telephone, then I'll finish my rounds. I'll be back as soon as I can. By that time Major Sangster should be home, and he can make arrangements for the funeral.'

When she nodded, he gazed at her for a moment. 'Will you be all right, left alone here for a while? There might be the occasional noise and movement from Mrs Sangster until her body settles down. That's normal, and nothing to be afraid of.'

'Yes, I'll be all right. I'm not afraid of Mrs Sangster. She was a lovely lady who wouldn't hurt a fly. I'm going to miss her.'

'Good girl.'

After the doctor had gone, Livia fetched the woman's best nightgown and some clean bed linen.

Soon, she and Florence had their mistress clean and tidy. There was a gold cross on the dressing table. Livia placed it on her arthritic hands, which were in an attitude of prayer. Between them, they cleaned and tidied the room.

'She looks ever so peaceful, like she's an angel in heaven already,' Florence said reverently.

Livia couldn't stop the flow of her tears.

They reported that they'd finished to Mrs Mortimer. She came upstairs to gaze at the still figure in the bed, and didn't bother to hide the faint smile as she taunted, 'Goodbye, Mrs Sangster.'

The stomach of her former mistress rattled.

Mrs Mortimer took a hasty step backwards and Livia became the recipient of a satisfyingly alarmed look when the woman said hastily, 'She made a noise . . . are you sure she's dead?'

'Doctor said she were dead. I've never seen a corpse get up and walk away yet, though I've seen them act a bit lively on occasion . . . of course, there's always a first time,' Florence said. 'Happen she might leap right off that bed and dance a jig after being confined to it for all that time. She might even find the strength to strangle you.'

'You've only been employed here for a short time, Hutchins. Be very careful if you want to keep your job.'

'I can't say I do want to keep it,' Florence said cheerfully. 'I was doing the doctor a favour when I came here, I reckon, not looking for a permanent position. He said young Livia here needed a bit of a hand.'

Livia gave a watery grin when Mrs Mortimer turned on her heel and stalked off, her mouth pulled tight.

Four

It was the kind of day when the sky would have vanished into a pale sheet of nothingness, had the land not been marked by a scribble of haggard winter trees.

The funeral was over. The service had yielded its last mournful note and Margaret Sangster's coffin accepted into the dark maw of the grave.

Livia paid her respects, standing behind the invited mourners with the cook and shedding her last few tears for her former mistress. Both of them wore black armbands provided by the major.

Nobody's grief was more than her own, Livia thought, for she'd genuinely liked Mrs Sangster, and had been saddened by her demise.

Major Henry was tall and distinguished in his uniform. He greeted his guests with a firm handshake and short, gruff, dog-like barks of words.

'Mr Phillips . . . gratified . . . Margaret would have been pleased. Ah yes, Peabody . . . so glad. A sad day . . . your presence most appreciated.'

He was socially elegant. 'Anthea Jennings, isn't it?' His glance wandered over the woman he was addressing and his tongue flicked out to touch his neatly trimmed grey moustache. 'You look well, m'dear. How's young Walter?'

'Gone, two years since. May 1916. He was one of the crew on the *Invincible.*'

'Jutland, was it? Lord, I hadn't heard. Sorry.' His hand closed over the woman's. 'So many of our boys . . . heroes, all.'

'Richard . . . is he here?'

'I sent word . . . the boy can't be spared, of course. A pity. He'll be sorry he missed his mother's funeral. They were very close. You don't look a day older, Anthea. We must get together before I go back to London . . . talk over old times, perhaps. Is Willie still abroad?'

When the woman nodded and gave a faint blush, Livia exchanged a glance with Connie.

Mrs Mortimer gave a rather conspicuous sob and swayed on her feet. She was elegant in a black, fur-trimmed coat, ankle-length skirt and deep-crowned hat. She wore a brooch of glittering red and white stones in the shape of a butterfly. There was no denying that she was lovely.

The major dropped the woman's hand and moved to Mrs Mortimer's side. 'Brace up, Rosemary, old thing. I'm relying on you to get me through the day.'

And Rosemary Mortimer, although already fully braced by the major's arm sliding around her waist, fluttered her sweeping black eyelashes over her large grey eyes and simpered bravely up at him. 'I feel so sad for you, Major. Margaret and I were such good friends. She always seemed like an older sister to me.'

'Lying hypocrite; I hope Mrs Sangster comes back to haunt her,' Connie whispered, and Livia, who felt exactly the same, wanted to jump up and down on the spot and shout the lie out loud at the disgust she experienced.

Then Dr Elliot – standing with his wife, a small, neat woman – caught her eye. He raised his eyebrow in a manner that said it all, and Livia gave a faint shrug. Getting indignant wouldn't change things.

Connie took her arm. 'Come on, let's get back. The wind is blowing up the legs of my drawers and my bottom is beginning to freeze.'

Livia tried not to giggle as they hurried back to the house. It didn't seem the right thing to do after a funeral.

'I'll wager that Florence is having her fill of the food I prepared for the guests, too. She'll be at the brandy bottle as well. I've smelled it on her breath once or twice.'

Livia told her, 'I like Florence. She does more than her share of the work, and she's not frightened to cheek off Mrs Mortimer. I hope she's allowed to stay on.'

'Not if Mrs Mortimer has her way. The only reason Florence is still here is because Doctor Elliot recommended her, and he's acquainted with the major.'

'So it's up to the major.'

'Mrs Mortimer has already got her claws into him. It's not decent . . . what with his wife hardly cold in her grave.'

Livia only half-listened to Connie's gossip, since it was really none of her business what people got up to, besides, she had troubles enough of her own. Despite the cold wind there was a restless feeling of spring in the air, though it was only halfway through March, and just a couple of weeks since a thin layer of snow had covered the ground.

But the sap was rising. The buds on the hawthorn exposed a tender and secretive tracery of green, while the periwinkle embroidered a twisting curtain of blue and white through the hedgerows to hide the nests of song thrushes and their young. An occasional early daffodil spread its yellow bonnet to the wind.

'With a bit of luck she'll go back to London with him.'

Livia jerked back to the present. 'What if the major decides to close the house up?'

'He won't do that, not until Master Richard comes back from the war. The house belongs to the son under the Sinclair legacy, don't forget, and he'll need staff.'

'But what will happen if he doesn't come back?'

'He will,' Connie said fiercely. 'He told me that army food was terrible, and the first thing he'd want when he got back was a good dinner. Nothing fancy mind, Connie, says he. I'll have good old roast beef and potatoes, with Yorkshire pudding, peas and carrots and lashings of gravy.' She gave a bit of a smile. 'He wants apple pie and custard afterwards. He always liked his apple pie and custard, did young Richard.'

They slipped in the back door, surprising Florence with her feet up in front of the fire sipping a glass of brandy.

'I knew I'd catch you at it one day,' Connie said, the satisfaction she felt at the thought spreading over her face like a dollop of melting lard. 'Mrs Mortimer will dismiss you for sure if she catches you with that,' Connie told her.

'She'll dismiss you and all if I tell her I got it from your pantry disguised as a bottle of Phillips' Milk of Magnesia.'

'I keep it there for medicinal purposes,' Connie said hotly.

'Of course you do, and thankful I am for it too, since I felt quite ill a moment or two ago.' Tipping the glass up, Florence downed the liquid in one long swallow, sighed, and said, 'I had a backache caused by Mrs Mortimer sticking her knife between my shoulder blades. The brandy has relieved the pain no end.'

This time Livia began to laugh.

Connie couldn't hide her grin. 'Have you set the table out like I asked you to, Florence? They'll be home before too long.'

'Don't you fret, it's all ready, and I've stoked up the fire so the drawing room is good and warm. Oh yes . . . and while you were all out a gentleman from London rang. Couldn't hear him very well because he whistled, as though he had false teeth that were a bit loose in his head. But he spoke really posh, and said his name was Sturgeon. He wants the major to telephone him as soon as he comes in.'

'Livia can pass the message on to the major while she's supervising the table. Better go and get your apron on, love. I want to inspect the table, because the major can be very particular. Florence, you go up to the landing on the stairs and keep a look out for them. Let me know as soon as you see them come down the driveway. I'll make the tea in the big teapot then, and carry it through, so it doesn't get stewed. You can bring the hot water jug.'

It wasn't long before the drawing room was thronged with people, all dressed soberly and talking in hushed tones. Most of them had come from the church and had traipsed dirt across the hall from their boots. Livia had a glimpse of Florence with dustpan and brush rushing to-and-fro so it didn't get trodden in.

When the major approached to get something to eat, his blue eyes gazed into hers. He smiled. 'It's Livia, isn't it? I've been given to understand that my late wife thought very highly of you.'

'She was a nice woman; a real lady. We got on well together, and I'm going to miss her.'

'Quite. You've grown into a beautiful young woman since the last time I saw you. '

A faint blush rose to her face and she didn't know what to say. She remembered the message with some relief. 'There was a telephone call for you when you were out, Major. It was from a Mr Sturgeon in London. He wanted you to call him as soon as you were able.'

'Sturgeon . . .?' He shrugged. 'I can't recall anybody by that name.'

Livia hoped she didn't give offence when she told him, 'Florence said the gentleman had a distinctive voice . . . an *impediment*. He lisped.'

His brow cleared and he gave a low chuckle. 'I imagine Florence meant Sir John. Thank you, young lady. I'll go to my study and ring him from there.'

He left, threading his way through the crowd and stopping for just a moment to speak to Mrs Mortimer.

She crossed to where Livia stood, frowning. 'You should have given me the message to pass on to the major. Do you know what it was about?'

'No, I don't, Mrs Mortimer. Perhaps the major will tell you if you go and ask him.'

She was the recipient of a hard look.

Dr Elliot edged Mrs Mortimer out and filled his plate with sandwiches, giving her an apologetic look. 'I'm sorry if I appear to be greedy. I've been flat out all morning and didn't have time to eat. Everyone who is suffering from spring fever imagines that they've caught the Spanish flu. How are you, young lady?'

'How do I look?'

'As lively as a flea on a dog. I heard from Denton yesterday. He asked me to say hello on his behalf if I happened to run into you, and he said that he hopes you found your sister and brother in good health.'

'You can tell him you nearly ran into me with your car.'

He chuckled at that.

Mrs Mortimer hovered nearby, clearly eavesdropping. Without the major by her side, nobody approached her.

Livia lowered her voice. 'As for my sister and brother, I'd wish for better than an overcrowded orphanage, but there are so many homeless children in London I should be grateful they have a roof over their heads. It was kind of Denton to enquire.'

'He also said to tell you that the pheasant's feather is his constant companion.' A dark eyebrow lifted in a query.

She laughed. 'He stole a pheasant's feather from my hat to take with him. He thought it would bring him luck.'

Dr Elliot grinned, and said over the muted conversation of the other guests, 'You're blushing, Miss Carr. Did my son flirt so very much with you? He has an over-abundance of charm on occasion.'

Like father, like son, she thought, and said, 'I am *not* blushing.' But nevertheless, her hands went to her cheeks and she lowered her voice. 'Actually, he did flirt a little . . . but I didn't take any notice. I'm a housemaid with two orphaned siblings to support, so I can't allow myself to harbour romantic notions about any man, especially someone of his standing.'

'That's very sensible of you, my dear, but war is a great leveller, and you can never tell what's around the corner. Is that some of cook's apple cake over there? A large slice please, Livia, since I can't resist it . . .'

His wife joined him. 'Behave yourself, Andrew. Give him a small piece of cake, dear; he's of an age where he must watch his waistline.'

'This is Livia Carr, Helen. I was just passing on Denton's message.'

A smile lit up her face. 'Andrew has told me a lot about you, so I'm pleased we've finally met. I understand that you're George and Eloise Carr's daughter.'

'Yes, Mrs Elliot.'

'Such a coincidence; I attended the same school as your mother, though we were in different boarding houses. Eloise James, she was then. I attended her wedding to George Carr. And met them again at a party in London. It was a long time ago, about fifteen years. They were a very popular couple, I recall . . . always entertaining.'

If they hadn't worked so hard at being popular they might have left something to help support their children, she thought, and vowed that she'd never be irresponsible with money if she married and became a mother.

Helen Elliot reached out to squeeze her hand. 'I'm sorry, that was insensitive of me . . . especially since you find yourself in such difficult circumstances. You would have led a very different life if they'd lived, I imagine.'

Livia shrugged. 'It's been six years, Mrs Elliot. Moping about it won't bring them back.'

'That's the ticket,' Dr Elliot said, and ambled off.

Helen Elliot lingered. 'I understand you have a brother and sister to support?'

Livia nodded. 'They've just turned eight, and they can't remember our parents, which is a blessing. When I have time, I'm hoping to find them somewhere near here where they can stay, so I can see them more often.'

'You must come and visit us one day, so we can have a proper chat.'

'I'd like that.'

Mrs Mortimer cut in, her smile so thin it could have skinned a tomato. 'You'll have to excuse the maid, Mrs Elliot, she has work to do. Go to the kitchen and fetch some hot water, Carr.'

'We have hot water.'

After Helen Elliot moved off, Mrs Mortimer frowned. 'You're being paid to work, not to stand and gossip. It was a good job the major wasn't here to see what was going on.'

As if on cue the major entered, looking shaken. 'You'll excuse me please, everyone. I've just received word that my son has been injured. Sir John didn't have much information, but it's a head wound apparently.'

Dr Elliot moved to the sideboard and poured him a brandy. 'Here, drink this. How bad is he . . . did they say?'

'No . . . just that he's being shipped back to England and will spend some time in the City Hospital before he's sent to a convalescent centre. I'm glad his mother didn't live to see this.'

So was Livia. Margaret Sangster had adored her son.

Sympathetic murmurs filled the room at the thought of this double tragedy. The guests' condolences were offered again, and they began to drift away, leaving their host with this extra trouble in his life, glad it hadn't happened to one of theirs, and hoping it never would.

Livia began to remove the dishes and leftovers, though most of the funeral feast had been consumed. Florence joined her and they soon put the room to rights.

Just before the Elliot couple left, the doctor said, 'Don't give up hope, Henry. If they're shipping him home there's a possibility that he's strong enough to survive the journey. And people do recover from head injuries.'

'Yes, of course . . . I'll go up to London right away . . . use the Rolls, since there won't be a train until morning. I'll be there for him.'

His gaze went to Rosemary Mortimer and his lids hooded sleepily as he contemplated her, the nature of his relationship close to the surface, despite his shock over his son becoming a casualty. 'You'd better come too, Mrs Mortimer. I'll need someone to look after my household while I sort out the legalities of my wife's estate. My London housekeeper has left my employ.'

Smug-faced, Rosemary Mortimer left instructions that the house was to be spring-cleaned from top to bottom. 'I'll leave you in charge, Livia. That way I'll know who to blame if the work's not done to my satisfaction.'

They watched the couple go, the major at the wheel and Mrs Mortimer by his side, her face snuggled against the blue velvet collar of a coat that had belonged to the late Mrs Sangster.

'Brazen . . . the pair of them,' Florence murmured, for the maid had soon winkled out the household situation. 'Good riddance to bad rubbish, I say.'

'Don't crow too soon. She'll be back, and I wager there will be a ring on her finger,' Connie commented gloomily.

To save any further speculation, Livia began to make plans for the task she'd been left with. 'We'll start at the top and work our way down. We'll clean the main bedrooms first, except for Mrs Sangster's rooms. We'll leave them until last . . .'

But as soon as the car drove off the three of them held hands and danced around the hall until they were dizzy and delirious with laughter.

Five

April arrived clad in soft showers, a fluttering of peacock butterflies, wood anemones and primroses. The pond was full of tadpoles, the birds sweetly sang their melodies, and, on high, a watchful hawk circled on silent wings.

The house had been scrubbed and polished, and Mr Bugg and Florence had washed the windows – one standing on the outside, the other on the inside. There was very little left to do, so they'd put dustsheets over the furniture in the main rooms, and could now relax.

On the very last day of the month, a letter arrived for Livia.

'Joseph Anderson and Simon Stone. It's from a solicitor,' she whispered, turning it over in her hands. 'I expect it's for the major.'

'Since when has the major's name been Miss Olivia Carr?'

'But why would a solicitor be writing to me?' Fear stabbed her. 'I hope my sister and brother are all right.'

Connie rolled her eyes. 'Stop thinking the worst. There's only one way to find out . . . open the damned thing!'

Livia used the sharpest kitchen knife and carefully prised open the flap, since it would be sacrilege to damage such an important and official-looking envelope. The letter was crisply typewritten on pale cream paper, the signature a crouching spider of a scribble that looked as though it might unfold its legs and sprint from the page. Simon Stone was typed underneath, in case his writing didn't do his signature justice.

Florence leaned over one shoulder to read the letter with her, painfully mouthing the words. Connie gazed over the other shoulder.

'Fancy,' Connie said. 'Mr Stone is coming here in person to see you. On Friday, at eleven.'

'That's only three days away,' Florence added.

'He has a matter of importance he needs to discuss with me.'

'He doesn't give much away,' Connie said, clearly disappointed.

'And to think I signed as a witness to Mrs Sangster's signature for him.'

'He's probably coming to hand over the money that Mrs Sangster left for you and Mr Bugg in her will.'

Connie looked aggressive. 'He should have written to me then, since I've been here the longest.'

Florence looked glum. 'I wish someone would leave me fifty pounds.'

'Do you now?' Connie's hands went to her hips. 'You haven't worked here long enough. Mr Bugg was employed by the family when he were a lad, and I've worked here for nigh on thirty years. As for Livia, she's been here for nearly five years, and she did a lot for poor Mrs Sangster that wasn't her duty to do, and from the goodness of her heart. She's never complained once. Mrs Sangster took a shine to her right from the beginning, and that's a fact. But she didn't get any legacy, so why are you complaining?'

'I'm not complaining. I just said—'

Livia broke in swiftly, 'But why would they need to see me for that when it's none of my business? All they need do is give the money over to Major Henry. He told you the amount was insignificant, Connie, and he'd hand over the money when it had been cleared by the lawyers.'

'It might be insignificant to him, but when you've got only a small wage coming in . . .'

Florence shrugged, clearly uninterested because she was not to be included in any bounty that the death of Mrs Sangster had brought to Connie and Mr Bugg. 'What shall I do with that personal stuff in the nurse's room?'

'Pack it into her suitcase. I can't authorize it to be sent on unless she's left some money to pay for it. I'll telephone Nurse Gifford and ask her what to do with it. Those nurses are run off their feet looking after the sick as well as the wounded. She doesn't deserve to lose everything she owns just because Mrs Mortimer got into one of her moods.'

'Mortimer is a spiteful cow . . . that she is,' Connie murmured, and thumped her fist into a mound of risen bread dough. 'I hope he doesn't marry her, but she doesn't give up easily. She was wearing Mrs Sangster's blue coat with the velvet collar and matching hat when she left, and I've got an awful feeling . . . In fact, I wouldn't be surprised if Mrs Mortimer hadn't done away with her.'

Florence's eyes widened.

So did Livia's, because she suddenly remembered the pillow in Mrs Mortimer's hands, and hearing her tell Mrs Sangster she could put her out of her misery. She made a murmur of distress in her throat. No . . . it was spite on Mrs Mortimer's part. And she must put a stop to this sort of speculation.

She sent Connie a warning glance before saying to Florence, 'Connie doesn't mean that seriously, so don't you go repeating it to anyone, else we might end up in court for slander.'

'What's slander?'

'Making a malicious statement about someone that isn't true and can't be proved. I was there when she died. The doctor told me that Mrs Sangster died because of that fall. It damaged a vein inside her head, and it ruptured.'

Connie embroidered Livia's explanation with: 'Perhaps she tripped over the cat.'

'Since when have we had a cat? Mrs Mortimer doesn't like them, they make her sneeze.'

'Then I might gather a few strays up and let them run around her room for a while, before she comes back.'

It was hard not to laugh at Florence, but Livia knew she shouldn't encourage her. Mrs Mortimer must have a good side to her, and she held a position of trust in the household. If Connie were to be believed, she might end up being mistress of the house. Florence's gossip would only make matters worse.

'We'd better stop this gossiping. Whether we like it or not, Mrs Mortimer is in charge of us, and we must respect that. She might have come back and be outside the door listening. And before you pack that suitcase, Florence, you can set the table for lunch if you would.'

Connie sighed. 'Livia's right, Florence. After you've done that, tell Mr Bugg that I've cooked his favourite steak and kidney pie, and he's to come in for it at one o'clock sharp.'

When Florence's stomach rattled noisily, Livia grinned. Florence liked her food, but she was a good worker. She hoped Mrs Mortimer didn't dismiss her when she returned from London.

'After lunch, we'll clean Mrs Sangster's room. With the bathroom next door, and the nurse's room the other side, they might need to use it for Captain Richard Sangster.' Livia looked down at the letter again. 'Perhaps Mr Stone is coming with instructions to do with his care . . . after all, I was put in charge of the household.'

Connie said reflectively, 'Poor lad. That will be it then. I just hope the solicitor brings my legacy with him. I'm of a mind to have a good day out. I thought I might go on the church outing in June. We could all go together and bathe in the sea and have fish and chips for dinner. We'd have to book a seat in the charabanc though.'

Chad and Esmé would enjoy doing that, Livia thought. But she didn't have any money to spare for pleasure. 'You two go. Someone will have to stay to mind the house. Besides, I'm saving up to go to visit my sister and brother in London again. I promised them I'd try and get there more often.'

Livia had built up a picture of Simon Stone in her mind, in which he was tall and thin with a long, serious face. In fact, he was middle-aged, rather rotund, and gave her a jolly smile as he took her hand between his.

She'd tossed up whether to use the drawing room, but he might think it a little pretentious. Instead, she took him to the smaller morning room – the one Margaret Sangster had used before the accident had confined her to her bedchamber, she'd been given to understand.

'Would you like some refreshment, Mr Stone?'

'That would be very kind of you, my dear.'

With that ordered, they settled down to business.

'Is this to do with Mr Richard Sangster?'

He gazed at her. 'Why should you think that?'

'Well . . . I'd heard that he'd been injured, and thought that he might be coming home soon, and you were here to give me instructions.'

'Dear me, no. Captain Sangster will be in hospital for some time to come, I imagine.'

'Oh . . . I'm so sorry . . . I hadn't realized his condition was so bad. His mother would have been upset had she known.'

'Then be happy she didn't survive long enough to find out.'

'Why are you here then, Sir?'

'I'm here at Mrs Sangster's instruction. You're probably aware that Mrs Sangster had a private income and one or two properties of her own.'

'No, I didn't know, Sir. That sort of information wouldn't be shared with someone of my standing, and should remain private. Major Henry wouldn't like it being discussed with me.'

'Quite. However, I've already been through the matter with the major.'

'What matter?'

'There's a sizeable cottage not far from here. It's furnished, and is available to you for a peppercorn rent while you have need of it. Maintenance will be paid by the estate.'

'I don't understand. Won't the cottage now belong to Richard Sangster?'

'He will agree to the arrangement she made. There's also a small allowance, and when combined with the wage you earn here, and the money you pay to help support them in the orphanage, it will be enough to provide for your siblings.'

'I still don't understand.'

'Come now, Miss Carr. You're an intelligent young lady, or so I've been led to believe. What don't you understand about it? Mrs Sangster wanted to carry out a charitable act, and this is a grace and favour cottage.'

'But why me?'

'Because she feels . . . *felt,* that you'd need help to meet your obligations over the coming years. If you marry during that time, then the agreement is null and void, as your husband would be expected to provide for you.'

Choked up by the thought that Mrs Sangster would extend such a generous hand of friendship to her, Livia promptly began to cry. 'I'm not worthy of this. There are people worse off.'

'Believe me, Miss Carr, your background was inspected thoroughly before you started work here. You are eminently suitable as a candidate for the charity offered by Mrs Sangster in her last will and testament. We cannot take into account your parents' lack of responsibility towards you, only the consequence.'

'They loved us.'

'Children need more than love, my dear. They need a home, and that's something you're already aware of.' Simon Stone extended his handkerchief for her use. 'There is more, Miss Carr.'

She mopped her eyes then gazed helplessly at him. 'What more could there be?'

'Your brother will be the recipient of a scholarship if he proves to be educationally worthy.'

'I'm given to understand that he's a clever boy.'

'Nevertheless, he's not trying hard enough to produce results at the moment. To that end he will receive extra tutoring, if you will permit it. He will be expected to apply himself, of course.'

Her sigh was tinged with relief, because this was the answer to her prayers, and at long last she could see a future ahead for her family. 'I'll try and make sure that he does. You've been thorough.'

He nodded. 'Last, but not least, there is the issue of Mrs Sangster's wardrobe. She wants you to have her clothing. Not the jewellery, of course, which will belong to Richard Sangster. But she did give me this keepsake for you, so you'll always have something to remember her by.'

It was a gold ring with small white stones clustered around one yellow one, in the middle. Livia smiled, remembering admiring it because it was unusual. 'It's a daisy, I think, and so pretty. I'll cherish it. Didn't Major Sangster mind?'

'He was informed of the arrangement out of courtesy, though his approval was not sought. He didn't voice any objection either, which was his right. However, he's made a request, which I will discuss with you in a little while. His son's condition is a great worry to him, you see. I believe the captain will be moved nearer home soon. They are waiting for a vacancy at the convalescent home at Brownsea Island.'

She poured the tea into delicate blue and white cups that matched the teapot, and offered him some fruitcake, her sudden bounty making her feel like the lady of the manor. 'How bad is Richard Sangster, Mr Stone? Can you tell me?'

'I don't see why not. Richard Sangster can hardly speak. He shakes and trembles, so he's too uncoordinated to walk unaided. He suffers from blinding headaches at times, and at other times he can hardly breathe. As well as his injuries, he was gassed. To be honest, he's not expected to live very long. He's expressed a wish that he be allowed to spend what life he does have left in his home.'

She gave a small, distressed cry. 'The poor man! I must think about this before I decide whether to accept the legacy or not. What will happen to my brother and sister when the Sinclair estate is eventually passed on?'

'You misunderstand. This arrangement has got nothing to do with the Sinclair estate. The cottage has become the property of Margaret Sangster's son under her will, along with everything else she owned. Richard has been consulted, and is prepared to accept the condition attached to that particular property for the time being. When he dies, I imagine the major will inherit it. He has verbally promised to honour the agreement by leaving the arrangement as it is.'

He smiled and slid a key across the table. 'The present tenant has agreed to allow you to look the place over while he's absent for a few days. If you're satisfied with it there are certain protocols to observe . . . papers to sign.'

She placed her hand on his arm and whispered, 'This is not a cruel joke, is it? You said Major Sangster had made a request. What is it?'

'I will emphasize that this isn't a condition. The major wants you to take on the overall responsibility of the household, and to make sure his son is looked after properly when he finally returns home. He feels it will be beneficial for Richard to have a permanent carer, and he wants him to be made as comfortable as possible. He feels that his son will respond better to a pretty young thing like you. The captain will, of course, have a man to see to his private needs. The same man will also be responsible for any heavy work around the house.'

'I see. What if I don't suit such a position?'

'I'm sure you will, Miss Carr. Doctor Elliot has observed the household as it stands, and has recommended you for the position. He tells me you are a caring and responsible young lady who will keep the patient's welfare close to your heart.'

'What about the rest of the staff, and who will look after my brother and sister? I can't do all things?'

'The cottage is of a manageable size. Also, the children will be able to come here when the need arises, since you'll have the housekeeper's quarters at your disposal. Besides, my dear, you have several months until the cottage becomes vacant.'

'And what of Mrs Mortimer?'

Distaste flickered briefly in the depths of his eyes. 'I'm given to understand that she and the major are to be married when a suitable time has elapsed.'

'Oh . . . I see.' She shrugged. 'We . . . the staff, that is, thought that might happen.'

He gave a twisted grin. 'You do understand that you work for the Sinclair trust, and not for Major Sangster. I expect he will stay here from time to time, though. After all, he will want to see his son.'

Livia hadn't questioned who'd paid her wages, mainly because there was little left by the time it reached her pocket. She smiled. 'In that case, I won't overstep the boundary of my authority if I tell you that you're welcome to stay for lunch, Mr Stone? There's steak and kidney pie on the menu, and Connie Starling is a very good cook. You can either join us in the kitchen, or dine in solitary splendour at the big table.'

He looked startled for a moment, before smiling in return. 'I'm partial to steak and kidney pie, and would very much like to join you all in the kitchen. I can then explain the changes to everyone.'

Where Livia had expected lime-washed cob, she got red bricks. Where she'd expected to see thatch, she saw grey slate. A clematis threaded in and out of a wire support around the door. The cottage was not far from the village, where she could walk to the small general store, or she could get a seat on a bus that drove passengers into Creekmore to shop once a week.

The sitting room had French windows looking out over a small terrace and the garden. The kitchen was big enough to eat in. There was a dining room and a laundry room with a clothes boiler, mangle and ironing table. The privy was outside.

Upstairs were three bedrooms with sloping ceilings. The

two at the back would be for the children. Livia would have the bigger one for herself. There was a downstairs bedroom for guests, though it was filled with junk. Should anyone care to visit her it could be cleaned out.

Her eyes began to shine. The place wasn't fussy, but it was roomy and comfortable, with patterned winged chairs and dark wooden floors with rugs here and there. There was gas lighting.

She gave a plant in a pot a drink of water from the pump in the sink. 'There, that should stop you from wilting,' she said.

'Well . . .?' Simon Stone asked.

Livia experienced a pride of ownership so fierce that she wanted to cry and laugh at the same time. 'It's lovely. I wish Mrs Sangster were here, so I could thank her. When can I move in?'

'Whenever you wish, after the tenant has vacated the place. I'll make arrangements for the children nearer the time, and I'll drive them down myself. I'll telephone you first to let you know when we're coming.'

Just in time for Christmas, she thought. They'd be together at last, a family again. Her siblings would get rid of that unhealthy pastiness, and she'd fill them with nourishing food and sweet country air.

'Will I be able to have a cat? The children would like that.'

He smiled. 'I don't see why not.'

She was full of happiness, yet uneasy, as if it were all too good to be true . . . a sweet dream while she slept, and when she woke up it would evaporate and remain unfulfilled. Simon Stone wasn't real. He didn't exist. So she pinched herself, and resisted the urge to pinch him, and her mood fluctuated between happiness and despair as she cleaned and sewed a pretty smock for Esmé to wear for best, out of one of Mrs Sangster's dresses. She went to the market and bought them an outfit each . . . and the weeks drifted slowly past.

Finally she received a call from Simon Stone, but it wasn't what she'd expected.

'I'm so sorry, Miss Carr. Your sister and brother have been taken ill,' he said.

Dear God! Let it not be the epidemic that had gripped hold

of the country and spread throughout the world. It was cutting through the population like a true servant of the grim reaper, leaving thousands dead in its wake.

'They have the flu.'

It was such a short sentence, but so much fear was stored in its scorpion tail. Livia's anguish was a raging twist of misery, fear and loathing, and she gave a sharp cry. 'It's not fair! It can't be true . . . I must go to them.'

'My dear. Please don't come. You won't be able to see them, since they're in the isolation ward. You must put your trust in God.'

She dropped the receiver, leaving it swaying back and forth on its cord. A fine thing to be given such hope, only to have it crashed down. Was this some sort of test to see if she was worthy? Livia went to her room and stared out over the wilderness of a garden with its secret places. The children would love the freedom of living in the country, and she'd promised them they'd all be together as a family.

She crawled on to the bed, curled up small and began to cry in big swooping sobs. Although her chest became sore, she couldn't stop sobbing until she was scooped up against someone's warm body. She became aware that somebody was rocking her. It was soothing, like she was a child again, and her mother was cuddling her close.

Only it wasn't her mother, it was Dr Elliot. 'It's not right, my poor sister and brother getting that horrible disease,' she whispered. 'I feel so guilty, and I can't bear it.'

'You can and you must, my sweet, brave girl,' he told her. 'Chad and Esmé have each other, and it doesn't mean they will die.'

'They're twins. If one dies, the other will, because they won't leave each other behind.' She gazed up at him, hope in her eyes. 'Do you think they will survive it? Will praying help?'

'I'm a doctor. I deal with broken bodies, and sometimes broken minds. I don't profess to have any special knowledge of the spiritual, except we are urged to have faith. I would like to think so, though.'

'It's such a cruel thing to do . . . allow me to have such hope after four years apart, then just when happiness is within my grasp, and that of my sister and brother, to bring this down upon them. They've hardly lived.'

'But they are not dead, so their bodies are fighting the disease. You mustn't think that way, Livia. There is still hope.'

'I feel as though I've been robbed of hope as well as a purpose in life.'

'Of course you do, but we have more than one purpose in life, and you will find another if need be, and will have the strength to carry that through.'

There came a knock at the door.

'Come in, Connie.'

The cup rattled on the saucer Connie carried. 'Is Livia all right, Doctor? I was that worried.'

He placed Livia on the bed and removed her shoes. 'She's had a dreadful shock, and must rest. I'm going to give her a sedative to take with her tea.' He gazed down at her. 'You'll feel stronger and more able to cope when you wake. Connie will help you into your nightgown, and I'll pop in again in the morning to see how you are.'

Sleep . . . yes . . . just for a while so she could forget this awful disease that travelled the world with the sole purpose of slaughtering the innocents. She took the pill and soon the outside noise had retreated past the curious fuzziness that surrounded her. She remembered a line from a prayer from childhood . . . one she'd taught the twins. *If I should die before I wake, I pray the Lord my soul will take.*

'They are so innocent and it was just words, you don't have to take heed of them,' she muttered, and tears trickled from under her lashes. She had been given the time to plan their lovely life together in that sweet little cottage . . . if they died she'd be left with nobody to love. Just herself . . . and she'd never pray for anything again.

What had the doctor said . . . that she'd find another purpose? Well, let it be soon, for she couldn't stand to lose the warm feeling inside her where love and hope for the future resided. Perhaps she'd been presumptuous by leaving her heart in the sweet cottage she'd fallen in love with, and had thought of as home. She'd certainly left her dreams there.

She was selfish, feeling sorry for herself, when it was her brother and sister who were in danger.

The next day she threw herself into her work, nearly dropping from exhaustion every night. There had never been a house so clean.

Six

The Spanish flu epidemic picked up pace. It spread across the globe like wildfire, killing millions of people, both healthy and ill. Sparing others.

It spared Chad and Esmé, but only just.

The world powers ran out of fight in the face of it. In September 1918, Bulgaria withdrew from the war, quickly followed by Austria, Turkey and Hungary. The troops were exhausted and short of supplies, and another winter in the trenches was beyond human endurance, as well as impractical. The Germans initiated peace terms and the armistice was formally signed on the eleventh of November 1918.

There was a weary relief in the air, and people looked to Christmas with muted eagerness, and some with joy, for there was now a new hope in the air that their loved ones would return intact.

Even Livia felt it, for her own lost siblings had been restored to her, at least in spirit. Soon she would make a home for them.

Her concern over their illness had taken her into womanhood, and although she was twenty-one she felt as though she was ten years older in maturity.

They had not seen hide nor hair of the major, though they'd heard that he'd married Mrs Mortimer. Towards the end of November, on a miserably wet day, the pair turned up without any warning, traipsing mud into the hall. The major stamped his feet all over the newly polished floor.

Rosemary Mortimer was very thin and very elegant, her face nestled in fur. Her grey glance went from one servant to another and settled on Florence. 'You may take my luggage up to my room, Hutchins.'

'And which room might that be, Mrs Mortimer?'

'My name is no longer Mrs Mortimer, but Mrs Sangster. You will address me as Madam . . . That goes for all of you. You may take my luggage to the former Mrs Sangster's room, Florence. Is that clear enough?'

So . . . she was going to rub their noses in it, was she? Livia thought.

'We were keeping the master bedrooms clean and ready for when Mr Richard returns home,' Connie told her.

She looked down her nose at Connie. 'Were you . . . were you indeed? On whose authority?'

Livia answered. 'On mine, since Mr Stone put me in charge of the household. It was on the advice of Doctor Elliot, since the rooms have already been adapted to suit the needs of an invalid and carer. The Sinclair trust will adapt it further to meet any special needs Captain Sangster might have. It has a bathroom and a room for a nurse adjoining it.' Livia nodded at Florence. 'Take *Madam*'s luggage to the best guest room, Florence.'

'Henry, did you hear that?' Rosemary said petulantly, and before Florence had found the time to move a step, 'Who does she think she is? Am I to be a guest in our own home?'

He turned a frown her way. 'Strictly speaking, this is Richard's home, Rosie. We are his guests.'

'But he'll need you to handle his affairs. I do hope you don't expect me to stay in this dreary house long term, because I won't.'

'Oh, do stop whining, dear girl. The arrangement sounds perfectly reasonable to me. Richard *will* have special needs. Off you trot now, Florence. The guest rooms it is.'

Major Henry came to where Livia stood. 'I heard about your sister and brother. It must have given you a fright, and they were lucky to survive.' He patted her on the shoulder as if she were a dog. 'You'll be glad to get them back, I imagine. Nutting Cottage will be just the tick to bring them up in.'

'Yes I will. I believe I have you to thank for that.'

'Margaret really, it's what she wanted.' He shrugged, and his eyes darted to his new wife as he lowered his voice and said with a candid honesty, 'She wouldn't have liked Rosie using her bedroom, and I owed her that dignity in death. It didn't seem right letting anyone else but Richard have it.'

She felt sorry for him. 'Thank you, anyway, Major.'

His glance fell on her mouth before lingering a while on her breasts. He gazed into her eyes and smiled. 'You've gained a little weight, but you're still a pretty, lively little thing. Always thought so, you know.'

Colour seeped under her skin.

His new wife snapped from halfway up the stairs, 'Do stop gossiping with the maid and come upstairs, Henry.'

'I'm the housekeeper,' Livia said, reminding the woman of her former status. 'Do let me know if there's anything you need . . . *Madam*.'

Henry managed a wry grin and tossed a wink at Livia before he said on a sigh, 'I'm coming, darling.'

'I'm going to be bored to death living here again,' Rosemary complained as they went off up the stairs. 'All that beastly country food clogging up the system.'

Connie sniffed.

It was obvious that Major Henry was beginning to lose his affable manner, for Livia heard him say with some impatience, 'It's only while Richard is still with us.'

'That could be years.'

'I do hope so . . . I thought we might give him a proper Christmas while he can still enjoy it. The poor boy's had a bad time of it.'

'It would be better if he'd died, rather than linger on like a rotting vegetable.'

'Rosemary, I rather think we've exhausted this conversation. If you're not prepared to be civilized and would rather spend Christmas in London with your fast friends, then by all means do so.'

'Perhaps I will,' she said sulkily.

Connie's grin could only be described as satisfied when she whispered, 'It sounds to me as though the honeymoon is over.'

Wrapped in a cosy red blanket, Richard Sangster arrived home in the Rolls, driven by his father. Livia had forgotten how blue his eyes were, and how fair his hair. She remembered him as being bigger, and more robust . . . and she remembered her heart fluttering every time he'd smiled at her.

Florence gazed at him with her mouth open, and Connie burst into tears.

Livia and Florence had prepared Richard's rooms and had lit a fire. Livia didn't know whether to address the invalid, or the silent man in whose arms he was secured. She decided on neither, instead saying to the major, 'Will Mr Richard be going upstairs to his room?'

The major nodded. 'Yes . . . I think so. What do you think, Beamish?'

'The captain is tired from the journey at the moment, and would welcome a rest. We'll work out a routine over the next few days.

'This gentleman with him is Mr Beamish, Livia. He will be Richard's man. Beamish, this is our housekeeper, Miss Carr.'

A searching glance came her way. 'How do you do, Miss Carr?'

'Please call me Livia. This is Florence Hutchins, and our cook, Connie Starling.'

'How do you do, Florence.' He gave the maid an easy smile that made her blush fiercely, then turned to cook. 'Ah yes, and you, Mrs Starling. The captain told me you were the most wonderful cook in the world. He used to discuss your Sunday dinners in the trenches, while our stomachs were as hollow as logs. I'm looking forward to my dinner.'

'He'll never go hungry again, not while I've got breath in my body.' Cook and Florence both dimpled smiles at him.

Rosemary made her way down the stairs in an ankle-length hobble skirt and finely pleated tunic under a long blue cardigan. She posed four steps up, her beringed hand fluttering against her chest.

'My dear Richard, how wonderful. Will you not greet your new stepmother?'

Livia saw the captain's hand tighten on his man's arm. Beamish smiled. 'He rarely speaks to strangers, Mrs Sangster, especially when he's tired.'

'Oh, how disappointing,' Rosemary drawled. 'I was hoping he'd tell us all about his daring exploits on the front.'

Richard Sangster began to tremble.

'Follow me, Mr Beamish,' Livia said quickly, and set off up the wide staircase, with Beamish and his burden bringing up the rear.

She closed the door behind them to keep the warmth in, and indicated the bed. 'This is Captain Sangster's room. I've had his own furniture installed so he'll feel at home. Your room is through that door.'

The trembles had become violent jerks and the man's teeth chattered. Beamish placed him on the bed. Out of instinct Livia gently rubbed Richard's hand, and felt the strength in the muscle spasm. 'Is there anything I can do to help?'

'These spasms don't last very long, but sometimes they make him cough, and that tires him. When he's angry he swears, or he might lash out. You must be prepared for that.'

'I will, but we mustn't talk about him as if his mind is elsewhere. I'm quite sure it's not.'

She gazed at the wreckage of this once golden and healthy young man. A scar tracked through his Adonis curls like a livid parting. His eyes were open, but she couldn't tell if he was looking at her or over her shoulder, or whether he even understood what she was saying.

When he winked she was uncertain of whether it was accidental or a twitch. Beamish remained impassive, gazing at her from his towering height.

She gave him a faint grin before turning back to the patient. 'I'm not as delicate a flower as I look, Captain Sangster, and neither am I stupid. I think I might swear too if I were in your position. But let me warn you of one thing . . . if you lash out at me I shall box your ears, because I won't put up with it.'

The shaking stopped and his bluer-than-blue eyes widened as they focussed on her. 'S . . . saucy mad . . . am.' A grin flitted around his lips.

She caught Beamish's approving glance on her, and was heartened by it. 'Now we all know where we stand, don't we? If you need anything to make life easier, let me know. I'll bring you up some tea in a little while. Welcome home, Mr Sangster. Mr Beamish, you'll be a welcome addition to the staff, and we'll do our best to make you feel comfortable here.'

'Thank you, Ma'am.'

When Richard Sangster stuck his tongue out and saluted untidily, Livia sighed. 'You've only just got here and already you're being a childish pest. Behave yourself.'

She left the room accompanied by the low chuckle Beamish gave. It was going to be hard keeping any sort of control over these two, she feared, trying not to laugh.

Old Mr Bugg disappeared one day, replaced by a much younger version, who informed her that he was old Bugg's grandson, just back from the war.

'Grandpa's rheumatism is playing up so he's decided to retire. I've come in his stead. Call me Matthew,' he said.

She didn't know whether to inform anyone or not – so she didn't.

'Mr Bugg said he'd find me a small Christmas tree for Nutting Cottage.'

'Aye, I'll see to it for you.'

She wondered if she should perhaps tell Mr Stone, then decided against it. The major could do that if it occurred to him.

Matthew Bugg stayed on, and along with Beamish was useful around the house when anything heavy needed lifting, or the windows needed washing.

'Who *is* that person?' the major said to her one day.

'Mr Bugg. He usually works in the garden.'

Vaguely, he said, 'Ah yes, so he does; I thought he was an older man.'

Livia had worked out her routine with Beamish. She would have very little to do on her shift, apart from relax, keep Richard company, and walk him around the garden in his wheelchair if he felt like some air.

Richard Sangster responded to her attempts at conversation with grunts and the occasional word. He stuttered badly if he tried to converse, swore and banged his hand on the arm of the chair before stuttering out, 'S . . . sorry.' She learned to handle his moods with calmness, for they stemmed from frustration.

In the week before Christmas Livia took possession of

Nutting Cottage. She made the beds, using painstakingly repaired linen that had been discarded for rags. It would do until she could afford some of her own.

She went there after dinner each evening and usually fell asleep in the armchair, waking cold and disorientated when the fire went out.

The new Mrs Sangster called her to the drawing room the next day. 'This is not good enough, Livia. I rang the bell twice last night. A housekeeper needs to be on call twenty-four hours a day.'

'I was at Nutting Cottage preparing for the arrival of my sister and brother. I've worked through my schedule with the Sinclair trust. As long as the kitchen staff are familiar with the menu and the housekeeping is kept up to date, my evenings are free to spend with my sister and brother, when they arrive.'

Her mouth pursed. 'You certainly managed to manipulate the former Mrs Sangster. Well, don't think you'll do the same with me. We're very different.'

Livia could say the same about her with the major. 'Yes, Madam, you most certainly are. Is there anything else?'

'You can take my underwear and give it to Florence to wash.'

'I understood it was washed yesterday.'

'It was not washed well enough.'

Raising an eyebrow, Livia gazed at her. 'You know how short-staffed we are. Florence has a lot to do, and I would suggest you wash it yourself if you're not satisfied. Florence has other tasks.'

'You're refusing a direct order. Be very careful, Livia. You might find yourself losing that cosy little home you're making for your family.'

Fear leaped in her chest, digging its claws in as she whispered, 'You wouldn't do that . . . be so mean towards two innocent children.'

'Wouldn't I?'

Yes, she certainly would . . . but could she? Livia thought. The cottage didn't belong to Major Sangster . . . yet. Out of habit she washed the underwear herself, otherwise the woman would make everyone's life a misery

Esmé and Chad arrived the next day, just after lunch. From

Richard Sangster's window she saw Mr Stone's car come up the driveway, and a pair of pale faces looking out.

Excitement fermented inside her. *At last . . . at long last!* Thank you, God. 'It's my sister and brother,' she said, beaming a smile at the two men. 'They've arrived.'

'You'll want to get them settled into the cottage, so we can manage without you this afternoon,' Beamish said.

Richard stammered, 'G . . . give them . . . something . . . eat.'

'Thank you.' She flew down the stairs and out of the front door. *'Esmé! Chad.'*

The pair huddled together, looking bewildered. They were pale and thin, and carried no luggage. How lethargic they both were. Again, Livia was kept at a distance by the blank gaze one usually gives a stranger. Esmé clung to Chad, and he said, 'It's all right, Es. It's our sister. She won't hurt you. Hello, Olivia.'

Both children took a step back when she approached, and Esmé began to cry. 'I want to go back to the home.'

Tears pushed against Livia's eyes. 'You won't have to go there again . . . not ever . . . come here, darling.'

Chad pushed her forward, and Livia took her sister's thin little body in her arms. The girl began to struggle and scream. Wrenching away from Livia's arms, she hurled herself against Chad, who put a protective arm about her. 'It's all right, Esmé.' He gave Livia an angry glare. 'She needs time to get used to you. Don't make a fuss and she'll come round.'

Connie came out. 'Bring them into the kitchen where it's warm. There's some broth to eat, and if you're still hungry after that, I might find a slice of roly-poly jam pudding and custard apiece.' She ruffled Chad's hair and took Esmé's hand in hers. 'Say thank you to Mr Stone and let's get inside, where it's warm.'

They did as they were told.

Simon Stone smiled benignly at her after they'd gone. 'I have a son and a daughter about their age. The children are tired and hungry, I think. I have some business to conduct with Mr Richard Sangster while I'm here.'

'I'll go up and inform him. If you'd like to wait in the small sitting room, Beamish will bring him down. Thank you so much for bringing the children. I hope they weren't too much trouble.'

'None at all. This is a big change for them, Miss Carr, but it won't take them long to settle down. I should be about an hour. If you're ready, I'll drop you all off at Nutting Cottage before I go home.'

'That's kind of you.'

'It was my pleasure. They said they couldn't remember being in a car before, and your brother was most interested.' He hesitated a little, then said, 'I thought your sister was a little lethargic. She slept for most of the way, and has a cough. Chad said she'd had it for some time. I do think it might be a good idea for the doctor to examine them both.'

'Thank you; I'll take your advice on that.'

'I'll leave the bags in the car then. I took the liberty of buying them some suitable clothing, since they only had what they stood up in.'

'It didn't enter my head that they wouldn't have clothing. Oh dear . . . you must allow me to reimburse you out of my wages.'

She was filled with relief when he smiled, saying quietly, 'You'll need your wage, which is little enough to manage on. I'm sure the trust can absorb the cost. How are you managing with Captain Sangster?'

She laughed. 'You'll have to ask him that. He's very brave, and I feel so sorry for his plight. I also like him. He has a sense of humour and doesn't feel pity for himself. All the same, he's a bit of a challenge, since I never know whether he's teasing me or being serious. I'll do my best to help make him comfortable, of course. Mr Beamish is very good with him.'

'They went through the war together. Beamish saved his life at the front. He came looking for him after he returned home to discover that his own wife had become a victim of the flu.'

Livia had not known. Poor Beamish, she thought, and felt so very glad that her own kin had survived it. Perhaps her prayer had helped after all.

A little later, she, along with the children, copious bags, a fruitcake and a freshly made loaf of bread donated by Connie from the Foxglove House larder, were deposited at the cottage. She had to admit that Mr Stone had been generous with the trust's money.

The little Christmas tree was in a bucket in the sitting room. She'd put some cotton wool on the branches to resemble snow, and had made an angel out of a paper lace doily for the top. It looked a little bare, but pretty, and the children could make some paper lanterns to hang on it.

After she lit the kitchen stove and collected the milk from the shelf in the porch, she went inside to find the children sitting on the settee. She smiled at them, feeling slightly awkward, because the reunion had not gone as she expected. 'Haven't you been upstairs to see your bedrooms yet?'

When the children looked at each other doubtfully, she said, 'You have a bedroom each, and you don't have to ask permission to go anywhere inside the house.'

'For ourselves . . . a whole bedroom each?' Chad said.

'They're only small, but if you go up those stairs you will find your rooms through the two doors on the right. I sleep in the one on the other side of the landing.'

'How will we know which one belongs to us?'

'Go and look. You'll know. Take a bag up with you so we can put your stuff in the chest of drawers.'

There was also a large trunk in the hall, which was too heavy to take up by herself. She'd unpack the contents later, when she had time.

She followed the children up to the rooms, which she'd freshened up with a couple of coats of whitewash. Esmé's room had a gaudy pink patchwork quilt Connie had bought from the market, and a kidney-shaped dressing table with a glass top and a front curtain of printed pink rosebuds that matched the curtains. There was a rag doll sitting in a wickerwork chair, which had also been given a coat of white paint.

'Florence made the doll for you.'

'For me?'

'You must thank her when you see her.'

Nodding, Esmé smiled and picked the doll up. 'She's pretty.'

'Isn't she?' Between them, the three women had crocheted squares and made a blanket quilt for Chad's room, in dark blue, red and white. Livia had found a telescope in the attic, polished it and set it up at the window. 'You'll be able to look at the stars through it,' she said.

'You might see the man on the moon,' Esmé said, giving a bit of a cough. Emptying the bags, Livia sorted out the clothing and folded it into drawers, thankful that Mr Stone had been practical in his choices. There were at least two changes for everyday, flannel smocks, a pretty velvet dress with a lace collar for Esmé, and for Chad, a suit for best and sturdy boots.

Chad's mind wasn't on clothing, though. He swung the telescope round, then shouted, 'I can see a big red bird in the garden. He looks jolly fierce.'

'Where?' Esmé said, joining him and jiggling up and down with impatience.

'Down there,' and he handed the telescope to Esmé.

Livia smiled when she looked out of the window. 'It's a chicken. I'd better go down and shoo her back into her pen, else the fox will have her for dinner tonight. Then we won't have any eggs for breakfast.'

'Can I do it?' the twins asked in unison.

'We'll do it together in case the others have escaped. We don't want to scare them.'

Only two of the five were roaming the garden. The children took a handful of bran each and enticed the chickens back into their pen. They'd got out through a hole in their coop. 'See if there's a hammer and nails in the shed, Chad.'

He came back with both, and an old tin tray, saying in manly fashion, 'The wood's rotten. We need another piece.'

'Chickens need . . . new home.'

They turned to gaze at Richard Sangster, who was rugged up and leaning on Beamish.

'I thought you had a meeting with Mr Stone. Have you followed us?'

'We did. Simon only wanted my signature . . . he's w . . . with Pa now.'

Beamish smiled at them all and shrugged. 'He was too curious to wait, and insisted I bring him.'

'You walked all that way in this cold wind? I could have

taken the children upstairs to meet you if you'd wanted, Mr Sangster.'

'Room . . . like prison.'

'He needed to get some fresh air, so I drove him in the Rolls.'

'Hah! Call that . . . driving.'

'Children, this is Captain Richard Sangster, for whom I work. And this is Mr Beamish, who looks after him.'

Esmé clung to her leg. Richard held out a hand and Chad took it. 'Your hand is shaking, Sir,' he said. 'Are you cold?'

'The war . . . made me ill.'

'Were you shot?'

'Chad, that's rude.'

'No, not rude . . . curiosity. War seems . . . an adventure to a boy. Yes . . . shot head and back . . . uncover scar for inspection, Beamish.'

Beamish removed Richard's hat and Chad's eyes widened. 'Crikey Moses! You were jolly lucky, Sir. Have you still got the bullet? Can I see it?'

A wry smile twisted Richard's mouth. 'No bullet . . . I'm afraid. I should have . . . ducked . . . but didn't see it coming. Beamish caught one in his arse and couldn't sit down for a week. S . . . sorry, Livia.'

'How do you manage to look innocent? Arse yourself, Richard Sangster.'

He laughed.

'It was merely a splinter, but it's not a war wound I can brag about,' Beamish said.

When Chad began to laugh, Richard and Beamish grinned at each other.

'Arse is a rude word,' Esmé scolded. 'Chad got the cane for saying that, and he cried.'

'It didn't really hurt, and I wasn't crying, I had something in my eye,' Chad said quickly.

'I beg your pardon, Miss Esmé. A man shouldn't speak like that in the company of . . . young ladies. Help you build henhouse . . . Beamish and me, next week. I'll . . . instruct. You and Beams . . . do the work. All right, Chad?'

'I'll say, Sir,' Chad said, adopting a man-of-the-house air.

'We don't want the fox to get at the chickens. In the meantime, I'll patch it up with this tin tray I saw in the shed.' He set to with a will, hammering nails through a rusty tray and rotten wood. It wouldn't last long.

'That's . . . the ticket.'

Livia was worried about Richard being out in the cold. 'Would you like to come in and have a cup of tea. The stove is lit, and it won't take me long to put the kettle on and put a match to the fire in the sitting room.'

'Good of you, Livia. Give me your arm. Beamish, fetch my . . . gift.'

Richard was trembling all over from the effort he'd made walking into the house. Livia seated him in a wing chair, struck a match and lit the fire. When she looked up at him his eyes caught hers. It was like looking at his mother; he had the same fragile vulnerability to his face.

'Go and see where Beamish . . . has got to,' he said to the children, and they ran off to do his bidding.

'The room won't take long to warm up,' she said, feeling suddenly awkward without the children as a barrier between them. She straightened up.

'Don't fuss over me, Livia. I've been in . . . colder places.'

She smiled. 'I didn't expect you to be quite so different. You were strong and healthy when you left . . . younger, of course, but less mature.'

'I've aged about a century in the last few years. I expected you to be the same too . . . a child bobbing . . . around the house in an apron and cap with dustpan and brush . . . trying to please everyone at the same time. I felt . . . sorry for you.'

'Now the boot is on the other foot. Hush, don't talk so much, Richard Sangster, you're running out of breath.'

His mouth twisted into a grimace.

Guilt filled her. 'I'm sorry . . . I didn't mean that how it sounded.'

'I know that too. Do you really feel sorry for me?'

She nodded. 'Yes . . . I suppose I do.'

'You're sweet, Livia.' He reached out to gently touch her cheek, but jerked his hand away when they heard the children.

Esmé had a purring black kitten with white socks, nose and whiskers cuddled in her arms. She wore an ear-to-ear smile on her face. 'His name is Whiskers. Chad's got a dog.'

Another two mouths to feed, Livia thought glumly, as a hairy white dog with brown patches came in, dragging Chad along on the end of a leather leash. 'He's fully-grown and yaps a bit. Beamish got him from the market. He's house-trained and will keep the rats down.'

'Watch this, Livia,' Chad said proudly. 'Sit!'

The dog sat and gazed up at him, his short tail sweeping the carpet.

'Can we keep him? Please, Livia. It's a moving-in present from the captain.'

A *fait accompli* if ever she'd heard one. Livia looked at the odd creature with its tufty hair, which already seemed part of Chad, and she didn't have the heart to say no. 'What's his name going to be, Chad?'

'Bertie.'

She offered Richard an accusing look when Bertie lifted his leg against the door frame. 'I thought you said he was house-trained.'

Richard passed the look on to Beamish, who shrugged slightly and turned an innocent glance through the window. 'That's what I was told.'

'I imagine he's just putting his scent around his new home. I daresay . . . Connie will give you the scraps for them, so they won't cost anything to feed.'

Beamish had a box in his arms. 'What's in the box? Not more animals, surely,' Livia asked.

'Christmas decorations,' Beamish said. 'I'll hang the garlands up, and the children can put the toy soldiers and baubles on the tree. That will make it look more like Christmas.'

'Come on, Bertie,' Chad said. 'I'll show you where we sleep.'

It was time to put her foot down. 'He'll sleep in the kitchen.'

Beamish placed the box on the settee. 'There's a basket for him in the car. Come on, Chad, we'll go and find it.'

'Would you mind moving that trunk in the hall, Mr Beamish? It needs to go upstairs on the landing, under the window will do.'

Esmé went with them. 'I'll show you where.'

Richard smiled warmly at her. 'You're not angry about the cat and dog, are you?'

Her cheeks began to glow. This man could charm the birds from their nests if he put his mind to it. 'Of course not, they've never had an animal to look after, so it will be good for them. It's going to be the best Christmas ever, now we're together again. I can't thank you enough.'

'I'll think of some way . . . I know. The next time I visit I'll bring . . . some mistletoe.'

He laughed when she blushed. 'Why, Miss Livia Carr, I do believe you've never . . . been kissed . . . before.'

Immediately, her thoughts went to Denton Elliot and the kiss on the train. A lot Richard Sangster knew! Trying to hide her grin, she said with mock severity, 'Don't get too personal. I'll go and make the tea.'

'Wait . . . this is for you.' He took a small carriage clock from his pocket and handed it to her.

Tears came to her eyes when she saw the pink enamelled face and the little monkeys clinging to the hands. 'This belonged to your mother.'

'Yes . . . I bought it for her birthday, just before I went away to war. It's a little too feminine for my taste, and I thought you might like to have it . . . a Christmas gift. It might amuse the children as well as tell you the time.'

'Yes . . . I would like to have it, and I'll treasure it as much as she did.'

Mrs Sangster had counted the minutes until her son had come home. Now, Livia would look at that same clock and count them until he left again – this time for good. It was too sad to contemplate.

'Richard . . . I'm so sorry. Your mother was so looking forward to your return. I'm glad she didn't . . .'

'No tears, Livia, what's done is done. It was dashed bad luck copping this, and just when the war was almost over, that's all . . . Oh, damn convention to hell! I'll kiss you without mistletoe, if you'd allow me to. Or you can kiss me.'

When she stooped to kiss his forehead she found her face cupped in his trembling hands and drawn down to his. She didn't resist when his mouth touched against hers and lingered there for a few tender moments. When he drew away, his eyes gazed into hers, intensely blue. There had been a world of longing in that kiss, and she'd enjoyed it. But she could feel the need in him to survive, and there was an incredible sadness inside her because they both knew he wouldn't.

She set the little clock on the mantelpiece, keeping her back to him in case he saw the tears in her eyes. 'I don't think it would be a good idea to do that too often, do you?'

'Probably not. I've made you cry, haven't I? Was the kiss that bad? I'm out of practice.'

'It was the best of kisses.'

'Then stop snuffling. How many times have you been kissed before?'

'Once.'

He chuckled. 'So you're experienced. First kisses are an agony, aren't they? You never quite know if you're going about it right. Tell me about it?'

'It was a stranger on a train, a soldier leaving for the front . . . it was very innocent and sweet. He just needed to kiss somebody goodbye, and I was handy.'

Wild horses wouldn't allow her to tell him it had been his friend, Denton Elliot . . . that he'd taken her by surprise and she knew now that she'd have welcomed a longer, less innocent kiss.

His father had told her that Denton had got his discharge and was doing his formal surgery training in a London hospital under a distinguished surgeon. He'd probably forgotten the girl on the train by now, and she wondered if he'd be home for Christmas.

'That soldier probably kept that kiss with him, and it gave him a reason to keep going.'

His speech had barely faltered once, and she encouraged him with, 'Why?'

'People who are stressed cling to symbols and luck. They p . . . provide hope when there is little left to hope for. Even if you never meet that soldier again, that kiss on the train will always be in your memory. You'll remember him at odd times, and without even trying, and wonder what happened to him. He'll do the same with you.'

Livia knew what had happened. Denton had survived and she was glad of it.

Hearing the kettle lid begin to rattle furiously, she drew in a breath to banish her tears before she turned. 'Would it embarrass you if I said you have a rather romantic nature for a man?'

'Yes . . . I imagine it would.'

She smiled widely. 'You have a rather romantic nature for a man, Richard Sangster.'

He chuckled. 'I fell into that one, didn't I? Go and make the tea . . . and if you happen to have any of c . . . cook's gingerbread, a large s . . . slice.'

Seven

Christmas came. The day was cold with an occasional flake of snow in the air.

'It won't come to much,' Matthew Bugg said, gazing up at the sky with a knowledgeable eye.

Now the war was over, the church was full of people giving thanks. The family and staff attended as one body. The Sangsters sat in the front pew, their staff behind.

Major Henry, Captain Sangster and Sergeant Beamish all wore uniform, as was their right, since, officially, none of them had yet been discharged.

Richard leaned heavily on Beamish's arm and was helped to his seat. He didn't seem to notice the averted eyes, or the curiosity in the various glances that did go his way. He smiled pleasantly at those who knew and greeted him.

Towards the end of the service Livia saw signs of tension in Richard's face, and he began to tremble. Beamish leaned forward and whispered something in Major Henry's ear. As soon as the Amen was said, Beamish carried Richard out to the car, and they drove away.

'The car is coming back, isn't it, Henry?' Rosemary asked, her displeasure at the thought that it might not written plainly on her face.

'As soon as Beamish gets Richard settled down to rest, m' dear. In the meantime we can walk. It's not far.'

'It's two miles and I'm wearing court shoes. Everywhere is so far from everywhere else in this Godforsaken hole. When are we going back to London? We're missing all the parties and celebrations.'

She sounded so peevish that Henry turned a frown in her direction. 'My son has just returned home. He's ill. Celebrating in such circumstances is unseemly.'

'So is wallowing in self-pity over him, since it won't change anything.'

Livia had never met anyone with less sympathy for her fellow human beings than the new Mrs Sangster.

'Can't we have a New Year's party . . . do something to liven the place up?'

'Enough, Rosemary. Allow me to enjoy the season in the company of my son,' he said wearily, and began to walk away, leaving her to follow.

For a moment she hesitated, then she followed after him. Her arm slid through his. 'Don't be cross, Henry. I was only suggesting we could invite a few people to dinner.'

'I know what you were suggesting.'

'Anyone would think you were ashamed of me.'

'Oh . . . for God's sake,' he said, under his breath, and gave her a measured look, as though he was considering it.

'I miss the theatre so. I wanted to attend Lionel Crawley's New Year party. He promised I could sing to his guests; they will all be from the theatre, and he's casting for a new show. It's an audition, of sorts, really. I won't get a chance like this again . . . a talent scout from an American film studio will be there. Imagine that. I might be discovered!'

'Then by all means don't miss the opportunity to be *discovered*. You don't need me along to hold your hand.'

'You won't mind if I go to London by myself then?'

'Not in the least . . . in fact, I'll ask Beamish to run you up in the car.'

The look she gave him was arch. 'The least you could do is to pretend you'll miss me, darling.'

'Why pretend anything?' he said shortly. 'Go if you want to. Now, can we please change the subject?'

Livia exchanged a glance with Connie. It sounded as though the major couldn't wait to be rid of his new wife.

It was half an hour before the car returned.

'Is Richard all right?' the major immediately asked Beamish.

'He had a disturbed night and he's tired, Sir. He'll soon pick up after a sleep. Matthew Bugg is keeping an eye on him till I get back.'

They piled into the car. Rosemary's perfect oval face was expertly made up and framed by grey fur. She gazed out of the window, giving the occasional sigh, like a misunderstood and martyred wife.

Her husband, grey-haired and handsome, was behind the wheel. Outwardly, they were a perfect couple, except Rosemary was a lot younger. Yet it seemed that now she'd got what she wanted, she was still dissatisfied . . . while marriage had not curbed the major's roving eye.

Beamish gave Florence a smile as he seated himself next to her, and she blushed. The children leaned against Livia. They were still clingy, but there was a sense of excitement about them because it was Christmas.

Their little Christmas tree was nothing when compared to the splendour of the one at Foxglove House. It stood in the corner of the drawing room, frosted with cotton-wool snow, glass icicles and tinsel. The light caught the baubles as they twisted and turned, sending out dazzling gleams. Gifts were stacked underneath.

Connie disappeared into the kitchen with Florence. Soon delicious smells began to waft through the house. Livia set the table, with holly arranged down the centre. If she'd expected any help from Rosemary she was disappointed; the lady of the house arranged herself in a chair by the fire and sipped sherry.

Richard came down in time for dinner. The major carved the turkey and made a toast to his son, then they tucked in. Afterwards, the gifts were opened.

The children were almost overwhelmed by receiving so many

gaily-wrapped parcels: there were knitted jumpers from Florence, socks and scarves, jigsaw puzzles and a toy aeroplane.

Richard had bought Chad a bicycle.

'How absolutely spiffing, I can't wait to ride it,' Chad exclaimed, giving Richard a look brimming over with hero worship.

'You can have a quick dash around the hall on it,' Richard told him. 'I'll come out and watch in a minute. Everyone is welcome to attend the event.'

Everyone except Rosemary Sangster joined in the fun as Chad wobbled around the hall, a self-conscious grin on his face.

Esmé received a doll's pram. Its superior-looking occupant had blue eyes, dark fluttering eyelashes and real hair.

It struck Livia that the pair were open to influences beyond her control when Esmé exclaimed, her voice a childish gush, 'She's so sweet . . . thank you so very much.'

They gathered round the piano to sing Christmas carols, and Rosemary Sangster suddenly came to life, her voice putting them all to shame. As a result, the voices of the others faded away. She gazed around at everyone with an entirely self-satisfied look on her face when they applauded, then said, 'Goodnight,' and left the room.

It was a blatant signal to everyone who had a home to go to, and there was a scramble to find coats, hats and scarves.

'Can I ride home, Livia?'

'Not in the dark, Chad, the bicycle can go on the back of the car. Mr Beamish will take us.'

'Are these things ours to keep?' Esmé whispered.

'Yes, and I'll expect you to write thank you letters to everyone. Place all your gifts in the pram, and we'll put it in the car.'

When they arrived at the cottage, Bertie set up a racket and leapt all over them. The kitten mewed pathetically when Esmé picked him up and made a fuss of him. There was a sense of homecoming.

Beamish stayed for a cup of tea after the children went to bed. They sat in the kitchen where it was warm. 'I enjoyed today,' he said.

'Yes, so did I. I was worried about Richard in church, though. He's not as strong as he'd like us to think.'

'The captain has these turns. Sometimes he'll go for days, then he thinks he's getting stronger and overdoes things.'

'Is Chad being a nuisance?'

'Chad's good for him. He has a child's honesty and Richard tells him little things about the war. It's good that he can talk of it.'

'Richard is a hero to Chad.'

'Make no mistake; the captain *is* a hero, Miss Carr. Ask any of the men who fought with him. He kept going, though his condition was threatening to let him down. He brought many of his men through and they looked up to him.'

'Including you.'

He nodded. 'Things could have been different for him if he'd sought medical help earlier. As it turned out he was in the wrong place at the wrong time.'

'And you were there for him. I'm sorry your wife didn't make it through the flu outbreak. That must have been hard to come home to.'

He nodded. 'Doreen was a nice woman, ordinary and good-hearted . . . but life goes on and we cope as best we can. We didn't have any children.' He smiled. 'I haven't got a great deal, just a small flat over an ironmonger's shop in Parkstone, but it's more than many have got. There's enough profit in the shop for a couple, and my father runs it. After my job finishes . . . well, perhaps I can start over.'

There was a small charged silence. 'And then?'

He shrugged. 'Expand. Repair bicycles, install a petrol pump for motorists, and perhaps buy a charabanc and take people on day trips to the seaside. I hope I'll find a nice woman and we'll make a life together. I'd like a family. What about you, Miss Carr? What are your plans for the future?'

'More of the same, I suppose. The late Mrs Sangster made generous arrangements for me through the Sinclair trust, and Major Henry and Richard endorsed it. They have been kind towards me and I'm grateful to them. I'll work at the house and live in the cottage with my sister and brother until Chad has finished his education.'

'You don't want to get married yourself?'

'Who would want me with two children to support?'

'You'd be surprised, a lovely young woman like you.' He stood, shuffling his feet. 'Would you do me a favour?'

'As long as you're not going to propose marriage to me.'

For a moment he looked startled, then he laughed. 'I can see the notion has no appeal. Well I don't blame you since I'm no oil painting.'

'Actually you have a nice face, Mr Beamish. You look dependable and trustworthy. We never see ourselves as others do.'

'That's true.' He cleared his throat. 'I wondered if you'd find out what Florence thinks of me.'

'Do you need to ask when she blushes every time you go near her?'

'I don't want to make a fool of myself.'

'There are worse things than making a fool of yourself, Mr Beamish. If you want Florence, be positive. She's straightforward and will appreciate knowing where she stands. You'd better not leave matters for too long, though. I have a notion that Matthew Bugg has his eye on her,' she lied, in a moment of mischief.

'The devil, he has!'

Livia grinned to herself after he left. She washed the cups, turned down the light and went to check on the children. There was a suspicious bulge under Chad's eiderdown. Peeling back the corner revealed a wagging tail. 'All right, just this once, seeing that it's Christmas.'

Esmé coughed in her sleep. Holding the candle high, Livia gazed down at her. Esmé's cheeks were flushed, and she tired easily. She laid the back of her hand against her sister's cheek and found it was slightly moist with perspiration. Her new doll occupied the chair and Whiskers was asleep in the pram. He opened one eye, looked at her then shut it again.

Livia stooped to kiss Esmé's cheek, reminding herself she should get the children checked over by Dr Elliot. She would ask him the next time he came to see Richard.

The atmosphere lightened a little when Rosemary Sangster left for London.

When the major wasn't with Richard he wandered around aimlessly, getting underfoot and putting the routine of the house out.

Connie scoffed, 'He never did know what to do with himself here. It's not as if Major Henry was born to be a country gentleman, and he's not really needed here. He likes the high life, and the attention of women. I reckon he should have gone back to London with *her*. At least they have that sort of thing in common. And he has his club to go to.'

After lunch the major decided to walk over to see the reverend. 'Wish him a happy new year . . . it's the done thing, you know.'

'Don't forget to wear your scarf, Major. It's cold outside.'

'I will. Where are the children?'

'In my sitting room.'

'I thought I might take them with me for a walk. They must get bored.'

It was a kind thought. 'Chad might like to go; he's got his new bicycle with him and is dying to show off on it to someone. I don't want Esmé to go out, though, she's got a cold coming on, I think. I'm going to ask Doctor Elliot to take a look at her the next time he calls. I'll ask Chad if he'd like to keep you company, shall I?'

'Do.' His face crinkled into a roguish smile. 'Tell Chad he'll be doing me a favour. He'll provide me with an excuse to leave when the man gets boring. Besides, the reverend is going to teach the boy Latin, so Chad will have the chance to look him over. We might go to the stables afterwards and inspect the horses.'

Chad jumped at the chance to go out with the major and swiftly donned his balaclava, scarf and gloves. He wove back and forth down the drive, showing off for the major who marched in an upright soldierly manner after him.

The doorbell rang later in the afternoon.

A smile touched Livia's mouth when she saw Denton Elliot standing there.

'You haven't changed a bit,' she said.

'Neither have you.' It was obvious he'd forgotten her name because he put a finger over her lips and smiled. 'Hello, Miss Pheasant Feather.'

She raised an eyebrow and laughed, feeling instantly at home with him. 'Don't be ridiculous. I knew you'd forget my name.'

'I have not. If it isn't that then you must be Miss Olivia Carr, mostly called Livia, though being instructed to call you Miss Carr, in a rather spinsterish manner.' He placed his hands against his heart. 'I'd forgotten what a beauty you are, though, Miss Carr.'

'Your memory is outstanding if you can remember the exact wording of a conversation all that time ago.'

'It is, if the subject matter is worth remembering. Are you going to make me wait on the doorstep in the cold?'

She opened the door wider. 'I'm sorry, do come in,' and she closed the door behind him when he did. 'You're exactly like your father. I think the pair of you have Irish blood and have kissed the blarney stone. I was expecting him to call in on Captain Sangster today, and wondered if he'd look at my sister while he was here.'

'I can manage that. What's wrong with her?'

'She has a cough, though it's not much of one, so it's not urgent. I expect the captain will enjoy seeing you. He doesn't often get visitors of his own age. Follow me.'

'How has he been?' he asked, following her up the stairs.

'Pleased to be home, I think. He rarely complains, and is very kind, sweet and thoughtful.'

'He seems to have made a good impression on you,' he said rather drily. 'I was talking about his health.'

'I'm hardly an expert on his health, Doctor Elliot. Oh, dear, I do hope I don't get you and your father mixed up.'

'On the train I distinctly remember asking you to call me Denton, and you did. What's changed?'

She blushed. 'On the train it was different. You were a stranger and I didn't expect to see you again. And what's more, I didn't know you were a doctor.'

'What difference would that have made, when I'm also a man?'

'I don't know . . . doctors know more about people than they know about themselves. You don't expect to be kissed by an anonymous one on a train.'

'So . . . you intended to kiss and run.'

'You know very well it was the other way round. You did all the kissing and running. Behave yourself. You're here professionally, and I'm the housekeeper . . . Doctor Elliot.'

He grinned. 'You can call me Doctor Anonymous then, though it sounds a bit on the racy side.'

'I can see you're going to give me trouble. Don't you dare say another word,' she warned him, and knocked at the door.

Richard was sitting in the chair, dozing. He was shaved and fully dressed, Beamish had seen to that before he left for London, where he had business to conduct with a mutual friend. He'd be back on the evening train.

'I must say you look better than the last time I saw you, Richard. Are you up to having a visitor.'

Richard's eyes snapped open and an unbelieving smile sped across his face. 'You came at just the right time. I was bored, and about to ring for Livia to come and annoy me.'

'Oh . . . and how does the young lady do that?'

'She argues with me a lot. But you haven't met Miss Carr before, have you?'

'I most certainly have . . . on a train. I nearly flattened her with my kit bag.'

Richard's gaze sharpened in on her and he gave a faint grin when she laughed. 'You didn't tell me the soldier you met on the train was Denton Elliot.'

'You didn't ask for a name, and it was none of your business.'

Denton laughed. 'I didn't have her to myself for long . . . the train was crammed full of soldiers and sailors.' He opened his bag and took out a stethoscope. 'I'm here in place of my father, and I'll be interested to see how my stitching held up. The very fact that you're still alive tells me the crack in your skull healed, though it was touch and go for a while.'

'So, the ghoul who poked and prodded me in the field hospital was you, Dents?'

'Yes . . .' He ran his fingers along the scar and made a noncommittal but doctorly humming noise. 'Not that you recognized me at the time.'

'No wonder, when you have a face that would shatter glass.'

His voice thickened as he choked out, 'Dents, old boy, it's been a long time. How the devil are you?'

'I'm only just holding up under the schedule of surgical training, but generally I'm hotsy-totsy. Open your shirt.'

'My hands shake when I concentrate.'

'I need to see how badly.'

'If you were a dog with fleas you'd beg me to give you a pat.'

Denton laughed at that. 'You still have a way with words, I see, but it's hardly a description for the official report. I thought I asked you to open your shirt, so get on with it.'

'He's shy,' Livia said. 'I'll go and make some tea . . . will half-an-hour be long enough?'

When Denton glanced up at her, his darkly greenish gaze brimming with amusement, her heart gave a serious flutter. 'Fifteen minutes will do,' he said. 'I don't want to put you to any bother.'

'It's my job, and no bother at all. There's some walnut cake to go with it. Besides, I'm sure your patient will want some, he always does, and the staff spoil him.'

Denton came down later, listened to Esmé's chest, then transferred his stethoscope to the girl's ears so she could listen to her own heart. A smile spread across her face. 'I can hear myself go boompity-boomp.'

'There's nothing wrong with your hearing then.'

He took his time examining her before asking, almost casually, 'How long was she in the orphanage?'

'Seven years.'

'And her appetite?'

'Not very good at the moment . . . and she tires easily and perspires at night. Chad told me she'd had the cough for about two months before they came to me.'

She was alarmed when Denton said, 'I'd like my father to take a look at her, but I think we might need some tests done before we can make a proper diagnosis.'

'What do you think it is?'

His eyes engaged hers. 'It would be better to wait until the tests are complete.'

'You must suspect it's something serious else you wouldn't want tests doing. I thought it was just an ordinary cough that had persisted.'

'There's no such thing as an ordinary persistent cough, Livia. And I have to take into account that your sister spent several years in a crowded orphanage.'

'Tell me, please, Denton. I don't want to live in suspense.'

'All right, but I doubt if you'll thank me. I hope I'm wrong, my dear, but there's a possibility she's suffering from tuberculosis. If she is, you'll all have to be tested, and if the tests are positive, arrangements must be made.'

'What sort of arrangements?'

He shrugged. 'Isolation, warmth, a routine of rest, good nourishing food, fresh air and gentle exercise.'

Eyes wide and her heart full of dread, Livia stared at him and whispered, 'You're talking about an institution, aren't you? That's not fair . . . Esmé's only just settled with me.'

'It hasn't got to be an institution. It could be the cottage. In fact, it would be ideal, and much better for her to have people she loves around her. See, I knew you'd start building this up in your mind.'

Livia felt stretched in all directions as worries darted through her mind. Would she still be able to live in the cottage . . . be able to work? What about Chad? He might have the disease too. She said out loud, 'Who will look after the captain?'

'He'll manage with Beamish, and they can hire someone else to take your place for six months, if need be. Now, stop imagining the worst and let's get past the first hurdle. Get your coat. I'll take your sister to see my father now.' He fished in his bag and came up with a muslin mask, handing it to Esmé. 'Here you are, Poppet. You've got an infection in your chest, so this will stop the germs from escaping when you cough, and other people catching them.'

'Am I going to die?' she said, her bottom lip trembling.

'Lord no, whatever gave you that daft idea?' He fished inside his bag and came out with a piece of barley sugar wrapped in cellophane. 'This is for my second favourite girl.'

Livia sent Florence to keep an eye on Richard. 'Tell him

I'll be gone for only a short while. And tell the major and Chad if they're back from their walk before I get home.'

'This is an awful start to the New Year,' she said.

Denton's hand covered hers for a moment. His palms were warm, his long, slim fingers a light caress over hers as he gave her a quick smile and reminded her, 'It's not the New Year, it's the end of the old year. Things will get better, I promise. Probably in half-an-hour's time when my father's had his say on the matter.'

Eight

Despite Denton's optimism, things didn't get better.

Richard had gone to bed early that night.

Esmé was asleep in Livia's sitting room, her small face hidden behind her mask. Chad was poring over a book.

He had been made aware of the situation, and he took it calmly when she told him, 'Captain Sangster thinks it might be a good idea to pack you off to boarding school early if Esmé gets the all clear. He thinks he can get you into the same school he and Doctor Denton attended, though you'll have to sit the exam first. You'd be home for holidays, of course.'

'What about my Latin lessons? The reverend said I seem to be grasping what he's teaching me, though it's hard. I want to be a doctor and Doctor Denton said I will need Latin.'

She smiled. Chad was influenced by the men around him. It was no bad thing, considering the calibre of them. In particular, Richard, Denton and Beamish were the finest of men, and they seemed to be organizing everything between them on her behalf.

'I had no idea you were aiming so high, Chad.'

'I don't see why not. Captain Sangster said I should take advantage of the offer of a scholarship, since not everyone gets the chance to go to a good school like King's Charter. I've been trying to improve my manners and be polite. And Doctor Denton said he'd take me under his wing if I wanted to become a surgeon when the time came. He said by that time he'll be old, and would have had plenty of experience.'

Denton would age well, like his father, she thought. And Richard? No, she wouldn't think about that. 'You'll be going to prep school first, and they will teach you Latin there. You can always have extra lessons in the holiday, if you need to. I expect you'll soon catch up. You don't mind going then?'

'A bit . . . but I know you'll look after Esmé until I'm old enough to do so.'

She hugged him then, despite his boyish resistance to anything he considered sissy. 'Chad, my love, you take your responsibilities too seriously. You and Esmé are my sister and brother. I love you both, and we're responsible for each other, though being the eldest, I hope you'll regard me as someone you can confide in as well. If you hate the idea of going to a boarding school, we'll find some other way.'

'Captain Sangster said that sometimes a chap has to do what's right for others, whether he likes it or not. I won't mind boarding school, honest, and I'll soon make friends. I miss having Billy as a friend. I just want Esmé to get better.'

She nodded. 'What are you reading?'

'*The Jungle Book*. Rudyard Kipling wrote it. It's a story called "Rikki-Tikki-Tavi". He's a brave mongoose who kills a cobra. Captain Sangster said I can borrow any book I want, but must show it to him first in case it's not suitable.'

'I'll leave you to it then. I'm going to clear the dishes from the dining room now. I shouldn't be more than half-an-hour.'

He nodded, his eyes already going back to the book.

As soon as she'd finished her work, Beamish would drive them back to the cottage. Richard didn't like them walking through the cold darkness of winter evenings.

When the phone rang, Livia answered it. It was Rosemary Sangster. 'Get Henry for me, and quick about it,' she said.

Major Henry had been drinking fairly heavily, and he raised an eyebrow when she said, 'The telephone call is for you, Major Sangster. It's your wife.'

'Tell her I'm not here.' He draped a heavy arm over her shoulder, his hand dangling an inch from her breast.

'Excuse me, Sir, I have to get my work done,' she said, and she slipped from under him and walked away.

He weaved across the hall, picked up the receiver and said angrily, 'It's about time you rang me. Been enjoying yourself without me, have you?

'What do you mean you're going to America? You know I can't leave Richard . . .' There was a chink of crystal decanter against his glass as he refilled it.

Livia walked across the hall and gently closed the door as the major began to shout. Like most of the rooms in the house, the door to the study was stout, the walls solid and the carpet thick. The room was almost soundproof, and it was best not to allow everyone to overhear Major Henry's business.

She had cleared the table and buffet and was sweeping the crumbs from the table when he came in, his face flushed. Swaying on his feet, he said, voice slurring, 'Any whisky in here? None left in the study.' He gazed at his glass then moved to where she stood. 'Well?'

'Only what's in the decanter, Major.'

'Bring it to the study, at least it's warm there.' He wandered off, leaving her to follow. Surely he could have carried the whisky decanter by himself.

He closed the door behind them when she went in, and took the decanter from her. Slopping the whisky into his glass he swallowed it down. 'The damned bitch said she's leaving me for a film producer . . .'

'I'm sorry.'

'Sorry . . . why should you be sorry?' He put an arm round her when she went to walk past him, drew her close. 'You're a pretty little thing, Livia. Have a drink.' He held the tumbler to her mouth and tipped it. She swallowed what went into her mouth and gagged. She pushed the glass away.

'You wouldn't deny a man a kiss for New Year luck, would you?'

'I'd rather not.'

'Rather not? Beggars can't be choosers, my dear.' His fleshy mouth covered hers and a wet tongue was inserted into her mouth. When she began to struggle he took her hand and slipped it into the opening of his trousers. 'Come on, Livia.

I've been good to you and your family. Just a little bit of hanky-panky to make the old major feel like a man.'

The major had kept himself fit and he kept her hand there while he rotated against it with his pelvis. She panicked when he hardened in her palm and tried to shout for help.

Borne to the floor and kept there by his body, one of his hands went over her mouth while the other fondled under her skirt. Her drawers tightened as his hand bunched round the fabric, and he ripped them.

'Stop it . . . please stop it!' she begged, her voice muffled.

'Too late, old girl. You've brought the old man alive and he won't be vanquished. Relax, my dear. If you're good I'll give you a nice bonus in your wage packet . . .'

Relax – when he had thrust himself into her and she felt as though she was being split down the middle. Horror of horrors, he was grunting like a pig as he kept thrusting into her. Tears ran down her cheeks as she tried to shove him away, but she'd lost the strength in her limbs.

It was soon over.

'Sorry . . . so sorry, m'dear, I didn't mean to hurt you . . .' The major relaxed in a shuddering heap on top of her, his breathing harsh.

There was a shout . . . 'Livia, where are you?'

Chad! He shouldn't see her like this. Using all her strength Livia managed to heave the major's body aside and pulled her skirt down. She shuddered in disgust when she noticed he'd passed out. Shakily, she got to her feet and tidied her clothes. Then she burst into tears – she couldn't help herself.

'Livia! What were you doing on the floor?' Chad gazed at the major, bewildered, then his eyes widened. 'Is he dead . . . have you killed him?'

Just at that moment Livia wished he were dead. 'He's had too much to drink. He's passed out and I can't wake him.'

'Why are you crying?'

'A gust of wind came down the chimney and blew smoke into my eyes.'

'Esmé is awake. Can we go home now? Bertie will be hungry, and the cook has given me some scraps to take for him.'

The sooner she got out of the house, the better. 'Yes . . .

Go upstairs and tell Mr Beamish while I find our coats and wrap Esmé up warm. I'll just take the dustpan to the kitchen.'

When she came back out with Esmé in her arms, Beamish was gazing down at the major. He looked up at her, at her dishevelled state, and his eyes narrowed. 'Are you all right?'

She avoided looking at him. Her ripped underwear was dangling from the elastic waistband, and she was sore, sticky, and bruised where he'd chaffed her between her thighs. She was worried that the remnants of her undergarments might drop to the floor. 'Of course I am . . . why shouldn't I be?'

'No reason, except you're trembling, and you look as though you've been crying. Your breath smells of whisky.'

She'd start crying all over again if he kept this up. 'I'll thank you to keep your observations to yourself,' she snapped, then immediately felt guilty. 'I'm sorry. I didn't mean to snap. I'm just tired. I want to go home, have a wash before I go to bed. I'm looking forward to a good night's sleep.'

She wanted several washes, in fact, and after that she wanted to sleep for as long as it took to forget what the major had done to her. And she wanted to gargle the taste of his whisky from her mouth. The thought brought the urge to retch . . . something she hoped she could keep from doing before she got back to the cottage.

Beamish shrugged. 'I'll move the major when I get back if he hasn't moved himself. Allow me to carry the youngster to the car for you. Take the torch and light our path, Chad.'

She stopped herself from retching long enough to get outside, where she rushed into the shrubbery and was sick.

Depositing the children in the car, Beamish returned, the ever-ready flashlight darting from side to side until he located her. He handed her his handkerchief.

'It must be something I ate.'

'Are you all right?' He gave the faintest of smiles. 'I don't think the major would appreciate you vomiting in his car.'

It would be poetic justice, she thought, with a sudden burst of anger. 'I'm all right now, Mr Beamish. I would appreciate it if you didn't say anything to the captain. His condition seems to be improving a little, and I don't want him to worry. I'm not ill, and nothing happened to be alarmed about.'

The expression in his eyes told her that Beamish had his suspicions. She'd never tell him – she'd never tell anyone. She was much too ashamed. So she seized on one of his observations. 'You were right about the whisky. I thought I'd try some, and it was too strong. I'm not used to it, you see.'

'Yes . . . I see how something like that would have upset your stomach. The major gave you it, did he.'

'I only had one glass. It wasn't very nice . . . I didn't like it and I won't drink it again, I promise.' Now she'd started talking she didn't seem able to stop as she followed after him to the car. 'I don't know what you men see in drinking whisky, honestly I don't.'

'Don't you, Miss?'

'No . . . I'll never drink it again.' In fact, if she even smelled whisky on a man's breath again, she was sure she would vomit. She fell silent as the enormity of what had happened hit her. How on earth would she be able to face the major in the morning?

She needn't have worried, the major made it easy for her, acting as though nothing had happened.

At first she thought he'd forgotten the incident, but then he called her into the study. Although she left the door open, he closed it.

'I'd rather it was left open.'

'What I have to say to you is private,' and he ran a hand across his brow. 'Listen, m'dear . . . I was rather inebriated last night . . . had some bad news . . . Rosemary said she's running off with some film producer chap. The point is, Livia, I seem to remember taking a few liberties. Wouldn't have hurt you deliberately . . . that goes without saying.' He hauled in a deep breath. 'The thing is, I can't remember much about it . . .' He spread his hands and grimaced. 'I don't know how far I went . . . you know what I mean, I expect.'

Livia felt nothing but relief that he didn't remember, and she was deeply embarrassed by the whole thing. 'No, I'm afraid not. Nothing happened, really, Major.' Perhaps nothing had. She wasn't sure now. A physical relationship with a man was something she'd never experienced before. 'You tried to give me a New Year's kiss, then fell over. Can I go now? I have work to do.'

He came towards her, a piece of paper in his hand. She backed away until the door stopped her. He came to a halt at arm's length, and held out the paper. The guarded expression was gone from his eyes, as though he'd manipulated her way of thinking to achieve the desired result. Instinct told her that he had, and she felt instantly dirty and experienced a strong urge to scrub herself again.

'The thing is . . . I'd be obliged if you kept this little episode to yourself, Livia. After all, we wouldn't like to upset Richard, would we? This is for you, a little bonus for your trouble. No damage done.'

'I don't want anything.'

'Nonsense.' He slid the cheque into her apron pocket and she panicked when he accidentally brushed his hand across her stomach.

Thrusting the door open, she ran without bothering about direction, nearly bumping into Florence who'd just descended the staircase carrying an ash bucket, dustpan and brush. 'Sorry.'

The study door clicked shut.

A few seconds later and she was in the drawing room. Pulling the cheque from her pocket she tore it into shreds.

When Florence followed her in, Livia hastily threw the pieces on to the cold ashes in the grate and stirred them in with the toe of her shoe.

'You look like you've just seen a ghost. The first Mrs Sangster isn't in the study, is she?'

Livia managed a tight smile. 'No, just Major Henry. I'm a bit under the weather. The cramps must be due.' It was a lie, since they weren't due for a fortnight.

Captain Sangster wants to see you,' Florence said, and her eyes were shining with happiness. 'I think he's going to propose to me.'

Livia knew very well who Florence was referring to, but she couldn't resist it. 'Who . . . Captain Sangster?'

Florence snorted. 'Beamish, of course. He wants to see me tonight, private like. He told me he had something special to say to me. Fancy me being Mrs Beamish. I won't know who people are talking to.'

'I expect you'll soon get the hang of it.' She kissed Florence on the cheek. 'He's a lovely man, very sincere, and has plans for the future, but I expect he's told you about them.'

Florence looked mystified by that.

'If he hasn't, I imagine he'll tell you to present himself in the best light possible. I'm sure you will suit each other very well, Florence, dear. I shall expect an invitation to the wedding.'

'Oh, it probably won't take place until after the captain . . . well, until the captain no longer needs him. Anyway, he hasn't asked me yet, and we'll get engaged first, I expect, like most people do . . . just in case someone thinks I'm in the family way. Not that I am, but you know what people are like when arrangements are too rushed.' She turned red. 'Well, I'd best get on, since the work doesn't happen by itself.'

'I'll go up and see the captain. I'll take some coffee and biscuits up with me.'

Beamish opened the door and his searching scrutiny made her avert her eyes. He knew nothing, only suspected, she thought.

Richard greeted her with a smile, which faded as he gazed through his delicious blue eyes at her and said, 'You don't look happy. Why?'

She wanted to cry at that, for he was good at tuning into her moods. 'Oh, I'm just having one of those down days. I'm trying not to carry the misery around with me.'

'You're not succeeding very well, since you look like a wet weekend.'

'Thank you very much. Stop being so beastly.'

He gazed at Beamish. 'Take a break, Sergeant. With a bit of luck you might run into that feisty little Florence of yours.'

Beamish raised a smile and left, humming to himself.

Making an effort, Livia summoned up a smile especially for Richard. 'How are you this morning?'

'All the better now you're here.'

'Thank you.' Her heart gave a little lift. 'Florence said you wanted to see me.'

'I always want to see you. I think I'm falling in love with you . . .'

That gave her a bit of a jolt. Richard was teasing, of course, but if he ever discovered what had happened with his father . . . She rolled her eyes, letting him know what she felt about such a silly idea. 'Behave yourself, Richard.'

'Yes, Ma'am.'

But was it so silly? She loved him too, but in her own way, for there was nothing about him not to love. Her affection for him, though motivated by pity, was strong. It was not inconceivable that he imagined himself in love with her, since he relied on her for many small comforts.

She began to pour the coffee, the liquid an aromatic darkness pooling within the white interior of the cup. Dropping in three sugar lumps, she added a good inch of cream to cool it, and placed a plate with a couple of iced biscuits next to it. 'Do you need any help?'

'I'm having a good day today.' To prove it, he ate the biscuits without dropping crumbs everywhere. Then he carefully looped a hand around the handle of the cup, the other supporting the other side, and took several sips before giving a satisfied sigh and replacing the cup on the table.

'Well done, Richard.'

He grimaced. 'You sound like my nursery school teacher.'

'Sometimes I feel like one.'

He laughed. '*Touché.* Arrangements have been made.'

'About?'

'Dents rang me. He'll pick you up and drive you into Poole hospital to get the tests done tomorrow.'

'That's nice of him to spend some of his precious time driving me around. I admit, I'll be glad when they're over and done with.'

'No doubt you will. By the way, I managed to get in touch with the headmaster at King's Charter and we had a little chat. They're willing to take Chad, as long as he's healthy, and depending on the results of the exam. They're sending a set of exam papers to the reverend for Chad to sit under his supervision, since the man used to be the school chaplain in his youth.'

'Chad will be able to ride to the rectory on his bicycle. He's worried about his Latin, though.'

He won't have to sit the exam for a week, and besides, they won't expect much at his age, especially from a boy who's been brought up in an institution. Tell him to come up at ten, with his book, pen and paper. I'll coach him in the basics for an hour every day. Between us we'll soon show the headmaster what Chad is made of. Mornings will be best, I'm more lively then.'

'So I've noticed. Your speech is good today.'

'My health has improved since I've been home, and I feel more confident. My aim is to walk around the garden unaided. The last time I tried it I nearly fell into one of the rose beds. Thankfully, young Bugg was there to catch me. What happened to old Bugg?'

'He retired and his grandson took over.'

'Yes, I suppose that makes sense, and it gives Foxglove House a sense of continuity.'

Something it wouldn't have for much longer. She wanted to wrap her arms around him, make him feel secure, but it would probably have the opposite effect.

'What happened yesterday with my father?'

She shrivelled inside at the reminder. 'I don't know what you mean.'

'Yes you do. Beamish said you found the major passed out on the floor.'

'Oh, that.'

'Yes . . . Oh, that. I'm surprised you didn't tell me.'

'Goodness, Richard, I've hardly had time. Beamish was there, he said the major had drunk a little too much whisky, and he'd see to him after he'd taken us home. I was trying to rouse him. Did Beamish think I was trying to pick his pockets?'

'He was worried about you . . . said you were *untidy*. He also said you were sick in the shrubbery.'

Crossly, she said, 'Beamish said a lot for someone I specifically asked not to say anything. I knew you'd worry. I drank some whisky too, and as for being untidy, one usually is at the end of a day's work.'

He drew her eyes to his with one glance. 'You wouldn't lie to me, would you, Livia?'

To which she forced out a smile. There was lying, and then there was lying by omission. 'It's entirely possible.'

He laughed at that.

She finished her coffee and placed the cup back on the tray. 'I'm going to get some work done. Would you like my biscuits?'

He nodded. 'It would be a shame to waste them.'

When she was halfway to the door, he murmured, 'Livia, would you really lie to me?'

'You've had my answer.'

'I know an evasion when I hear one.'

'You have a good imagination then, for you obviously know an evasion when you don't hear one as well. Enjoy your biscuits, Richard.'

'Don't forget to send Chad up.'

She nodded. 'He'll appreciate your help.'

Richard watched her go, his eyes narrowing. What he hadn't said was that Beamish had mentioned that his father's trousers were open and his undergarments disturbed, so he was exposed.

Richard had become aware of his father's philandering ways at an early age, when he was a teenager, in fact. He had not been aware that Rosemary Mortimer had been his mistress before his mother's death, and that she had been working here while his mother was still alive. Beamish had ferreted that snippet of information out of Florence, who had an inclination to gossip.

The result was, his father had sunk low in his estimation. He was pleased the woman had left his home.

But surely Livia wouldn't be susceptible to any advances his father might make? He could always question the boy, since Chad had been there before Beamish.

No . . . Livia would never forgive him if he encouraged Chad to spy on her. She was already as mercurial as the weather this morning.

'Anything?' he said, when Beamish came back.

'There's this. Miss Carr threw it on to the ashes. Florence said she was a bit furtive about it, which she thought strange, so she picked it out.' He dropped a pile of dusty paper scraps on to the plate vacated by the biscuits.

Richard's hands began to shake. 'What is it?'

'A cheque for ten pounds made out to cash, and signed by the major.'

The blood began to pound in his ears. Surely not . . . not Livia! But why had she torn it up? It was no use trying to get it out of her. She was as closed as an oyster when the occasion suited . . . and it suited her now. 'I'm going to get to the bottom of this, Beamish.'

'Do you want my advice?'

'Not in particular, but go ahead.'

'I can see the way things are going for you with the fair Livia.'

'Damn it, man, I think . . . *I know* I'm in love with her.'

Beamish gave a faint smile. 'Is that wise?'

'Not in the least, but emotion doesn't often listen to wisdom, my friend. If I have her by my side for the little time I've got left, then I'll die happy.'

'What's stopping you?'

'You know what. It's not fair to her.'

'Let her decide that for herself. Wait until the right opportunity presents itself . . . you were always good at that. Livia is in a precarious position. She's dependent on your family for the roof over their heads and the food in their stomachs, and she has a sick child on her hands.'

Had his father used that to manipulate her?

The thought of him using Livia for such a purpose was abhorrent to Richard. Something stank, and he intended to find out what it was.

A thought punched into his mind. Would he be prepared to manipulate Livia to his own ends if the opportunity presented?

If it were to her benefit, yes.

'You're right about her, Beamish. I'll let her decide when the time comes. Do me a favour and keep your eye on the situation, would you?'

'You expect me to spy on your father? I'm surprised.'

'So am I. What I'm actually asking is for you to keep him away from Livia if you can. He's bored and he's looking for a diversion, preferably in the form of a woman. It's time he went back to London.'

Nine

Denton picked them up on the dot of nine. The morning was misty. The frost melted into the shafts of weak sunshine that filtered through the tree branches and drifted upwards as wisps of cold smoke.

The children were excited.

Denton aimed a smile Livia's way as he gave the handle a turn to start the engine. He jumped in beside her. 'The Humber is rather a come down after the Silver Ghost, I imagine.'

'The Rolls is glamorous, but this is a nice car with a friendly rumble to it. I like the colour. It reminds me of burgundy . . . and it smells like lavender.'

He chuckled. 'That's a typical woman's answer. Actually, my mother used to polish the seats with lavender-scented beeswax. Watch out when we go round a corner because I slide down the seat and it's quite likely we'll collide and I'll knock you flying out through the door.'

She laughed. 'You'd better not.'

He called over his shoulder, 'You're very quiet in the back. Are you still in there.'

'I am,' Chad said.

'What about your sister, we haven't forgotten her, have we? Look out of the window and see if she's running after us, trying to catch us up.'

Esmé giggled. 'Of course I'm not, Doctor Denton. I'm here, being good, like Livia told me to be.'

'Good for you, Poppet. That deserves a reward.' He drew a paper bag from his pocket and handed it to Livia. 'There's some humbugs and barley sugar in the bag. Have one yourself if you like.'

'Not for me, thanks, how about you?'

'I'll have a humbug.'

Taking one from the bag, she held it to his mouth and his

tongue curled round it and drew it inside. A bulge appeared in the cheek nearest to her.

She handed the children the barley sugar and said, 'Chad, tuck that blanket round Esmé so she keeps nice and warm.'

'I want to look out of the window so I can see everything.'

Denton removed his humbug and said firmly, 'You may look out of the window on the way back, my dear. I want you rested when you see the specialist, that's why I made you up a little bed in the car.'

A defeated sigh issued from behind her mask. 'Yes, Doctor Denton.'

He took the sweet back into his mouth. Soon, the sound of contented sucking filled the car. Her eyes met Denton's and he crunched his confection up and swallowed it. 'Rude of me to suck a humbug, but I can't resist them.'

'They're quite noisy humbugs.'

They grinned at each other.

'Have you had the car long?' she asked.

'I had it on order before the war started, and I took delivery of it just before I joined up. It cost me sixty-three pounds, and my father found room for it in his garage for the duration.'

'So it's practically new.'

'Yes.'

'Was it bad? The war, I mean.'

'It wasn't too bad for me. I was in a field hospital, and though I saw the result of the conflict, I wasn't really in the thick of the fighting and was able to detach myself from it a little. I wouldn't have been able to do my job otherwise. As it was, I learned my practical surgery the hard way, taking a hands-on approach.'

After a reflective silence, he said, 'You saw what Richard was like when he arrived home, though at least his condition was stable. My father is pleased by his progress.'

'Is there any chance that—'

'None whatsoever, I'm afraid. A cold winter could finish it for him. But I shouldn't be discussing Richard's condition with you, especially since he's my father's patient.'

'Sorry . . . I like him . . . a lot. He treats me as though

I'm a friend, rather than an employee.' She shrugged. 'I worry about him.'

His hand covered hers for a moment or two and he said evenly, 'I'm sure he considers you to be a friend, but he wouldn't want you to worry about him. The best that can be done for Richard is to keep him warm and happy, and allow him to live as normal a life as his condition will allow.'

Then she could never confide in him about his father's attack on her. Not that she wanted to, of course. It would be too embarrassing.

'I'll do my best.'

'With you and Beamish looking after him I see no problem about that. I just don't want you to have any false hope.'

'I'm worried. I will need to take time off to look after Esmé if she's ill. I don't know how I will manage.'

'Richard and my father will sort something out between them.' His profile set into a firm line. 'Let's not talk about the war or illness. I like to think there's a better future ahead of us.'

'May I just say that I'm glad you came home in one piece.'

'I'll let you into a little secret . . . so am I. Luckily I had my pheasant's feather to protect me, and the thought of a lovely young lady waiting for me at home. I never forgot you, you know.'

'Now who's having delusions, Denton Elliot. That pheasant's feather had nothing to do with it . . . and I wasn't waiting for you to come home.'

'My father said you asked after me often.'

'Once or twice, actually. I was being polite, that's all.' She slanted a look in his direction. 'Did you really think of me? You looked so important standing there on the station, talking to that officer. As soon as you turned your back I imagined you'd never think of me again.'

'Then you'd be wrong, Livia, since I thought of you every day. Having a girl to come home to gives a man something to look forward to.'

'I would imagine you looked forward to coming home to any number of young women.'

A smile played around his mouth, and she suddenly

remembered the kiss he'd given her – such a fleeting touch, like a butterfly alighting. How tender it had been. He was a tall man, decisive in his ways and sure of himself. A void opened inside her as her heart seemed to slow down, then it gave a thud. She blushed. 'You're still a flirt. Stop it at once.'

He seemed not to hear her. 'I can remember what you were wearing the day we met . . . a suit as grey as the day itself, and a hat that looked like an upside-down bucket.'

'A bucket!'

'Well . . . a flower pot then, complete with drooping pheasant feathers.'

'The day was cold, but lovely, and my hat had a turned-up brim. It was you who broke the feather and made it droop.'

'Like I said in the first place; a bucket.' He chuckled. 'You also had a hole in the sole of your boot.'

'How did you know that?'

'I noticed it when you fell backwards on to the seat with my kit bag on top of you. It's not often I get to literally bowl a girl over the first moment we meet.'

She began to laugh. 'You noticed too much. A gentleman wouldn't have pointed that out.'

'It's your turn now. What did you notice about me?'

'That you were the only other person in the carriage.'

'Ouch . . . can't you do better than that?'

'I suppose I could. Let me see . . . you were in uniform and your eyes were sort of devil-may-care, and were the greenish-brown colour of pine trees.'

He flapped his eyelashes at her. 'Tell me more.'

'There was a moment, just a small one it was, when I mentioned that Richard was in France. The laughter in your eyes was replaced by intense sadness. It was a poignant moment, one that said you cared, and for that alone, I'll never forget you.'

'My dear, Livia, you are almost reducing me to tears. Of course I cared. The trick is learning not to care too much, lest you end up like Richard. He always took things to heart.'

'You know, you're very much like your father, Denton.'

'Really . . . in what way?'

'You tease a lot, but underneath is a confidence that's

disconcerting. You're aware of who you are, what you are and where you're going. Your own sensitivity is tempered by good sense.'

'Then perhaps this is a good time to ask. Would you wait for me?'

She hadn't expected that, and fell silent. It was not possible now, and she couldn't tell him why . . . that she was no longer worthy of him – of any decent man.

'I . . . I really don't know what to say, except I feel . . . 'How did she feel? Different to what she felt for Richard. She was attracted to Denton in a less protective manner, and totally aware of him as a man despite her negative experience. Her reactions towards him were so positive she almost felt like part of him.

'It's too soon, huh?'

She grabbed at the straw he offered. 'There's that . . . Also, I have the children to consider, especially Esmé.'

'If my father proves to be right – and he's an excellent diagnostician – Esmé is suffering from bronchial pneumonia, which has been left untreated. As a result, she's now prone to a cough that's become a habit. She might well grow out of it.'

'I do hope so.'

'Then will you at least think about me now and again. In another year I hope to be working locally, and I'll be back again in about six months.'

She nodded. 'I'll probably think of you a lot more than now and again.'

'Thank you for that. If I wasn't driving, I'd kiss you.'

'Kissing is rude,' Esmé observed from behind them.

'Only if somebody doesn't want to be kissed . . . and I'm sure your sister does . . . don't you, Livia?'

She felt the colour seep under her skin. 'I'm disinclined to answer that question.' Of course she wanted to be kissed. The awareness pulsed back and forth between them like a spark of lightning, and he knew it.

'Mrs Starling said kisses have got germs hiding in them,' Esmé persisted.

'Not mine. I'm a doctor, and I haven't got any germs. Besides, I've just eaten a humbug.'

Chad began to laugh. 'That's bum hug backwards.'

Esmé giggled.

'Ah . . . the minds of juvenile males,' Denton said. 'Actually, humbug backwards isn't bum hug, it's gubmuh, which sounds rather oriental and grand. Using your cruder method of translation, Chad, it would come out as bug hum.'

Livia snorted. 'Actually, it's muh gub backwards. Can we put an end to this ridiculous conversation?'

With great seriousness, Esmé said, 'I know the name of a hum that bugs. It's called a bumble bee.'

Livia and Denton shared a glance and dissolved into laughter.

Beamish made himself scarce when the major arrived.

'Hello, son.' Richard's father went to stand at the window, hands in pockets and jiggling on his heels. He was a handsome man settled into late middle age. He observed rather vaguely, 'A nice day, isn't it?'

'Is it, Father?'

With a sudden shock, Richard recognized that he didn't really know this man who was his father. He'd gone to boarding school at an early age, and spent most of the holidays with his mother, here at Foxglove House. Then it had been a law degree, something he'd earned comfortably, though never practised before the war had claimed his attention.

He'd always regarded and respected his father from afar. The major had never been the sort of man Richard could get close to because he'd been his mother's son more than his father's. He realized now that the pair had been estranged long before his mother's accident.

His father turned. 'No, I don't suppose it is a nice day, really. Rosemary rang to tell me she's going off to America with some film chappie. I should never have married her. It will cost me a pretty penny to get out of it, I suppose.'

'Why did you marry her?'

He shrugged. 'When your mother died I had no excuse not to. A man needs a woman.'

'But you had a relationship with her long before mother died.'

'Yes, well . . . Your mother was an invalid.' He cleared his throat.

'Rosie wasn't like the others. She did things – things no respectable woman would even imagine doing. Damn it, Richard, surely I don't have to explain to you. She was exciting, and I always did like the chase.'

'I don't want to know. You were weak, you've always been weak where women are concerned.'

He gave a faint smile. 'It's true that I was able to attract women easily . . . apart from my wife, who didn't seem to need me once she'd provided the Sinclair estate with an heir.' He shrugged. 'But why not take advantage of women, when they are one of the great pleasures in life? They seem to enjoy a man who knows what he wants and who can gently coerce them into wanting the same. I imagine you know all that without us needing a father and son *tête-à-tête* at this stage in your life.'

Coerced was an odd sort of word to use. Richard had never considered that his mother might have been an indifferent wife. But then, one didn't usually regard one's parents in a sexual context. But he admitted that by being reluctant, his mother might have contributed to the situation. 'Have there been any women who didn't enjoy being coerced?'

His father looked uneasy, and his eyes didn't seem able to settle on anything, least of all Richard. 'I'm not sure where you're taking this conversation, my boy.'

'Oh, I don't think you'd have to stretch your imagination too far back, do you?'

Henry grimaced. 'Did the girl tattle on to you about it? I paid her to keep quiet about it, the silly creature. How was I to know she was inexperienced? She should have said.'

'Ah . . . so you remember that about her.'

He shrugged. 'If I were you I'd get rid of her.'

'You're not me, and Livia hasn't said a word, because she wouldn't have wanted to upset me. What happened?'

His father shrugged. 'I'd been drinking heavily . . . Rosemary's phone call, you know. The girl was clearing the table, a pretty little thing. Nice hips, I thought. A girl like that would be snug. I tried to kiss her. She objected, but it was too late for me. She struggled and we fell on the floor . . . I'm not sure what happened then. I think I got the business over and done with quickly, then passed out. Didn't wake up until that man of yours practically dragged me upstairs to my bed by the scruff of my neck.'

'Beamish told me.'

'When I spoke to the girl the next day she said nothing had happened. I gave her a cheque for the fright I gave her, you understand. You say she didn't complain, so how the hell did you learn of it?'

'The cheque was found ripped to pieces and thrown into the ashes of the drawing room fire.'

'There you are then, that proves I'm innocent of any hanky-panky. Don't worry your head about it, Richard, it won't happen again. Odd, I always thought her to be a nice girl . . . but she's the same as all the other women, accepts money for favours. It's no good complaining about it after she's accepted payment, is it?'

Richard's blood began to boil and his throat constricted so he could hardly speak. 'No . . . it won't happen again. Not to my staff. Not in my home.'

'I say, old boy, was I treading on your turf there? Sorry, and all that. I understood you were past that sort of thing.'

'Be quiet, Father.' And for the first time in a long time, Richard began to stutter. 'I have s . . . something to say to you.'

His father gazed at him, surprised by his tone.

'Pack your f . . . fucking bags and get out. Go back to London and sort out that woman of yours if you want to keep her. Follow her to America if you need to.'

'I say, old chap, there's no need for that sort of language. I'm your father, after all.'

'There is every need. Livia Carr is a decent young woman, who I happen to have a great deal of affection and respect for. I won't have you mauling her whenever you feel the need. Get out. Go back to your tart and stay there.'

'Look, Richard . . . I can understand your anger. I'll apologize to the girl.'

'You won't go near her again . . . not while I have a b . . . breath left in my b . . . bloody useless body. I don't want to see you again.'

'Don't be silly, Richard. You need me to look after you.'

'I don't need you at all. I have Beamish and Livia. For Christ's sake, stop being a bloody nuisance, and leave me to d . . . die in peace.'

Richard reached for the bell on the table, but his arm jerked and everything went crashing to the floor. It sounded like a shell exploding and he cowered in the chair, his chest tight, so he found it hard to breathe. He didn't want to die, not now. His breath came harshly as he was surrounded by stinking yellow mist, the stuff that had caused the damage to him.

Beamish came in. He swept him up in his arms and laid him on the bed. Richard's men came, the ones left behind in France. They crowded around the bed, wearing their gas masks. Their eyes behind the glass eyepieces were anonymous as well as accusing.

'I'm s . . . sorry,' he murmured, his body beginning to shake and his hands plucking at the eiderdown.

His father hovered behind Beamish, watching wide-eyed as Beamish prepared an injection and administered it. As Richard's muscles relaxed one by one his breathing became easier. He began to float.

'I'm all right . . . leave me now . . . get the men to safety, Sergeant.'

'They're safe, Sir, and so are you.' Beamish removed Richard's shoes and tucked the eiderdown over him. 'You rest now, Sir. You'll be all right in a little while.'

'He wants me to go back to London,' his father said.

Beamish had a fierce look on his face. 'He can't afford to be upset, so it would be for the best.'

'Who will manage his affairs?'

'Captain Sangster is quite good at managing them himself, he always has been. But the Sinclair trust lawyers have his power-of-attorney, so you needn't worry that he'll be taken advantage of. Do you need any help packing, Major?'

'Perhaps it would be better for him if I did go back to London. Richard seems to be distraught. I had no idea he jumped at the sight of his own shadow. This sort of thing shouldn't be pandered to. He needs to learn that the war is over, and to straighten his spine and be a man. But then, he always was his mother's son.'

Beamish's voice was deceptively mild. 'He needs to be a man, does he? Let me tell you this . . . a better man you couldn't wish to find.'

'Don't be impertinent. As for you, Beamish, I don't know what you thought you saw the other night, but it would have been better if you'd kept it to yourself, then this wouldn't have happened.'

'And better for you if you'd kept your dick inside your trousers, Major. Well, let me just say this to you, and with the respect it deserves. You're a desk soldier who doesn't know how to salute without knocking his cap off. You don't know the first thing about war, or about the loyalty shared between soldiers-at-arms. You just enjoy a kiss-arse relationship propping up the bar and grunting with the rest of the desk officers.'

'I think that's enough insubordination from you, Beamish. Were you still enlisted I'd have you up on a charge.'

Richard grinned widely. The sergeant didn't usually say much, but when he did it was a corker of a speech. He opened his eyes to exchange a smile with his men, to find they were no longer there.

Beamish was in full flood. 'No doubt you would. You know, you're a poor excuse for a man, Major. If Captain Sangster told you to make yourself scarce, then be quick about it. As for Miss Carr, if you as much as look at her sideways again, I'll knock your soddin' head off your bleedin' shoulders, officer or not, and kick it all the way to Land's End.'

Thank you, Beamish, Richard thought, and he began to chuckle.

An hour later a knock came at the door and his father cleared his throat before whispering against the panel, 'I'm off then, Richard . . . we'll let bygones be bygones, shall we? Keep in touch.'

'Goodbye, Father. Get yourself sorted out.' Despite everything, the man was his father and Richard couldn't shame him by disowning him altogether.

'I will. I promise.' Henry's feet trod heavily down the stairs, and Richard's door rattled when the front door closed behind him.

When the car drove away, Beamish said, 'I forgot to fill the tank with petrol. I hope he checks the gauge when he gets to Bournemouth.'

Richard chuckled. 'You know, Beamish, we should buy ourselves a car, something practical like Dents has got. You could teach Livia to drive it.'

'Yes, Sir, I suppose I could, though I don't go much on women drivers in general.'

'They were driving buses in London during the war, or so I was told.'

'With respect, Sir, may I point out that you're not a bus company?'

'With respect, Beamish, somebody has wound your little clockwork spring up and set you in motion, and you're talking too much today.'

Beamish grinned. 'It must be true if you say so. Do you want me to see to the car?'

'I'll telephone Simon Stone tomorrow and tell him to expect the account first. I don't want him to have a heart attack.'

'How are you feeling now, Sir?'

'The gremlins have gone, thank God.'

'Good. How are we going to handle Miss Carr's problem?'

'We're going to forget it ever happened, unless she decides to raise the matter with me. I hope she'll confide in me.'

'She's a nice girl and she won't want to take it any further and worry you with it, Sir. Something like that would be too hard for her to live with.'

'I hope not, because if it gets out it will go against her. After all, we don't really know for sure.' Even his father had been too inebriated to remember the details. 'Whatever happened, she needs to deal with it in her own time. I don't want her to feel ashamed, and if she thinks people know about it, she will. Does Florence know?'

'I haven't told Florence anything, except that the cheque had the wrong amount on it and Livia was told to burn it. Luckily, Florence doesn't read very well, and she didn't question it.'

Ten

It was a blustery afternoon late in March, when Dr Elliot came.

His smile broadcast the positive nature of the news he carried, before he had time to get into the house.

'It's as I thought, a bronchial complaint. In addition, the girl is anaemic, which accounts for her pallor and most of her other symptoms. That's what fooled Denton.' Dr Elliot plunged his hands into his bag and placed two bottles of liquid on the table. 'I've brought her an iron tonic, as well as some cough medicine.'

Esmé pulled a face when she saw it.

'I only bring the best medicine for my best girl. It tastes like cherries,' the doctor told her. 'It should get rid of your cough. You won't need the mask any more, so you can take it off.'

'Can I go and tell Chad? He's in the garden.'

'You most certainly can, but put your coat on first, then off you go.'

He turned Livia's way after Esmé went skipping off. 'If she gets a cold in the future we must be careful it doesn't go to her chest. The trouble with being in an orphanage is that they only get the bare essentials, and they don't receive enough nourishment. It can't be helped, of course. She was lucky she didn't end up with her legs bowed from rickets. Many children do.'

'Yes, I remember the orphanage food. It was a choice of thin oatmeal for breakfast, pea or cabbage soup and potatoes with Anything stew.'

'Anything stew?'

She grinned. 'The meat could have been anything. It was marginally worse than the food in the boarding school I attended before that . . . though at least I had parents then, and they sent hampers now and again.'

'Ah yes, I'd forgotten you'd spent a few years in the orphanage.'

'Two years. I was sent here to work when I was sixteen.'

'That must have been hard after your former life.'

'The orphanage prepared me well for it. I was an expert at scrubbing floors when I left. I've discovered that it doesn't pay to dwell on what might have been, and complaining about your lot in life just makes you unhappy. You have to get on and make the best of what comes your way.'

'You've got a good attitude towards life, Livia. I've noticed that you're looking a little tired yourself of late, though. Perhaps it's time I checked you over.'

She tried not to panic at the thought. 'I'm fine, really. I've been worrying about Esmé. Now I won't have to.'

A careful gaze scrutinized her face. 'Hmmm.'

'Denton told me that when a doctor makes a humming noise, he only does it because it makes him sound like an expert, as though he knows something the patient doesn't.'

'That could be true. All the same, I'm going to ask you to take some of that iron tonic in the other bottle. The same dose as Esmé, a teaspoon each a day until it's all gone. By that time the roses should be back in the cheeks of both of you.'

Now it was her turn to grimace. 'That concoction looks dreadful. You're not out to poison us, are you?'

He laughed. 'Actually, it's not as bad as it looks. Try to build Esmé's strength up with eggs and milk . . . and broth made with red meat, if possible.'

'She doesn't have much of an appetite.'

'Then only give her small meals. Praise her when she finishes it, so she'll get a sense of achievement. Gradually increase the amount, a spoonful at a time so she doesn't notice. You'll have her eating like a horse in no time. When the medicine is finished we'll have her blood tested again.'

'Thank you, Doctor Elliot, you couldn't have brought me better news.'

'Talking about news, I've got something else for you.' He stooped and kissed her cheek. 'That's from Denton. I left him a message telling him the news, and he rang me back when he was free, and asked me to tell you he's delighted to hear he was wrong and I was right. He said he's writing you a letter.'

'That's kind of him. I'll look forward to receiving it. Is he all right?'

'When you write to him in return, you'll be able to ask him yourself, won't you? Where's Richard, is he upstairs?'

'Captain Sangster is in the drawing room. I was just about to bring him some tea and a custard tart. Would you like some?'

'I most certainly would. I'll see myself in.'

'Tell him Esmé's good news if you would.'

As the door closed behind him, Livia's smile faded. How kind everyone had been to her. And just as things were going so right . . . She took a quick glance in the hall mirror as she went to the kitchen. The doctor was right; she did look washed out. Perhaps it wasn't what she feared, and all she needed was the iron tonic. She could only wait and see . . .

There was a knock at the door and Richard looked up to see Doctor Elliot.

'I hope I'm not disturbing you, Richard.'

'Of course not.' Richard placed the paper he was writing on to one side, and smiled at him. 'It's not my day for being poked and prodded, so to what do I owe the honour?'

'I was visiting little Miss Carr.'

'Livia has been looking a little off-colour lately, I thought. Is she all right, d'you think?'

'I imagine she'll manage to consult a doctor all by herself if she isn't,' the doctor said rather drily. 'I meant Miss Esmé Carr. No doubt you'll be pleased to learn it's not what we feared.'

'Splendid. Perhaps Livia will stop wandering round with a long face now. Have you seen the new car? I bought an Austin tourer for Livia. Beamish is teaching her to drive it. He says she's doing well, despite being a woman and not knowing anything about cars.'

'You bought a car for Livia?'

'Well, not exactly. As you know, my father has returned to London, and he's taken the Rolls with him. I thought that if we had a car, Livia could take turns with Beamish driving it, then I'll be able to get out a bit once the warmer weather arrives. And we need a bit of room to fit the children in.'

The doctor gave a frown. 'It sounds as though you've adopted the whole family.'

'They're nice children and I like them. Hearing them play and laugh . . .' He shrugged. 'The war has changed my perspective towards many things. In the normal way of things I would have enjoyed having a family of my own, and a future to fit them into. Those two children would have been raised by their parents had they not died, and Livia would be living a different sort of life, not sacrificing her own youth to care for them by herself. Now I snatch little bits I can have, and I try to make them my own for the now I've been dealt. I can't change the course of my life, but I can compress inside its smallness every scrap of happiness I can glean, and perhaps be useful in making another happy. You have no idea how much joy a child's laughter can contain.'

'Of course . . . I'm sorry, Richard. May I now ask if you're practising for a sainthood?'

Laughter filled him. 'Did I sound like a pontificating bore?'

'No . . . you've always spoken from your heart, and you haven't changed.'

'Have you heard from Dents lately? He promised to write.'

'He said he's about to write to Miss Carr, when he can find a moment. I think he may have taken a shine to the young woman.'

Richard tried not to allow his dismay to show. 'Ah, so that was what the frown was about. Do you disapprove?'

'Of Livia, no . . . but to take on a family as well might prove to be an imposition?'

'It might never happen. Dents would never allow his heart to completely rule his head. He has his training to complete, and besides, a letter isn't a proposal of marriage.' Though somehow Richard knew it was.

'You're right, and I'm worrying unnecessarily. I thought he may have confided in you about her.'

'Not a word, and neither has he shown her any undue attention, apart from indulging in some mild flirting, which we all indulge in, including you. Luckily, Livia is too sensible to take much notice of it.'

Having said that, he remembered his conversation with his

father over her, and his lack of remorse over the way he'd treated her. He must make it up to her for that.

'You'll have to ask Livia for Denton's latest news when his letter arrives.'

As if on cue a knock came at the door and Livia wheeled the tea trolley in. She offered them both a smile, but it was too wide and it lacked spontaneity. Richard wished she'd tell him what was bothering her.

'Oh goody, custard tarts,' he said.

She laughed and placed one on a plate for him. 'You're worse than the children for liking sweet things. Fork or fingers?'

'Fingers.' It was safer when one had visitors. She nodded and cut the tart into quarters so he wouldn't make a fool of himself with a face full of custard if his arm jerked.

There was an irresistible little curve of red-tinted dark hair behind her ear that Richard wanted to kiss, and her jaw was a delicate sweep away from it. Usually the skin of her cheek possessed a delicate bloom, like the down of a peach-tinted rose. Now it had a shell-like translucence.

It was a long time since he'd been this aware of a woman. He seemed to have lost any manly urges he'd possessed, and in any case, he doubted if he'd have the strength to carry them through, which was a pity, since she smelled faintly of something sweet and velvety.

He drew in a breath, thinking he might marry her himself if she'd have a cripple who could guarantee nothing except an early widowhood. It would be the ultimate make-believe for him. Her family would become his the house would ring with the laughter of children, and Livia would be his wife. It wasn't make-believe that he loved her. He did.

She felt something for him too, he sensed it . . . and even if it turned out to be pity, he would use it for his own good.

He had an estate that wasn't part of the Sinclair trust. He had to leave it to someone, and that would guarantee her an income for life.

Her perfume reminded him of his mother and he pictured the almost empty bottle on her dressing table, with its shoulders and the heart-shaped glass stopper. *Guerlain L'Heure Bleue.*

'That means the blue hour of dusk, just before the stars

appear in the sky,' his mother had told him, and he'd gone off to seclude himself in the rose arbor to watch the stars come out and write a poem he'd titled less than romantically, 'Blue Dust'. He recalled that his mother had left Livia her wardrobe. The perfume would have been part of that.

When Dr Elliot cleared his throat and said, 'How are your driving lessons coming along, Livia?' Richard tore his eyes away from her and chuckled.

She gave a light laugh. 'I'm enjoying it, though Mr Beamish isn't. And I do manage to steer around the puddles.'

'You're never going to allow me to forget that dousing I gave you on the day we met.'

'Probably not. Would you like milk in your tea, Doctor? There, I think that's all. Do ring the bell if you need anything more, though I'm sure you can manage to drive a teapot across the table without mishap.'

Now the thought of marriage to Livia had entered his head, Richard knew he'd act on it. But what about Dents? They'd always had the same taste in women and his father had said he seemed keen on her.

A small niggle of guilt beset Richard. Yet he'd made more than his fair share of sacrifices of late. Denton had time on his side. He didn't, and it wasn't as though his friend would call him out. Denton could wait!

Richard waited until Chad had been delivered to his school.

As co-sponsor, Denton came with them that day, and they sat either side of Livia, with Chad next to Beamish.

Denton gazed at Richard across Livia, and they smiled at each other, slightly challengingly, and each took one of her hands in his.

'I thought Chad was the only schoolboy in this car,' she said as she disentangled herself. 'Behave yourselves, gentlemen, else I'll swap seats with Beamish and do the driving.'

Chad was slightly nervous, but excited. Richard had dismissed the offer to be carried through his old school in the arms of Beamish, and the invalid chair had been left behind, so Denton took Chad to meet his housemaster.

Richard shook the boy's hand, wished him luck, and watched

his friend walk into the hallowed halls with Livia and her brother. Denton smiled reassuringly at her, because she looked glum, and on the brink of crying over the parting. Chad was looking around him with interest, and by the look of his suitcase, the cook had weighed it down with goodies.

He smiled, remembering that school had usually had a feast or famine aspect to it. Denton would probably slip the boy some extra money to spend at the tuckshop, when Livia and the housemaster weren't looking.

Livia and Denton looked as if they belonged together, and his smile faded when Denton ran his fingertips across her knuckles, as if he'd entwine her fingers with his, should the occasion allow.

Livia took the passenger seat in the front on the way back, and remarked, 'You can hold each other's hands if you get lonely.'

The next morning Denton caught the train back to London.

Richard waited a while until it was Livia's day off and Esmé was at school. Rags of clouds chased each other across the sky and the trees creaked in the wind like arthritic old men doing a Morris dance.

'I'll wear my new lounge suit today,' he told Beamish.

'Waistcoat?'

'No, a pullover . . . that fancy Fair Isle one that Livia gave me for Christmas.'

'But you said you didn't like it?'

'Today, I do.'

Beamish donned his suspicious face. 'Are we going somewhere special?'

'You can drop me off at Nutting Cottage, Beamish. Collect me in two hours.'

He intercepted a grin on Beamish's face, said, 'Before you ask, mind your own business.'

'Going courting, are we?'

'We are not, I am. Now shut your clack, Beamish.'

'Yes, Sir.'

It was a perfect day, despite the wind. The cottage had always been a pretty sight in spring, and this one was no different.

The elms were dotted with white and purple blossom, the garden threaded with golden celandine, blue periwinkle and sweet violets. There was a clump of early daffodils near the door. As Richard's eyes drank in the beauty of it, a thrush opened its beak and poured out an exquisite song.

He'd found a sweet ring amongst his mother's jewellery, an oval sapphire surrounded by small white diamonds on a white-gold band. It was exquisitely flawless, like the stars in that blue dusk.

He caught a glimpse of the cat on the upstairs windowsill, gazing out, its mouth opening in a silent meow at the sight of him. The dog set up a yap at the back of the cottage. Released, he clattered to the front door and made a furious assault on it.

'Stop it, Bertie, you bloody idiot, it's me,' he said against the door panel. 'Go and fetch your mistress. Tell her that her knight has come on his white charger to carry her off.'

Beamish snorted.

The noise diminished to a yappy whine of excitement and he heard Livia reprimand it with: 'Where are your manners, Bertie?'

'Right-oh, you can go now, Beamish,' he said when he heard her footfalls, and Beamish made himself scarce.

The despair in her face when coupled with eyes red from crying couldn't be disguised by the brilliant smile she gave – one that nearly broke his heart.

'You look a total mess, my love,' he said, by way of greeting.

'I know.' She held out her arm for him when the car drove off. 'Come in, Richard, I can't leave you on the doorstep. To what do I owe this pleasure?'

'I missed you.'

'Oh!' She gave a watery giggle as he shuffled to the settee and patted the seat next to him. 'I'm not very good company, I'm afraid.'

'I know.' He'd not meant to blurt it out, but he did. 'I'm here to propose marriage to you.'

Her eyes widened. 'Why?'

'Because I'm madly in love with you.'

'Oh . . . is that all?' She drew in a shaky breath and tears began to course down her cheeks.

'Don't cry, my darling. I know I won't be much of a husband, in fact I don't know if I *can* even be a husband to you. But if I can have you just for a little while I would die happy.'

'I can't marry you, Richard. It wouldn't be fair. You've always done so much for me. And I don't want you to die happy – I don't want you to die at all.'

'Just hear me out, Livia. I don't know what will happen to the Sinclair trust. In fact, the whole thing is a bloody nuisance, and it can go to charity as far as I'm concerned. If that happens, you and the children will have nowhere to go. I've got money of my own, and have nobody to leave it to except my father, and he's got enough of his own to keep him comfortable. If you marry me you'll always be secure.'

'I still can't marry you, Richard.'

'Why not? Is it because of what my father has done to you?'

Her head jerked up. 'How did you know about that?'

'Beamish told me about the state my father was in, and gave me the torn-up cheque. I put two and two together and spoke to my father about it. He confessed to what he'd done, so I sent him packing.'

'And now you feel it's your duty to marry me.' She placed her hands to her face and tears trickled between her fingers. 'I'm so ashamed . . . he was drunk and I couldn't fight him off, and couldn't shout for help because he had his hand over my mouth. I didn't want you to know, Richard . . . didn't want you to worry . . . or think I led him on. He . . . he hurt me.'

When he pulled her hands down and gazed into her eyes he could hardly breathe for the bewildered hurt he saw there. 'Believe me, Livia, it's got nothing to do with duty. I've thought it through.' He placed a kiss against her temple. 'Nobody need know about the assault. I love you . . . and I thought you cared for me a little.'

'I do care for you . . . I care for you a lot. I just can't marry you. It wouldn't be fair.'

'Why the hell not?'

The tears began to flow again. 'Because . . . I'm not sure, but I think I might be expecting a baby.'

Her words came as a shock to him. He hadn't considered . . . no wonder she'd been down in the mouth lately. He considered it now, but only for a few seconds. Nobody could accuse him of not being decisive, he thought wryly as he summoned up a smile. 'So, if we marry I'll have a legitimate heir to pass on the Sinclair estate to. That will solve that problem.'

She looked shocked now. 'But it wouldn't be your child, so that would be dishonest.'

'Nobody but us would know that . . . and dishonesty doesn't come into it. I'd be related to the child by blood, and since he'd be my brother he'd be my heir anyway, even though the Sinclair strain would be well diluted. He wouldn't inherit if he were born on the wrong side of the blanket, though. As it stands, my name can go on the birth certificate and everything will be hunky-dory.'

'I don't know, Richard. I don't feel right taking advantage of your kindness.'

'Kindness, be damned! Haven't you been listening, woman? I adore the hell out of you. Did you have a better plan for the infant, my dear? A visit to some grubby woman in a backstreet who calls herself a midwife, perhaps?'

She placed her hands over her ears and shuddered. 'Don't, Richard. I won't listen.'

He pulled her hands away, kissed the soft skin at each temple. 'Marry me and we'll all have our needs met. Your respectability will remain intact. The Sinclair trust will have an heir, the baby a name as well as a home, and you and the twins will have a future together.'

He knew she was going to agree when the tension drained from her body. He held all the cards and she had nowhere else to turn. She knew it, too. Her brown eyes engaged his, still wounded, but considering the possibility. He turned the screw, just a little.

'To be honest, my dear, I'd quite like people to believe I was manly enough to be a proper husband and father a child, even if it turns out that I'm not.'

A delicious blush dusted her face and a smile edged across her lips as she gazed at him. All the same, she looked troubled, and she had reason to be. Damn his father for ruining this girl with his bullishness. She was *his* girl!

He took her face between his hands before she could turn away, and engaged her eyes. 'I wouldn't insist on anything physical between us.'

'I know you wouldn't, Richard. But yes, I'll marry you, and I wouldn't deny you anything that would make you happy . . . not you, my dear.'

He kissed her mouth very gently and pulled away, doubtful of whether the question of intimacy would arise, and in more ways than one.

'There is something I haven't asked you, but need to, Livia. Can you bring yourself to love this baby?'

'How can I not love an innocent baby? Will you?'

'Yes . . . I'll love him, just as long as I can.'

'There's one thing I'd like to say, Richard.'

'Which is?'

Her hands went to her stomach in a protective manner. 'You talk about this infant as though it's going to be a boy. It could quite easily be a girl, you know.'

He chuckled. 'Better still, especially if she looks like you. It wouldn't make any difference to the trust.' He took the ring from his pocket and slid it on her finger. 'This belonged to my mother. I didn't have time to go into town before I came here, but I will buy you one of your own if you prefer.'

'You needn't, this one is lovely, and it fits perfectly. I won't wear it at work, though.'

He laughed. 'You won't be working for me for much longer. I shall have to find a new housekeeper. I was thinking that Beamish and Florence might like to live in the cottage until Beamish is no longer needed. They've planned to wed, and he has long-term plans of his own.'

'I'll be sorry to leave this cottage when we've just settled in.'

'We'll have to do the legalities quickly, and privately, though I'll have to inform Beamish. I'll make an appointment with the bishop to obtain a special licence and we can be wed in three or four days.'

'What will we tell him?'

'The truth.' He chuckled at the alarm on her face. 'Half of

it, anyway. I'll tell him that going through the usual rigmarole will be too gruelling for my condition. Then we'll alert the reverend. We'll go to the church, and the staff can act as witnesses. Will that suit you?'

Denton came into her mind and she was beset by unease as she wondered what he would say in the letter he intended to write to her. He didn't seem like a man who would be put off easily. But then, he was unaware of all the circumstances surrounding her, something she wasn't about to tell him. If he found out, she hoped he wouldn't feel too badly of her.

'Can we invite Doctor Elliot and Helen, since he's more of a friend than a doctor, and we can't invite one without the other. He can let Denton know . . . afterwards.'

He nodded. They were both taking the coward's way out where Denton was concerned. He hoped his childhood friend would understand when he discovered the reason for the hasty marriage.

Livia needed him, when it was usually the other way round. He liked the feeling.

Eleven

Livia had been tempted to wear the gown the late Margaret Sangster had given her, the one her mother had designed. But the wedding was to be a quiet one, so a ballgown would be out of place. Amongst the rather old-fashioned wardrobe she'd inherited was an unfussy but elegant pink suit with a tunic top. The skirt had a handkerchief hem, the points of which reached her ankles, and she found a pair of kid shoes with Louis heels and a strap across the instep.

Esmé helped, choosing from a variety of hats a wide-brimmed cream creation weighed down with pink silk roses.

'It's rather large; hats are smaller now,' Livia told her.

Esmé looked disappointed. 'But you're a bride, and the hat looks pretty with the suit.'

It seemed as though Esmé was developing their mother's fashion sense, and Livia smiled at her. 'Yes, I suppose it does. All right, I'll wear it just for you.'

She removed half of the flowers, which made the hat lighter, and sewed them on to a pink velvet ribbon to wear at her wrist.

She hoped the frantic gasps of the mad March wind wouldn't carry the hat away.

'You look like a princess,' Esmé said, unable to keep the excitement from her voice.

'So do you.' Livia had kept Esmé home from school for the occasion, and had made her a pretty pink-flowered cotton frock with puffed sleeves, using the sewing machine that lived in the back room. She'd bought her a pink mohair cape with pearl buttons to wear over it, and in her hair she wore a large pink satin bow.

They telephoned Chad at school to tell him the news. Cautiously he asked her, 'Does that mean the captain is going to be my stepfather?'

'No, since I'm your sister, not your mother. Richard will be your brother-in-law.'

'Super, I wouldn't mind having a big brother. I mean, girls are all right, but sometimes they don't understand a chap as well as another chap. Good luck then, Livia. How is Esmé keeping now?'

'Her cough has almost gone and she's eating more and has more energy.'

'Oh, jolly good. And Bertie? I expect he misses me.'

'I expect he does, but he's sprightly, and we keep him busy so he doesn't pine. Whiskers chases him around the cottage and we take him for walks every evening. Oh, by the way, we'll be moving into Foxglove House.'

'Wizard! Mrs Starling is a much better cook than you are. I say, Livia, would you send me some of her gingerbread. They starve us half to death in this school.'

Livia doubted it. 'How's your Latin going?'

He said casually, 'Oh, not so bad. I came fourth in class in the exam, thanks to the captain cramming me.'

'Well done!'

'It was nothing really. I don't know why I was so worried about it. You can tell the captain if you like. He should be pleased, I imagine.'

'He's here if you'd like to talk to him yourself.'

'Rather!' And the comment was voiced with such enthusiasm that she nearly laughed.

'Hello, Chad, I hope you don't mind me marrying your sister.'

Their faces touched as they shared the earpiece, and Livia heard the conversation clearly.

'No, I don't mind, if you don't, Sir. Congratulations.'

'How's school treating you? Have you made any friends yet?'

'Crumbs, lots of them . . . I've made a best friend, too. His name is Peter Laker. He's a spiffing chap, and is going to teach me how to play tennis when summer comes.'

'I'll have to buy you a tennis racquet then.'

The conversation became a man-to-man of sports and school, including the fact that Richard had been the captain of the first eleven in his final year, while Denton had merely won the biology prize by dissecting a cow's eye.

'I wonder if he killed the cow first; I must ask him,' Richard said, and laughed. 'I don't suppose you've seen any one-eyed cows wandering around the school grounds?'

Chad burst into howls of laughter.

'It wasn't *that* funny,' Livia said. 'As for you, Richard Sangster, ugh, you're horrid. I shall never look at Denton the same way again.'

'Never mind. Look at it this way. I expect he needed to develop his sadistic side.'

'Men! I shall go and make us some tea while the pair of you are playing at being magnificent males,' she whispered, and Richard drew her to his side, kissed her ear and whispered, 'I love you,' before allowing her to go.

Livia smiled, thinking how confident Chad was becoming since he'd left the orphanage. She would never do anything to spoil his progress, and Richard had known that, and had used it. But in her own way she loved Richard, and nothing would ever change that.

Sliding the engagement ring on to her hand, she waited for Beamish to pick them up for the church.

The letter from Denton arrived just before Beamish, conveyed on a post office tricycle with a huge wicker basket on the front. It was in a pale blue envelope, addressed to Miss Livia Carr, in firm, clear handwriting.

In half-an-hour she would no longer be Miss Livia Carr, but Mrs Richard Sangster. Nerves sang along her spine as she wondered again: was she doing the right thing?

She had no choice. Without opening the letter she pressed her lips against the seal and whispered, 'Forgive me, my Denton,' then reluctantly slid it unopened into the desk drawer when she heard the car. She didn't want to think of Denton and feel guilty on her wedding day.

Beamish smiled at her. 'May I say you'll do the captain proud, Miss Carr. You look as though you've dressed for each other . . . and you as well, Miss Esmé. The pair of you are as pretty as a picture.'

'Thank you, Mr Beamish. Did everyone get to the church without any bother?'

'Yes. It caused quite a stir when they realized what was going on, and their tongues have been clacking ever since. Florence isn't speaking to me because I didn't tell her . . . I must be thankful for small mercies, I suppose.'

Livia laughed.

'Some of the villagers have turned up, too, though God knows how they got wind of it. From the reverend's wife, I expect.'

Livia handed Esmé a little basket of silk roses to carry and smiled at her sister, thinking, if it weren't for Richard the girl would still be in the orphanage, and probably ailing from lack of nourishment. 'Come on then, Esmé, let's go and get married.'

She had half expected that Richard would have worn his uniform, but waiting for her was a dapper young man in an almost flamboyant cream suit. He looked like a young God with his fine-featured, boyish face, his golden curls and exquisite blue eyes. He had a sprig of pink blossom pinned to his wide lapel. No wonder Beamish had said they'd dressed for each other.

He looked handsome and healthy, as though he was about to spring from his seat, take her in his arms and dance a foxtrot. Then he stood painfully and shuffled into position, breathing heavily and supported on Beamish's arm, before eventually being transferred to hers and a walking stick. Fine tremors wracked his body. Beamish took a step back so he was within reach should he be needed.

She drew in a breath when Richard gave her a wide, happy smile.

She was less sure of this marriage, and tried not to think of Denton's letter waiting for her. She was very aware of the fact there was probably an infant growing inside her, a little being, who in innocence and ignorance would have a claim on her time and her love. It was the ultimate lie, she thought. The child could never know its creation was less than immaculate, and would probably never know, or remember, the man who'd unselfishly offered his name as a birthright. Enabling the child to grow within the security of his name as it lived its life was the ultimate proof of Richard's love. She would tell the child his father was a hero.

The sun chose that moment to briefly illuminate the window behind the altar, and they were bathed in colour as though the marriage was being blessed.

The reverend gently coughed and the ceremony began.

It didn't take long to dispose of her blemished spinsterhood. Richard repeated the vows in a clear, calm voice, as if absolutely certain that what they were doing was the right thing in his eyes.

Resentment flooded through her at the thought that this beautiful man had made his sacrifice, and was standing in the queue waiting for God to collect him. Short of a miracle, there was nothing anybody could do about it. Meanwhile, he was trying to snatch just a little normality and happiness out of his suffering.

She felt every word of the ceremony with acute but useless anguish.

Now it was her turn to give account of herself, and her voice reflected the emotion in the moment.

'I take thee, Richard Sinclair Sangster, to my wedded husband, to have and to hold from this day forward, for better for worse, for richer for poorer in sickness and in health, to love, cherish and to obey, till death do us part . . .'

There was a poignant moment in the ceremony when her voice faltered and tears pricked against her eyelids. She wanted to shout out: It isn't fair! Richard's hand gently squeezed hers, strengthening her as she completed the vow, '. . . *according to God's holy ordinance; and thereto I give thee my troth.*'

As they left the church a boisterous gust of wind snatched off her hat and sent it bowling across the field.

Richard laughed when Beamish was about to run after it. 'Let it escape. By the time you catch it, it will be covered in mud. I'll buy her a new one.'

Dr Elliot arrived to join his wife. He waylaid them to give Livia a kiss and to shake Richard's hand. 'The best of luck you two. I can't see your father anywhere, Richard, couldn't he make it?'

'I'm afraid not. Are you coming back to the house, Doctor? We have champagne.'

'I can't, I have my rounds to finish. How lovely you look, Livia. I'm almost tempted to make my patients wait . . . though I don't think Mrs Miller's baby will appreciate it. Hmmm . . . I've missed one cheek, so you look a little lopsided.' He kissed her again on the other cheek, laughing, 'There, that's better.'

'May I point out that kissing Livia is now my privilege,' Richard said.

'And kissing you is mine, Doctor Elliot,' Helen reprimanded, and the doctor laughed and surprised his wife with a kiss on the lips.

They crowded into the Austin, the staff squashing into the back seat, laughing and making jokes as they splashed through the potholes.

Tomorrow would be different. Tomorrow Livia would interview a new housekeeper, and she, who'd not long ago been the maid-of-all-work, would take her place as the mistress of the house.

Beamish had arranged for a photographer to record the

wedding. They posed in the conservatory, Richard seated, Livia claiming him, standing with her ring hand on his shoulder so the platinum band was obvious. Esmé was at the front, clearly loving being dressed up, but looking self-conscious at being noticed.

The photographs would be a reminder for her in the years to come, the players gazing stiffly out at her from silver frames lined up on the piano. Except for Richard, who looked as though he was about to burst from happiness. It was humbling to realize that a man like Richard could love her.

He began to look tired when they got to the champagne toasts. Livia stayed by his side while Beamish made a short speech. Richard responded, his voice shaking a little. He flinched at the end when Matthew Bugg popped the cork from a second bottle of champagne prematurely, and she witnessed a moment of fright and panic in his eyes.

She stooped, taking his hand in hers and whispering in his ear, 'Richard, you're fatigued.'

'Yes. Ask Beamish to take me upstairs so I can rest before dinner, if you would.'

After he'd gone she accepted the congratulations of the staff.

'You're a dark horse, I must say,' Connie told her with a touch of acid. 'I told Florence something was up, though I don't know what all the secrecy was about. We could have done a proper wedding feast with guests, a cake, and all the trimmings.'

'Thank you, Connie, but it would have all been too much for . . . for my husband.' There, she'd said it for the first time. 'Richard didn't want a fuss made.'

'Aye, there's that I suppose.' Connie sighed. 'Still, we didn't expect this. We all thought you were interested in young Doctor Elliot.'

Livia didn't indulge her in that observation. 'The agency is sending out a new housekeeper tomorrow.'

'Aye, well. Now you've gone up in the world I doubt if you'll want to get your hands dirty.'

Gently, she said, 'Connie, we'd best get one thing clear right from the start. Whatever my role has been in this house in the past, I've always given of my best and treated everyone with respect. There's no reason why this shouldn't continue. This reversal of roles is as hard for me as it is for you, and I think it might be a good idea for you to think about that a little.'

'Aye, you're right. I'm sorry, it's just . . . well, it's going to take some getting used to, isn't it? What would you have us call you?'

'If Captain Sangster had married another woman and brought her into the house as mistress, how would you expect to address her? It shouldn't take the staff long to work that out, and adjust. Including you.'

'Yes, *Mrs Sangster*.'

Leaving the staff to the celebrations, and taking Esmé with her, Livia went upstairs to see if Richard was comfortable, aware she was leaving a small smudge of resentment behind her. Champagne had given Connie a false sense of courage. The cook had decided to see how far Livia could be pushed, and had got her answer. She would soon get over it.

Beamish had moved out of the connecting room, and it was now Livia's domain, though she hadn't yet moved her things from the cottage.

Esmé would be in the smaller room across the hall, and the room next to that would be Chad's when he was home. Beamish had found himself a room a discreet distance away, on the other side of the bathroom and within easy reach of the bell.

Looking round, she thought, This is now my home . . . this big house with its air of shabby gentility, its ageing creaks and groans, its constant dust and the stale aura of birth, life and death. It was passed down through the Sinclair family and supported by the original Sinclair, who had made his fortune from whisky, and who'd gone to his grave keeping tight control of both fortune and tradition with typical Scottish thriftiness. She didn't envy her child the responsibility of it in the future.

'We need some nightwear, so Esmé and I are going to the cottage to collect it.'

Half asleep, Richard took her hand and gave a faint smile as he snuggled his cheek into the palm.

She pressed a kiss against his mouth. 'I won't be long, and I'll see you at dinner.' But Richard's eyelids had already closed over the brightness of his eyes. Gently, she withdrew her hand.

'He'll be out for a couple of hours and Matthew will come up and keep an eye on him,' Beamish said. 'I'm going into Poole to send some telegrams on his behalf. I can drop you off at the cottage and pick you up on the way back if you like, Mrs Sangster.'

'Thanks. I'll be able to pack a couple of boxes to bring back.'

The first thing she did was pluck the letter from Denton from the drawer. The contents beckoned her; the firmly stuck-down flap mocked her. She must forget him. She threw the letter on to the cold ashes, then, suddenly remembering that the torn cheque had been snatched out of the same, she plucked it out again. Brushing the ash off, she slid it back into the drawer and under the lining. Instinct told her it wasn't time to open it yet, but one day . . .

When Livia got back, carrying everything she could pack, including the cat and dog, which Esmé took upstairs to her room, Richard was awake. He'd been brought down to the drawing room and looked rested. He put his book aside. 'Come and talk to me, Livia.'

'I've got to put my things away and make Esmé's bed.'

'Florence can do that.'

'She has enough to do. Look, Richard, you might as well get used to me doing things in the house. I'm used to it, and I don't know how to act the mistress.'

When he rang the bell Florence appeared, her eyes merry and her smile a champagne glitter. 'Yes, Sir?'

'Put Mrs Sangster's things away please, Florence, and make her bed up, and that of Miss Esmé. Oh . . . and tell the cook we'd like some afternoon tea.'

'Yes, Madam . . . Sir.' Florence went off with a slightly sideways gait, humming Mendelssohn's wedding march tunelessly under her breath.

They looked at each other and laughed.

'There you are, it's easy being the mistress of the house,' Richard said.

Livia threw a cushion at him.

Twelve

The disruption over, they settled into a new routine. The replacement housekeeper was called Ellen Anstruther. She was a widow of fifty years of age with a grown-up son and daughter, both married. She was quiet and efficient and soon had the household running to schedule. The rest of the staff got on with her, too.

A couple of weeks later Livia suffered her first bout of morning sickness, and her suspicions were confirmed. Luckily it only happened a couple of times so she was able to avoid detection.

It had become a habit for her to get into her nightdress and robe and go through to say goodnight to Richard after Beamish had retired for the night. Quite often they talked until Richard was ready to sleep.

This particular night she found his room lit by candlelight.

'Does your gaslight need a new mantle?' she said. 'I'll ask Matthew to fix it in the morning.'

He gave a bit of a chuckle.

'I'm sure now about the baby, Richard, though I'm not going to tell Doctor Elliot until I'm about three months gone. It should be due halfway through October.'

He smiled and kissed her, then placed a hand against her stomach. He'd become more affectionate of late, and she was growing used to the familiarity of his touch. Now he lightly caressed her cheek. 'Would you do me a favour, my love?'

She nodded.

'You don't know what it is yet.'

'Then tell me.'

'You once said you wouldn't deny me anything.'

'I meant it.'

'Then I'd like you to sleep in my bed so I can hold you in my arms, like a normal husband would with his wife.'

She thought about it, then grinned and kissed him. 'I think I'd like that too.'

Removing her robe she slid under the covers and snuggled against his warm body. 'Tell me if you're uncomfortable.'

He slid his free hand down over her hip and bunched the material of her nightgown in his fist. 'What the devil is this garment you're wearing?'

'My nightgown.'

'It's as bulky as a circus tent.'

She tried not to grin. 'It used to belong to your mother, though I never saw her wearing it. I was going to cut it up and make some nightgowns for the baby from it, but I only had one nightgown of my own, so it seemed like such a waste.'

'It's certainly a waste to cover yourself up in it. You feel like a rabbit in a sack.' He began to laugh. 'And if you need another reason to get rid of it, I don't want a reminder of my mother in bed with us. As a passion killer it's a very effective tool. Would you take it off so I can ravish you?'

'Stop being so mean. I'll go and put another one on, shall I?'

'To be honest, I'd prefer you to be as bare-arsed and naked as I am.'

'Oh, I didn't know you were . . . naked.' She covered her shock with a light laugh. 'Good Lord! Now you've made me blush, and me a married woman.'

'Unfortunately, you're not married enough yet, and by now you must realize it's my intention to get up to no good. Why else do you think I'd light all these candles? My hands were shaking so much it was a wonder I didn't burn the house down.'

'I thought—'

'So did I, and that might yet prove to be the case. But anyway, I would like to get to know you better if I can. Taking a hands-on approach seemed the best way to encourage a little romance between us . . . literally.'

She didn't know whether to encourage him by laughing or not. She did know that putting his manliness to the test like this had taken a great deal of courage on his part. Her mouth dried up a little and she pretended to be shocked. 'Richard Sangster!'

'Oh, don't sound so prissy.' Taking her face in his hands he tenderly kissed her, then gazed into her eyes, laughing. 'If you don't fancy getting down and out dirty with me then I won't insist, but a little bit of naughtiness wouldn't go astray.'

'I won't know what to do.' But because he'd made her laugh and she was relaxed in his company, she did fancy it. 'I admit that the thought isn't too outrageous, and I suppose you can teach me how to go about things.'

He crossed his eyes and curled his lip, drawling, 'Mostly it's instinct, Livia, my lascivious wench.'

'Don't leer like a villain in a melodrama, it's a most unattractive trait.'

Stepping out of bed she undid her nightgown, bunching it at the neck and saying before her courage completely deserted her, 'Now you see it . . . and now you don't.' When she opened her hand, the material slid down her body and pooled around her feet. 'Is this naked enough?'

His gaze lingered on her rapidly cooling flesh. 'You're perfection . . . like all my imaginings, only better.'

'You've imagined me naked?'

'Often. You have a little round bottom that bobs when you walk.' He took her hands and pulled her down into the bed and against him. There was a moment when their eyes met and the laughter between them became charged with an intensity of emotion – when flesh touching unfamiliar flesh seemed to meld and melt them together, as though the heat from the flickering candles had dissolved them one into the other.

'I do love you,' she whispered, not knowing whether she was trying to convince him or herself.

He stooped to kiss the hollow at the base of her throat, then on he went, his mouth nibbling a trail to her breast. When his tongue gently circled the sensitive nub, shivers wracked her spine and she arched against him with a small, frenzied cry. He abandoned it in favour of the other breast, which swelled willingly into his mouth as if offering itself as a sacrifice.

She'd never imagined that making love would be so pleasurable, so frustrating, so exquisitely unashamed and so . . . so abandoned, as his hands created magic in her and she opened to his touch.

She dared to respond, her fingers gently stroking him, until a little groan came from his mouth. He'd begun to perspire, and the salt on his skin against her tongue had the tang of the ocean about it.

She became aware then of the subtle change in him . . . of his need . . . of her own need in the moisture of their loving. But his breath was coming harshly, and she instinctively knew they'd lose the magic of what was happening between them unless she helped him achieve what he'd set out to do.

Her hands closed around him, the silky shaft, half-aroused, gradually grew rigid. 'I don't think . . . I can manage this . . . no strength,' he panted.

'I have some to spare, just help me a little.' She moved astride him and poised over him because it seemed the right thing to do, her moist centre just touching and teasing him.

His palms slid one over each buttock and he brought her sliding down his shaft. His murmurs were contented as she began to move, his hands guiding her. Eventually he found enough energy to allow his pelvis to rise and meet her.

She leaned forward, feeling the need to kiss him, but his breath was laboured now. Instead, she took his golden curls loosely in her fingers and looked into the brilliance of his eyes, flickering in the candlelight.

'You smell of rose-musk and arousal,' he murmured, and he closed his eyes as she tightened her muscles around him. It didn't take long, and he gave a heartfelt groan when everything came together into a climax of sorts. He reached the point of satisfaction, but Livia still felt a little keyed up, as though she was on the outside looking in. She'd wanted more, and still did, but thought that it might be a different feeling for women.

Afterwards, he drew in a storm of harsh, ragged gasps, his chest heaving and his heart beating rapidly against her palm. It scared her.

'Do you feel all right? Should I fetch Beamish?'

'Not needed . . . be all right . . . soon.'

Gradually his breathing calmed, and he said, 'I never thought that would happen. Thank you, my love.'

'I'd better go back to my own room.'

'No . . . stay with me tonight . . . please.'

'I'll blow the candles out.'

'They'll blow themselves out.'

She cuddled into him and he kissed her ear. 'I adore you, my darling, wonderful Livia. Goodnight.'

She watched him fall asleep, and contemplated the fragile fey beauty of his face. It was as if he'd been marked by his fate since the beginning of time. A tear crept down her cheek and fell on to his, where it glistened like a diamond.

She watched over him while, one by one, the candles drowned in hot wax and sputtered into extinction.

He would go like that too, his blessed flame snuffed by his last breath, she thought. And she'd miss him beyond measure.

Beyond the window was a false dawn, the thin threads of yellow light dividing the darkness into bands. Downstairs in the hall, the clock struck four. It was one of the witching hours when souls were most likely to leave the body – or so she'd heard.

Richard murmured something in his sleep when she rose from their warm nest. They won't get your soul tonight, my love, she thought, as she pulled the curtains across.

Livia woke to find Richard gazing at her from the chair by the window. Light streamed in from behind him, forcing her to screw her eyes up. He was fully dressed.

'Are you up already?'

He laughed. 'It's ten-thirty.'

'Esmé!'

'Don't worry, everything is organized. Mrs Anstruther took her to school. I've ordered breakfast for eleven; that gives you half-an-hour in which to get bathed and dressed. Florence has run your bath.'

Her eyes widened. 'Florence knows I slept with you?'

'The whole house will know by now, I expect. We are married, after all.'

'No wonder you look so smug.'

'I feel extremely smug. I slept well. You?'

'I watched you sleep until the candles went out.' She looked round for her robe, found it on the end of the bed and slid into it.

'No wonder you slept late. We're going into Poole to see a dressmaker after breakfast. I can't have my wife walking around in my mother's cast-offs, and wearing circus tents to bed. You can choose your patterns and fabrics from their catalogue.'

'I didn't wear anything to bed.'

'Except me.' He grinned. 'It was fun, wasn't it?'

She kissed his cheek on the way to the bathroom as a reply, even though she was blushing rosily all over at the thought of what had taken place between them.

'Livia.'

She turned.

'What happened between us . . . you enchanted me last night, and it makes me feel as though I've made the child mine.'

She returned to where he was seated and her eyes searched his. 'But that wasn't the reason behind it, was it?'

'No . . . it was because I adore you, and wanted the intimacy of us being part of each other. I don't know if that can ever happen again. I don't know—'

She placed a finger over his mouth. 'Don't say any more, Richard. Let's love each other the best we can, while we can, and take each day as it comes.'

'Will you stay in my bed?'

'Is that a request or a question?'

'You know which it is. Well?'

Her head slanted to one side and she gave him a faint smile as she touched her stomach. 'Yes, I'd like to . . . at least, while there's still room. And while it's comfortable for you.'

Poole was in its usual bustle. It was a busy port, the quay a hive of activity. The berths were full of ships, their masts swaying with the movement of the water. Seagulls wheeled and shrieked overhead. Brownsea Island dominated the harbour.

'Didn't you spend some time at Brownsea recovering from your injuries before you came home, Richard?' she said.

He nodded. 'It depends whether you regard a mental condition as an injury. They treated the bullet wounds before I went there. They nursed soldiers suffering from shell shock and nervous breakdowns. Some people classified it as cowardice . . . including my father. He was ashamed of me being there, and only visited me once, on the day I came home. Luckily,

I have the scars from the bullet wounds to redeem my worth in his eyes.'

He was brutal about his condition, and about his father, and she tried not to flinch.

'Mrs Van Raalte, who owned the island, was very good to us all. Beamish joined me there. He insisted on looking after me and refused to leave. In the end he was found a room and became an honorary nurse. They found him useful for lifting us about. I don't know what I would have done without him.'

Beamish shrugged. 'Neither do I.' He placed Richard in a wooden chair with wheels, to trundle him around town in.

They found an establishment with a discreet shop front, which was very superior. Livia went through the patterns and fabrics, and was measured from head to toe. She ordered several outfits, and bought a couple of frocks that were already made up.

She would still wear Margaret Sangster's legacy to her, though. Longer skirts were still in fashion, and she could always alter the length if need be.

They had lunch in a hotel, where the men supped on a glass of ale. After they'd eaten the two men exchanged a glance, and Beamish grinned when Richard handed Livia a wad of money and said, 'Why don't you go off and buy some frilly bits and pieces? We'll wait here for you.'

She gazed from one to the other, suspicious. 'I smell a conspiracy. I'll be back in one hour, and I'll expect you both to be sober.'

She was exactly one hour. They weren't sober. Richard's smile was so wide it threatened to swallow his ears, and she couldn't smother her laugh at the thought. This man had so much charm he could get away with anything with her, and she suspected he knew it.

She glanced at the half-empty glasses. 'Are you nearly ready, gentlemen? I have the car outside.'

Their hands reached out for the glasses, Richard's shaking slightly as it folded round the glass. The liquid disappeared down their throats in one smooth swallow apiece.

Richard and his wheelchair were stowed in the back amongst the parcels.

'There isn't any room for my feet, Beamish old boy,' he said.

Beamish offered a solution. 'Stick them out of the soddin' window, Captain. That's what it's for.'

Beamish gazed to where Livia had taken her place behind the wheel. He looked as though he were about to argue, until she said, 'Say one word, Mr Beamish, and you can walk home. Give the handle a turn, would you please.'

Behind her, Richard deflated himself with an authoritative belch and lay down, saving himself the bother of trying to arrange his feet.

Beamish scrambled into the front passenger seat, banging his head on the roof on the way in. He tried to look casual as she set the car in motion. Soon his head was nodding on his chest as she drove sedately through the countryside. Both men began to snore.

'The pair of you are a disgrace,' she said, giggling because she couldn't find it in her heart to blame them for their transgression. They all needed to unwind now and again.

It was four p.m. when they arrived home, and she was a bit peeved that her passengers hadn't stayed awake to observe her driving prowess. Beamish had recovered his wits, and he gave her a sheepish grin. 'Sorry.'

'Don't be. You should take Richard to the local inn for a pint sometimes. It will do him good to mix with other people.'

'We have to be careful with his medication.'

'Perhaps it's something I should learn to manage. After all, you'll be married soon and will want to spend more time with Florence.'

Beamish's face assumed a slightly stubborn expression. 'Captain Sangster's welfare is my responsibility.'

'I rather think the doctor is in charge, don't you?'

The huff of laughter he gave was derisory. 'Your husband would tell you otherwise if you asked him.'

Though instinct told her not to, she pursued the subject. 'I'm sure Doctor Elliot would teach me how to give Richard his injection if I asked.'

His eyes came up to hers. 'Injection? I think you're mistaken, Mrs Sangster. The only medication the captain is prescribed is a sedative to calm him down on occasion.'

'I'm sure I saw a hypodermic needle in the bathroom once.'

'With respect, it would be better for all concerned if you forget about what you saw. That's your husband's business, and he knows what's best for him.'

So that's why Beamish went on day trips to London now and again. 'What is he addicted to?'

'Cocaine.'

He leaned into the car and brought the wheelchair out before giving Richard a gentle shake. 'We're home, Sir.'

Richard woke with a grunt and gazed around him. 'We got home safely, despite having Livia in the driving seat, then?'

Her sigh was exaggerated. 'Less of your impudence, Sangster.'

Taking Richard under the armpits, Beamish slid him out of the car and into the wheelchair. 'Upstairs or downstairs?'

'Up. I want to see what Livia has in all those parcels, though it will take a week to get them all out of the car.'

'Are you sure you've got your feet with you, Richard?'

'My feet?' He gazed down at them, then at her with some bewilderment. 'I do have a vague recollection . . . did I lose them?'

Beamish chuckled. 'Mrs Sangster's mind is as keen as mustard today, so if I were you I'd leave the matter right there, Sir.'

Knowing the advice was for herself, not for Richard, Livia decided it might be wise to take it.

From then on, and as the weeks carried them on towards summer they made love in a rather one-sided manner. Richard's ability to function fully as a man had not returned after one further brief exchange, although he still appreciated and enjoyed the intimate, sensory exchange between them; saying it was relaxing.

Livia thought it was rather that he wanted to please her. He'd learned when the moment was right for her, and she for him, so they didn't leave each other in need.

'I don't want a frustrated wife who will look to be satisfied in bed elsewhere, so tell me if you need more attention, and don't be shy.'

'What about you?'

'This is as good as it will get for me. I'm thankful you were too inexperienced to know the difference between myself and a man who has his health and strength, and love on his mind.'

Now, he brushed the hair back from her brow and kissed her eyelids. 'You look lovely when you're aroused. Your eyes are seductive and your mouth trembles. Am I making you happy?'

'I couldn't be happier.' She could only think of one thing that would make her happier . . . but his complete recovery was impossible. Living intimately as she was now, she'd noticed his breathing deteriorating, and she knew he needed to rest more. He seemed driven, trying to cram more and more into his day, and sometimes seemed too exhausted to speak.

'My love, you should rest more,' she said.

'I haven't got time to rest. I was thinking it would be nice to have a supper party and invite everyone. The end of June might be a good time. It's my birthday about then, so we can use that as an excuse. If it's a nice evening we can open the French windows and use the patio off the drawing room for dancing. I'll write the guest list and send out the invitations.'

She didn't ask him if he was up to it. Richard was a law unto himself, and she'd do anything to make his life more comfortable and enjoyable, and the small tasks involved with the arrangements would occupy his mind.

Mr Stone paid a visit and he and Richard spent two hours talking together.

That same evening Richard placed his mother's jewellery box in her hands. 'You might as well have these. I've cleared it with Simon Stone, and none of them belong to the Sinclair estate. My mother didn't have a lot of jewels, but what she did have are of exceptional quality. She would have wanted my wife to have them. '

'Thank you, Richard. I'll put them back in the strongbox for safe-keeping.'

'I've told Simon Stone about the baby.' He placed his hand against her stomach. 'You're not showing yet, but isn't it time you consulted a doctor?'

'It is time, but I don't know if I can fool Doctor Elliot. I've worked out that the child is due on the eighth of October. But I've got to take another six weeks into account for it. I was thinking I might go to his partner.'

'Doctor Bramble? He's nearly retirement age, and he's getting a bit absent-minded.'

'Yes, I know, but I'm not a very good liar, and Doctor Elliot is so thorough.'

'Which is why I'd rather you saw him. I don't want your health put at risk.'

'But what if he realizes?'

'He's a man. He'll think we had a bit of something going on before we got to the altar. Most of the people in the village speculated on why we married in such haste, and in secret, so they'll expect the child to arrive early anyway.'

Her hand went to her mouth and her eyes widened. 'How utterly embarrassing. Say it's not true!'

He drew her face down to his and kissed her, his lips tender against hers. 'If I said it wasn't true, would that make you feel better about it?'

'Only if it's true that it's not true.'

'It doesn't matter if it's true or not since nobody will ever ask you outright. I'll ask Doctor Elliot to see you the next time he checks me over. We'll fudge the dates. I'm a wonderful liar, so would you like me to stay with you?'

She nodded. She hadn't thought much about the coming infant, just put it to the back of her mind. She wouldn't be able to do that for much longer, so she might as well see the doctor and get it over with.

Dr Elliot hummed and briefly felt her stomach through her clothing. 'It seems as though you're correct, Mrs Sangster.' He made a few calculations on his notepad. 'From the dates you've given me, the baby is due to arrive in the first week of December, a lovely Christmas present. Congratulations to the pair of you . . . though don't be surprised if the little chap arrives early; first babies often do.'

He knew! Yet the smile he gave them both was impersonal and non-judgemental. 'Mrs Sangster, I'll need you to come to my surgery for a blood test and a proper examination, just to confirm it. My nurse will be there for the examination, and she'll give you some information leaflets so you'll know what to expect in the coming months. You might like to sign on for her maternity clinic, where a monthly check can be made on your progress.'

'Thank you, Doctor, I will.'

'Good. Now, I'd like to have a private word with Richard, if I may, and to be quite honest, I could do with a cup of coffee if you wouldn't mind.'

'I'll make you one.'

As Livia closed the door behind her, the doctor was saying to Richard, 'Your blood pressure is elevated. I might have to put you on medication if it hasn't normalized in a couple of days, and I'll make sure you have a tank of oxygen at hand to help your breathing if need be . . .'

Thirteen

Within days an oxygen cylinder took up space in the corner of the room. It was an unwanted reminder to both of them that he might need assistance to breathe before too long.

The days went by fast. Beamish and Florence celebrated their wedding at the church and there was a party in the staff quarters. Richard, who'd been his friend's best man, made a short speech, then he and Livia left them to it.

Life went on as usual. Beamish and Florence had refused the offer of the cottage.

'Beamish and I have plans of our own,' Florence told her. 'We'll be leaving when . . . well, before long, anyway, so there's no sense in going to the effort of moving.'

Richard began to die before her eyes, and she thought each coughing spasm might be his last. She was thankful for the oxygen and for the stalwart Beamish. There was nothing Livia could do about Richard's suffering. At his urging she moved back into her own room, and the closeness between them reverted to a supportive friendship.

The day of Richard's supper party arrived. Livia intercepted Beamish in the hall when he came to dress him. 'He's very tired, Mr Beamish. I hate seeing him like this. I think we should cancel the supper.'

'It's too late for that. Besides, it's his birthday and he's looking forward to it. We both know he's not going to celebrate another. You go and dress up in your very best for him, Mrs Sangster. The captain is proud of you, and he loves seeing you looking pretty. He needs your support. Leave the rest to me. I'll give him some oxygen and he'll be as lively as a lop in no time at all.'

Livia had already decided to wear the gown her mother had designed for Margaret Sangster, though she'd shortened it to just above the ankle and removed the train. The overskirt hid the growing signs of her pregnancy, and the salmon pink suited her colouring. She'd had her hair styled into a bob that morning, and the curls sprang about her neck.

In Margaret Sangster's jewellery box Livia discovered a necklace glittering with a spray of diamonds, and she wore her engagement ring.

Esmé was excited because Chad had come home for the weekend, and the pair had been allowed to stay up for an extra hour and mingle with the guests. Chad had changed a lot. He was quite the gentleman, quiet and polite, and self-assured for his tender years.

Livia waited for Richard at the bottom of the stairs by the wheelchair. Eventually, Beamish carried him down. Richard had lost a lot of weight and his dinner suit hung loosely on him.

His smile broke her heart as her eyes met his, for his had lost their tiredness and regained their brilliance, though there was something desperate about them. She wondered for a moment if Beamish had given him an injection to bring about this transformation. Whatever it was, Richard would have sanctioned it. 'You look exquisite, my lovely girl,' he said.

She kissed him, whispering against his ear, 'Happy birthday, Richard, I love you.'

He bore her hand to his mouth. 'Ready?'

They made their way through to the patio, which was decorated with coloured lanterns. A long table was set out with drinks and glasses and was tended by Matthew Bugg. Florence and Connie wove in and out with trays of food.

Claps, cheers and shouts of happy birthday went up. 'For those of you who have never met her, I'm proud to present the love of my life, my beautiful wife, Livia.'

There was more applause, then a man detached himself from

some half-a-dozen men and stepped forward to take a hold on the wheelchair.

Livia put a hand on his arm to stop him.

'It's all right, Livia, this is Corporal Anderson. We fought side by side in the war together.'

She smiled at the man. 'How do you do.'

Richard pulled her down so he could whisper against her ear, 'Look, Dents is skulking behind the pot plant. I think I put his nose out of joint when I took you to the altar. Go and be sweet to him, my darling, and I'll work my way round to you.'

Straightening up, she turned. Immediately her eyes were drawn to the enigmatic green of Denton's. They stared at each other while her heart fell out of her chest like a star deserting the sky. She was poignantly aware that she still loved him. She wanted to laugh. She wanted to cry. She wanted to run to him, have him hug her tightly against his strong, warm body, and tell him she loved him.

How could she love two men at once? It wasn't decent. She couldn't . . . she mustn't allow herself to.

She did none of the things her turbulent mind suggested. Instead she pulled on her Mrs Sangster smile and began to close the gap between them, making sure her feet touched the ground between steps.

Denton watched her approach, a smile playing about his lips, his eyes filled with an unguarded mixture of condemnation and love, so they scorched as well as caressed her.

That look turned her resolve to mush and her knees to water. Suddenly she was standing in front of him, defenceless, gazing up at his tallness. His name whispered from her lips like a caress, giving away her feelings to anyone who happened to be listening. 'Denton.'

'You look absolutely breathtaking, Livia.'

'Thank you, Denton. I'm so glad you came.'

A tender kiss grazed across her cheek to her ear, and left a little shiver there. 'Are you happy, Livia?'

Across the patio she heard Richard's laughter ring out. If he was happy then so was she. 'Richard is a wonderful man.'

'Yes, he is, and if you're happy, so am I. You didn't answer my letter. You broke my heart, you know.'

'I'm sorry, I didn't intend to. The letter? I haven't opened it yet . . . I couldn't bring myself to.' She drew in a breath to steady herself. 'It arrived on our wedding day, just as I was about to leave for the church. I thought it would be better to put it away until . . . later.'

'And it's not later yet.' A wry smile touched his lips and he folded her hands into his. 'Obviously the letter was bad timing on my part. How has Richard been keeping?'

'Some days are better than others. I'm sure you have noticed how much he's deteriorated. We live for the present, and for his sake I'm trying not to despair.'

He glanced over her shoulder and released her hands, leaving her palms glowing like the colour of rubies. His smile came, full of its usual warmth, but a little forced as he directed it behind her. 'Oh, there you are, Bernice, what took you all this time?'

Bernice was of average height, with a pert nose, slightly pouting lips and sculpted dark hair cut to perfect points against each cheek. Her dark blue satin frock had a crossover bodice that left her arms bare, and floating chiffon side panels on the skirt, which finished at mid-calf. She looked fit and well-muscled.

'I needed to comb my hair and renew my lipstick. If we had to come to this party, the least I can do is dazzle the peasantry. I've picked up a plate of food on the way through. The vol-au-vents are divine.' A pair of midnight blue eyes fell on Livia, followed by a frown. 'Do we know you?'

The possessive plural wasn't lost on Livia. Denton and this woman were involved, and she had to deal with an almost lethal stab of jealousy. Be content, she told herself. You made your choice and married Richard.

Had there been any choice? Would she have married Richard if it hadn't been for . . .? God, she hoped Richard hadn't invited his father as well. That would be too much to bear.

'Where are your manners, Bernice? This is our hostess, Livia Sangster. Livia, this is Bernice James. I study with her brother, Nicholas, and we live in the same boarding house.'

'Whoops! Sorry, Livia. Trust me to put my foot in it.'

Bernice held out her hand, and after a moment of hesitation Livia took it. 'Are you studying surgery, too?'

'Lordy no, men are a bit disapproving about women poaching their professions. I suppose they're frightened that women will outshine them . . . don't you think so, Denton?'

Denton looked bored, as though he'd heard it all before. 'If you say so.'

'I'm a dress designer. At least, I'm trying to be one. Mostly I sew seams for a living. I hope to open my own business before too long.' She slid her arm through Denton's and gazed archly up at him. 'Though I expect to get married one day?'

Denton didn't seem to hear her, instead asking, 'Didn't your mother design dresses, Livia? I seem to recall . . .'

'Yes, she did. She designed the one I'm wearing. Her name was Eloise Carr.'

Bernice became animated. 'Hey . . . I've heard of her. Do you take after her?'

'I'm afraid not. I haven't got an artistic bone in my body. I leave the drawing to my little sister.'

Denton gazed around him. 'Where is Esmé? Is she in bed. If not, I must say hello to her.'

'She's with Chad somewhere. He tells me the school we sent him to is starving him to death, so they're probably hanging around the buffet table.'

'They starved us to death, as well. It's a feature of boarding schools. There's a tuckshop in the village, though.'

'There's Bertie. He's supposed to be in the kitchen. Chad can't be far away.' The dog pawed at Richard's leg, then leaped into his lap when he patted it.

The children appeared and Livia called them over. Chad shook Denton's proffered hand. 'Wizard party, isn't it, Doctor Denton? Richard said I can put the records on the gramophone and keep it wound up when it's time for the dancing.'

Esmé gazed up at him and quietly waited to be noticed. Denton disengaged himself from the clutch of Bernice and took her in a hug. 'Hello, Poppet, how's my favourite girl now?'

Esmé hugged him. 'Doctor Elliot said I'm better now and I don't have to take that awful medicine any more.'

'Was it horrid?'

'Chad said it was poison, and made from boiled mud and bat's blood.'

'Chad has a wild imagination. My father wouldn't be so mean as to give you a concoction like that.'

'I've missed you, Doctor Denton.'

'I've missed you too. But I'm here for a whole week. I'll come over and visit you tomorrow, after I see my guest off at the station. Perhaps we can arrange a picnic.'

Richard wheeled himself across. 'Hello Dents, old man, I'm glad you made it. Who's the lovely lady with you?'

'I have three lovely ladies with me, two of whom you already know.' He introduced Bernice as the sister of a fellow student, who was at a loose end.

Bernice looked annoyed by being put in her place a second time, and fluttered her eyelashes at Richard. 'Are you related to Livia by any chance?'

Richard's eyes swept over Bernice and he offered Denton a fleeting grin. 'Not by chance, by design. I just happen to be her husband. Has Livia told you our news yet, Dents?'

Denton's delicious green eyes settled on her, an enquiry uppermost in his expression.

Up until now she'd avoided discussing the coming baby with anyone, because it brought back the shame of its conception – an act so quick and furtive, that had been forced on her without thought of the consequence. It was as if that grubby moment was ground into her changing body as well as her mind. She'd told Richard she'd love the child. She would try. But the nearer she got to the birth, the more she doubted herself. The baby was somehow anonymous . . . as if it had taken root in her womb like a tenacious weed, without really being part of her. She couldn't imagine it as a child.

'I'm going to become a father by Christmas,' Richard said, making the infant his creation, making the lie part of them. Only he wouldn't be here to be a father to it, would he, she thought, with an unexpected itch of resentment.

Shock exploded in Denton's eyes and he gazed at the alien, hardly discernible swelling under her dress. 'Congratulations, Livia . . . Richard.'

'I'm surprised your father didn't tell you.'

'I haven't seen him yet. We came here straight from London. Besides which, he would have taken your privacy into consideration and left it up to you.'

He sounded stiff and formal, withdrawn into his hurt.

Bernice dropped into the conversation, 'So, you're in the pudding club, Livia. Lord, how utterly dreary. I never want children.' She lit a cigarette and a cloud of acrid smoke drifted into the middle of the sudden silence. It caught in Richard's throat and he began to cough, his breath a harsh, painful rattle.

Denton said irritably, 'Do get rid of that gasper, Bernie . . . or go off and smoke it elsewhere.'

'Sorry . . . I didn't realize.' Shrugging, Bernice wandered off towards the group of men Richard had just left.

Denton let Esmé go and bent to Richard, holding a handkerchief against his mouth and gently patting his back as he struggled to regain his breath. 'I'll go and ring my father, though he's probably on his way.'

Richard shook his head violently. 'Will be . . . all right . . . soon.'

Livia took charge. 'Take him into the study, Denton . . . I'll fetch him something to drink. Chad, go and find Mr Beamish and tell him he's needed in the study. He'll know what to do.'

'Bring some brandy in milk. If he sips it, it will help him to relax.'

They got him quickly away and were joined by Beamish who took over. 'Breathe in through your nose and hold it. One . . . two . . . three. Gradually release it . . . one . . . two . . . three. Good. Again . . .' Richard's coughing became less frenzied as he concentrated on his breathing and took control of it.

Beamish's eyes came up to hers. 'You can't do much to help, Mrs Sangster. He'll be all right. It might be best if you go and attend to your guests and the children. I'll take him upstairs and give his back a bit of a thumping to help get the loose phlegm up. It's not something the captain would like you to see. Come if you like, Doctor. I'd appreciate your help.'

Livia nodded, and left the men to it.

Bernice had a glass of champagne in her hand when Livia

went down. 'Look, I'm sorry,' she said. 'I seem to have a habit of putting my foot in it. I've embarrassed Denton in front of his friends, haven't I?'

'Oh, I don't imagine so. Denton is a very self-possessed type of man, and most of the people here are Richard's friends. Have you known him long?'

The woman looked amused. 'Not long. My brother invited him to a party one weekend, about six months ago. We started going out together. We have an understanding, but we're keeping it a secret until he's been accepted into the Royal College of Surgeons. He's been pushed through because of his war service.'

Livia didn't want to know what that understanding was, though Bernice had made it clear that she expected to have a ring on her finger before too long. She was relieved when Bernice asked, 'What's wrong with your husband?'

'He was injured during the war.' And that was all she would tell her. The details were Richard's business.

'A pity. He's a good-looking chap.' Bernice drained her champagne then looked around her. 'Have you got a piano?'

'Just inside the French window.'

'Great. Will you mind if I get this party going?'

'I'll be relieved. I'm not very good at this sort of socializing.' She stopped, suddenly struck by the thought that Richard seemed to have organized his own farewell party. Thrusting the chilling thought from her mind with a faint shudder, she opened the instrument.

Bernice took her place at the piano and began to sing, *'You have loved lots of girls in the sweet long ago . . .'* By the time she started on the chorus, '*I wonder who's kissing her now . . .*', Richard's friends had drifted over. They joined in the next chorus with great gusto. That was followed by 'For me and my Girl' and 'Roses of Picardy'.

Bernice sang in tune, her voice loud and husky rather than sweet, and without a shred of nerves in evidence.

More guests arrived from the village, including Andrew and Helen Elliot and the reverend and his wife.

Richard came out into the garden again, a smile on his face, and nodded to Chad. Chad applied himself to the gramophone with great enthusiasm, while, Richard spun out into the middle and manoeuvred his wheelchair round and round in a circle, calling out, 'Come on, Bernice. Shake your tail with me.'

She swung into his orbit, clicking her fingers in time to the music and shaking her hips.

Denton chuckled, 'She'll dislocate herself if she's not careful.'

Beamish shook his head gloomily, though he was laughing along with everyone else. 'I don't know what's come over him lately. The daft bugger will make himself dizzy.'

The party suddenly took off, and a little while later, Livia found herself dancing a slow waltz with Denton.

'Richard's animated tonight,' he said.

'Yes, he is. It's nice to see him enjoying himself. He must get bored.'

'Believe it or not, Richard was never much of a gadabout, and he always managed to behave himself, even when he was tipsy. He had plenty of friends at school. He's got one of those personalities that attracts people, and he hasn't got a mean bone in his body.'

'He never complains about his condition or gets angry, but he tires easily. I don't know what he'd do without Beamish . . . or what I'd do, come to that.'

'The man is extremely competent and Richard is lucky to have him. And he's lucky to have you, Livia. He told me he'd never felt happier. He's pleased about the baby. I hope all goes well for you.'

'Yes, he is . . . we both are. I imagine all will be well, since babies are born every day. Your father is making sure I do all the right things to prepare for the birth.'

He danced her back to her husband and handed her over. She kissed Richard's forehead. 'I'm going to take the children up to bed and settle them down now. I won't be long.'

'Good, we don't want them too tired. We're all going on a picnic tomorrow.'

The party continued for the next couple of hours, after which people began to say goodnight and drift off. Bernice was cajoled into playing the piano again and there was another sing-song. Livia tried to stifle her yawn.

Richard kissed her knuckles. 'Go on up to bed if you're

tired, angel. I want to yarn with the lads for a while. I'll be up later.'

She said her goodnights to everyone, and left.

In the hall she found Denton waiting for her. He drew her into his arms and kissed her willing mouth until she thought she'd run out of breath. She thought she ought to protest, so murmured against his mouth, 'Denton, stop.'

He did, saying, 'You owed me that one, woman. Sleep well, my love.'

The music stopped five minutes later and she heard Denton's car drive away. There was the chink of glasses and the sound of muted male voices, with the occasional outburst of laughter ringing above it. They would be swapping stories about the war, she supposed, and wondered where Richard's companions would sleep. Should she get up and arrange something? No, she thought, Beamish was one of them. He could make the arrangements.

She fell asleep before she could argue herself out of bed to perform the task.

Richard woke early. He'd taken a dose of Andrews liver salts before he'd gone to bed, shuddering at its tart taste. Even so, he had a filthy headache.

'It serves you right,' Beamish said. 'You know damned well you shouldn't drink to excess, especially beer. You'll be peeing all day.'

'No I won't. It wasn't drink that gave me a headache . . . it was the other stuff. It packed quite a kick, and I thought my heart was going to leap out of my chest.'

'I know. You had your wheelchair standing on end.'

What happened to my men, Beamish?'

'Phipps offered to drive them home. Five of them took him up on it. Phipps was cross-eyed, so they either got home safely, or they ended up in a hedge between here and Birmingham.'

'Birmingham . . . who lives in Birmingham?'

'Nobody, but that's where Phipps said he was going. A couple of wiser chaps took the milk train to London. Odd that, since one of them lives in Bristol, which is in the other direction. It could be something to do with the company. Miss Bernice caught the same train.'

'She was a cracker, wasn't she? Good old Dents.' Richard laughed. 'Did I make an arse of myself?'

'Your lady will forgive you if you did. Here, drink your coffee, Sir. You'll soon feel better. Doctor Elliot the younger is coming over and you're going on a picnic this afternoon.'

Richard groaned silently. 'Not too far, I hope.'

'We can stay in the grounds. There's that clearing near the stream, where the oak tree is. You can admire the bluebells while I act like a butler.'

'I used to go there with my mother when I was young. Old Bugg hung a knotted rope from a branch and I used to climb up it. Mother called it the magic tree, and she told me stories about the elves and fairies who lived in its branches, while she painted flowers.'

'I would like to have met her. Mrs Sangster said she was a lovely lady.'

'Yes . . . she was. I'm sorry I missed her, but at least she didn't see me looking like this. She was proud of me, you know. Her little hero, she used to call me when I was small.' Richard put the reminiscences away where they belonged, in the past. He and Livia had agreed that they were only going to live for the day.

'Shall I prepare a pick-me-up?'

'Not today, Beamish. I feel strong, and the oxygen will suffice.' He didn't tell Beamish that it was a bit of an effort to breathe, and his heart was pounding along with his head. Beamish would insist on him staying in bed, and he was sick of seeing the inside of four walls, especially on such a nice day. 'Have the day off. Take Florence into town so she can spend some of your hoarded cash. I don't feel like being babysat today. Besides, Dents will be there if I need him.'

The feeling of strength accompanied Richard to the picnic.

Denton played hide and seek with the children. Livia stayed by Richard's side. She was wearing a summery flowered dress. He touched her hand. 'You're enchanting, like a freshly picked bunch of flowers. I adore you, my Livia.'

She looked as though she were about to cry. 'Oh . . . Richard,' she said, and her glance flickered towards Denton, who was stalking through the long grass on his hands and knees. The dog gave Chad's position away, and Esmé's giggle signalled hers. Livia laughed when Denton pounced on them, and Esmé went leaping off across the grassy tufts like a grasshopper.

'Go and play games with the children,' he urged.

'Denton isn't a child.'

'He is when he allows himself to be. Have I told you how much I love you today?'

'Don't change the subject. Someone should be with you.'

'Last night is catching up with me. I'm going to have forty winks. Go away and play.'

She plumped up his cushion, kissed him and said, 'I love you too.' Then she was gone.

For a while Richard watched the game as the sun moved around the sky, pushing the shadows before it. The dragonflies skimmed across the pond, wings flashing with iridescence. He loved his home and would rather be here than anywhere else on earth. He felt well, and there was a huge sense of euphoria about him – like the buzz he got from the cocaine he indulged in now and again.

The day took on a diffused edge, as though he was gazing at it through smoked glass. Richard saw a movement by the pond. There was a man standing there . . . more than one. He recognized them without their gas masks as the fallen from his regiment. He stood, his pain gone, and made his way down the slope towards the pond to greet them.

He stopped to kiss Livia on the cheek as he passed her. 'I love you,' he whispered against her ear, 'but we always knew I'd leave you.'

He looked back when he reached his men. Livia, her hand against the cheek he'd kissed, was gazing back at the crumpled figure seated under the oak tree. She called out to him, her voice coming from far away, slightly panicky. *'Richard . . .'*

She would never be alone, he thought. Denton would always be there when she needed him.

The mist thickened, blotting the scene. Turning, he smiled at his men as they crowded around him.

Fourteen

Even while knowing her husband didn't have long to live, Richard's death seemed sudden to Livia, and losing him was a great shock.

They'd live one day at a time, they'd said. Now Richard had run out of his days.

'It's as though the sunshine has left my life,' she told Denton, who had decided to stay on until the funeral was over. 'Everything seems to have been leached of its colour. I can't even cry.'

'It's delayed shock. You'll weep eventually.'

Beamish did everything, and although beset by his own grief, he was in a better state than she was and became her rock to lean on.

'Has Richard's father been invited to attend the funeral?' she said, when she asked him what she should do.

'He's been informed of Richard's death. The captain didn't want you to be worried, and told me exactly what he wanted done, and who to contact. I expect the major will attend. After all, Richard is his son. I'll make sure he doesn't bother you.'

At her insistence, she saw Richard again before they closed the coffin. Denton and Beamish came with her. Tears in his eyes, his jaw tense from holding in the sadness he felt, Denton paid his respects first. He left to wait by the car, leaving her with Beamish.

Richard was dressed in his uniform, except for his cap, which would go on top of the lid. He looked healthy, and she could have sworn he was wearing rouge. He fitted into the coffin without an inch to spare.

'He's lying to attention,' she said, giving a watery smile. 'I hope he doesn't want to turn over.'

Beamish grinned at her, but it was a guilty grin they shared, in case smiling in the presence of the newly dead might offend the undertaker.

'Thank you for everything, Mr Beamish. You've been an absolute brick.'

'So have you, Mrs Sangster. He would have died long ago if you hadn't taken the emptiness from his life and allowed him to live in as normal a manner as possible. You gave him back his self-esteem.'

'He did more for me than I did for him. He was a wonderful and generous man. He knew the end was near. He arranged his own farewell party, didn't he?'

Beamish nodded. 'It seems so.'

'It is so. Would you mind leaving us now? I won't be long.'

When Beamish had gone, she ran her fingers through Richard's golden curls. His scalp was cold and waxy under her fingertips, so she formed the impression that he'd been changed from a living, breathing man into a beautiful marble statue. She wished she could see his intense blue eyes once more, but his lids were closed and his lashes feathered against his skin. She kissed the tip of her finger and touched each of the closed eyelids.

She heard a faint footfall behind her.

'I just want to tell you again that I love you, Richard Sangster. You're my tall poppy, along with Denton and Beamish. But I don't think I'll ever forgive you for leaving me. Goodbye, my love, I'm going to miss you.'

She took a step back, nodding to the undertaker who had entered, and who stood a respectful distance away, then went out to join Denton.

Outside, the comrades-in-arms who'd been reunited with him just a week ago had formed ranks, with Beamish at the head. They moved through the bright day with Denton and herself a short distance ahead of the hearse, so they could be at the church before Richard arrived. The soldiers came on behind. They would carry the coffin into the church then on to the burial ground afterwards, to honour their officer.

Denton took her hand in his, and she was comforted. Chad and Esmé came to the service with the cook and Mrs Anstruther. They were subdued by the event, but Chad couldn't wait to get back to school, and Esmé had accepted Richard's death and had already shed her tears. She was too young to grieve for long.

Livia had thought that Major Henry might not come. But tradition died hard, and duty was duty. He was waiting at the church, and seated himself next to her in the pew. Immediately she became rigid with tension, but was thankful Rosemary was not with him.

At the gravesite she moved to where the Elliots' stood, leaving the major alone. The less time she spent in his company, the better. They stood on opposite sides of the neat oblong hole that had been made ready to receive Richard's body. It was next to his mother's grave. Denton stood behind her with his parents, so close that she could almost feel his breath warm against her neck.

Under Livia's sober black dress and concealing tunic, the baby quickened. She'd been told what to expect, but nothing could have prepared her for this soft fluttering of new life in the midst of death. It was as though Richard had sent her a reminder that life moved on – that he'd claimed this child as his own, and she must treat it with the respect it deserved.

Her face softened. Richard had trusted her to do the right thing by the child, and she would, but she would have liked to have shared this moment with him, and watch his smile come once more.

The major didn't gaze at her once, but for the sake of convention he came back to the house for refreshments afterwards.

He approached her then, his face desolate. 'I did love my son, you know.'

'Yes, of course you did. You're Richard's father and he was a wonderful man.'

'Are you well, Livia?'

'I'm expecting an infant.'

He looked startled for a moment. Then he gave a faint frown, as though he'd recalled the incident and had calculated the possibility. He laid down his own terms. 'So . . . I'm to become a *grandfather*.'

He was making it clear what relationship to the child would

be acceptable. She wasn't going to argue, but she wasn't going to encourage him in that role, either. She was too numb to be angry. Did she want Henry in her life in the future? Not really, but the infant might.

'Yes, I suppose you are . . . since you're kin to Richard.'

'We should forgive and forget,' he murmured, giving a faint, cajoling smile.

She had no intention of falling for his charm, especially on this of all days. Forgiving him was out of the question. Her loathing for him was buried too deeply. Forgetting would be impossible when she had the child to bring up.

When he patted her hand she jerked it away and took a step backwards. Beamish appeared at her elbow, his gaze steady on the man like a dog waiting for the command to attack.

Henry edged away, collecting condolences on the way to the door and murmuring to anyone who was listening, 'I must go now. It's such a sad thing to bury one's only son.'

Livia couldn't help whispering as she moved away to talk to the reverend, 'Perhaps you'd see the major off, Mr Beamish.'

The amused twitch of his lips was only just discernible. 'It would be a pleasure, Mrs Sangster, but I think I'll allow him to leave without that particular indignity.'

Denton crossed to her side. 'How are you holding up?'

'It doesn't seem real. I expect to hear Richard's laughter, and I keep putting two cups on the tea tray.' She gazed up at him. 'You'll be going back to London soon, I imagine.'

'In an hour or so. I've come to say goodbye.'

'Would you like anything of Richard's to remember him by?'

'We were friends throughout our childhood and into adulthood. I have my memories to draw on. You should keep his personal effects for his child.'

'Yes.' She smoothed a hand over her stomach. 'This doesn't seem real to me either.' Livia was moved to share her special moment with him. 'I felt the baby move when we were at the gravesite, and I wanted to share it with him.'

He grinned wryly at her. 'You've shared it with me instead. Usually a baby doesn't quicken until between the fourth and fifth months.'

Alarm nudged at her, she'd forgotten Denton was a doctor. 'Yes, you're right, of course. It was probably my stomach gurgling.'

'Then again, it might be a baby with long legs who needed to stretch them a little.' He gazed silently at her for a moment, his eyes contemplative, then he brushed a kiss against her cheek. 'I'll be back in time for Christmas.'

The urge to hug him was strong, and had to be avoided. 'I'll see you then. Keep well.'

He walked away, tall, straight and strong, and her heart reached out to him, willing him to turn.

He did, and their eyes met for one precious second before he was gone.

A little later, when the mourners had departed and the children were in bed, Livia went into Richard's room.

It was neat. His personal goods were packed away, his clothing folded into the drawers in which Mrs Anstruther had placed lavender bags. Livia packed Richard's clothing into a trunk. Beamish could have them if he wished, though he was more sober in his dress than Richard had ever been.

She placed Richard's personal effects – his diary, gold cufflinks and a gold watch with an inscription in it, a gift from his parents for his twenty-first birthday – into the safe with his mother's jewellery.

The next morning, Simon Stone came to read Richard's will. There were small legacies made to the house staff, depending on their length of service; nothing more than an acknowledgement really. They were dismissed from the room.

'Mr Beamish, will you stay please,' he said. 'Richard Sangster was appreciative of your comradeship during the time you spent in the defence services together. He was grateful for your ongoing loyalty, and your unstinting service during his illness. He has requested that you will accept as a legacy the sum of one thousand pounds.'

Beamish swooped in a breath and turned pink. Livia had never seen him in such a flap before, when he stammered out, 'But I can't . . . it's too much . . . a fortune.'

Livia gave a little grin, even though it wasn't really the time or place for it, and placed a hand on his arm. 'You'd better let Richard have the last word this time, Mr Beamish, else he'll likely come back and haunt you.'

'But one thousand pounds,' he spluttered. 'The captain must have been mad when he made his will. I can't accept it.'

'I will attest that he was totally sane, Mr Beamish. He said he hoped you would see it as a reflection of the trust he placed in your discretion, your honesty and your friendship.' Simon Stone slid a paper across the desk. 'Don't be embarrassed about this sign of his appreciation, Mr Beamish. I'm sure you've earned every penny. Sign on the dotted line, if you would.' When Beamish's signature was exchanged for a cheque, Simon Stone shook his hand. 'Thank you, you may go.'

When the door closed behind the stunned Beamish, the lawyer turned her way. 'Mrs Sangster, how are you? I'm sorry we meet again under such tragic circumstances.'

'Richard's death was a shock, even though expected.'

'Quite . . . Your husband has left everything else to you, a mixture of trusts and property, with money set aside for the coming child . . . who is, of course, the Sinclair heir. Richard Sangster was comfortably off in his own right . . . and that estate is now yours. But there's one problem. Major Sangster has decided to challenge his son's will.'

She felt as though she'd been punched in the chest. The hypocrite! He'd been nice to her the day before, when all the time he'd been plotting her downfall.

'He will cite that you took advantage of his son's weakened physical and mental state and used your . . . and these are his words, Mrs Sangster . . . *womanly wiles to entice Richard Sangster into marriage, so as to gain monetary advantage from his imminent death.*'

She stared at him, dumbstruck.

'Moreover, he's claiming custody of the infant you are carrying.'

'My baby? He was unaware of its existence until yesterday.' Surely he wasn't going to shame her by confessing to having fathered the child. 'Because?' And she whispered, her mouth dry, for this double blow had left her reeling.

'He said he wants his grandchild to be raised in the manner

it should be, not brought up by a former maid. What are your thoughts on the matter, Mrs Sangster?'

The child suddenly became very precious to her. Richard had defended the right of this child to live a life free of guilt. In his generosity he'd given the child his name, and to both of them, his support. Now she would fight for its very identity. It was with a strong motherly instinct that she stated, 'Major Henry is entitled to put in a claim for his son's estate, but he's not getting my child without a fight.'

'Good, I was hoping you'd say that. On the strength of that statement I'm going to fight for your rights, and those of the child. With your permission I'll send my clerk down, who will take statements from yourself and your staff. We will then prepare our case to present to the court.'

She nodded.

'In the meantime, you can continue to live in Foxglove House.'

'Richard wanted the child to be born here. He said it was his birthright. He was determined that it would be a boy.'

'Quite so. A man always likes his first child to be made in his image.'

Only this one might be born in the major's image, she thought.

Simon Stone rose and patted her hand. 'These things take time. The major has yet to prepare and lodge an objection. Indeed, his solicitor has only just received a copy of the will. Do you have the means to support yourself and your sister?'

She had a bank account of her own, into which Richard had deposited money that would give her a private allowance for at least a year. She nodded, and told him the source of the account.

'Fine. That should last you a while.'

'Richard gave me his mother's jewellery as well.' She twisted the sapphire ring on her finger. 'I'd rather not part with this. Richard was so sweet when he proposed with it.'

'He consulted with me about the jewellery to determine that it wasn't part of the Sinclair estate. It's best you don't dispose of any of it until the will is proved. Wear the ring by all means, but bear in mind that if the major's case is proved, you will have to hand it over. Is the rest safely locked away?'

'Yes, it's in the safe.'

'Then I'll check it against the inventory before I return to London. Try not to worry too much, my dear. If the major goes ahead with this it's possible the court will see it as an attempt to assassinate your character, and it could easily bounce back at him.'

It most certainly could, she thought, it would blacken them all. She smelled Rosemary Sangster's hand in this. 'By any chance, would the major be in debt? I noticed at the funeral that he wasn't driving the Rolls.'

Simon Stone's eyes sharpened. 'That's something I'd never considered. I'll make some discreet inquiries in that direction.'

Livia alerted her staff as to what had taken place, and told them a clerk would take statements.

They were indignant on her behalf, but Connie had an I told you so expression on her face.

Livia remembered Richard's diary. Taking it from the safe, she carried it through to her own room. The page fell open to a loose leaf with a poem written on it.

Livia

Could I but sing as once I sang
When love and life and laughter rang
A girl adored inside my mind
My cherished one, heart soft and kind.

Tenderly, the spring curls back
Ashes of poppies in its track
Through summer, precious tho it be
Each breath steals my integrity

My love

This then is my reward, to yearn
And love my love in sweet return
I'll steal your mouth's blush when you sleep
And whisper words your heart will keep.

Your feet will walk where once I led
Sad tears for me your eyes will shed
Your heart will sometimes reach for me
A thread stitched tight in memory.

For eternity.

'Oh, Richard,' she whispered, and she curled up on his bed and began to weep as her heart, which she'd kept carefully glued together until then, shattered into a million pieces. The summer twilight was absorbed into night before sleep finally claimed her.

Fifteen

Rosemary Sangster was spitting fury.

Fists resting on her jutting hipbones, her slender figure clad only in a black lace-trimmed slip, she turned on her husband.

'You fool, Henry. Are you telling me you're broke? If I'd known I'd never have come back.' She gazed round her at the luxurious London mansion apartment. 'What about this place?'

'I had to use it as collateral for a loan to cover my gambling debts. The trouble is, I've got no income now to service it with, so the bank might foreclose.'

'And the Rolls?'

'Gone . . . sold. Bought a cheaper one.'

'But didn't you have an inheritance from Margaret?'

'She left everything to Richard, who left it to that serving maid he married.'

'So you married me under false pretences. You told me we'd be comfortably off.'

'I did expect to inherit. Margaret knew about our relationship and changed her will just before she died. She cut me out. You can thank yourself for that. You would keep goading her. Besides, I think it was the other way round, m'dear. You were an illusion. God knows why I fell for you.'

'I didn't marry you only for your money, if that's what you think.'

'Are you telling me you loved me?'

'No. I'm telling you that you were exciting, and wicked, and that pleased me. You also promised to take me to America. You know how much I wanted to become an actress.'

Henry laughed. 'Let's be honest, Rosie. You wanted a comfortable life, one that would enable you to mix with people of influence. I don't blame you for that, since we're two of a kind. I wanted exactly the same when I seduced Margaret. The difference between us, though, is that I'm in love with you, even knowing you're rotten to the core.'

'There was no comfort or influential people in that dreary country house you dumped me in.'

'You didn't want to stay in London and risk catching the flu, as I recall. And Foxglove House needed a housekeeper. What else was I to do with you?'

'Your wife wouldn't let me near her, and the staff would have poisoned me if they could have got away with it. Did you see their faces when you turned up with me on your arm and introduced me as your wife?'

'Actually, Rose, yes, I did. It served you right for thinking you were better than them. What happened to your gentleman friend . . . the one who was about to turn you into a film star in return for your services in the sack?'

Her face filled with fury. 'The bastard was trash. He left me. He was an accountant, not a film studio executive. His prowess in bed didn't live up to his promise either. As I told his wife; he was rather on the small side.'

'The world is full of deception, m'dear. Not many men would put up with a wife who has affairs. You should count yourself lucky that I don't throw you out on the street. I still might.'

'Then why don't you, Henry?'

She slapped him lightly when Henry laughed, and he pushed her on to the bed saying, 'We're good in bed together, if nothing else.'

A smile played across her face. 'I must admit we like the same perversions. The man wasn't a patch on you, and he shocked easily. Don't you care about my affair?'

'Not really . . . I haven't been faithful to you either. I like variety in my life.'

'You bastard! I still intend to become an actress.'

'You're lovely, Rosie, but from what I've seen, you have no acting talent. That's hardly surprising for a woman who was in the chorus line of a second-rate burlesque show for a living. You should take acting classes, or do something with your voice. At least you can sing.'

'Lessons require money.'

Henry smiled.

'Richard left you something in his will, didn't he?'

'No . . . he left everything to that delicious little doll he married. She had him wrapped so tightly around her finger that he even gave her his mother's jewellery. But don't worry. I've managed to put the brakes on everything until I get a solicitor. I'm going to enlist the services of Philip Conrad, since he owes me a favour. By the way, the girl is expecting a baby.'

Rosemary's eyes widened. 'Livia is? But I thought your son couldn't father a child?'

'His doctor told me it would be extremely unlikely. Something to do with nerves being severed by the bullet he got in his back.'

'Well, I'll be damned. So who fathered the brat?'

He shrugged, and avoided her eyes, fussing with his cufflinks. 'To all intents and purposes, Richard did, and we won't be able to prove otherwise. But why should we want to? What matters is that the Sinclair legacy comes with the child.'

There were the beginnings of a smile on her face. 'So?'

'I'm going to challenge Richard's will, and I'm going to apply for custody of my grandchild.'

'Who will look after the brat?'

'You will of course, Rosie.'

She began to laugh. 'That's what you think. I'm not looking after another woman's smelly brat.'

'With the Sinclair legacy, we'll be able to afford a nanny until it's old enough to send off to boarding school. You're right, though, you're certainly not the motherly type.'

'But Livia is. She couldn't do enough for your late wife, or your son, and she adores her ghastly brother and sister. You don't know her very well if you think she'll take this lying down, Henry. Given half the chance, she'll tear your throat out rather than part with her child.'

'Then I won't give her half a chance.'

'What about the scandal?'

'There won't be one, I promise. I'll be very surprised if Livia fights me on this. The thing is, m'dear, I'll need you to help me pull it off. I'm not very popular at Foxglove House. Go down and make friends with the staff. Not now, when they'll be sympathizing with the tragic young widow, but in a month or two. See what you can find out. There were some undercurrents of resentment when Livia and Richard married, I hear, especially from that Florence creature. I think she expected to be offered the position of housekeeper, though she and Beamish were planning to move. Try and catch Florence alone. Be nice to her.'

'I can't stand the sight of the woman.'

'You can always look on this as a role you're playing. You say you can act, well now's the time to prove it.'

'I suppose I could go and offer my condolences to the grieving widow. Besides, I left a few things behind, so I can use that as an excuse to be there.'

'I'll tell you where the key to the safe is. You might have a chance to open it.'

She laughed. 'I put my time there to good use, Henry. I know where the key is kept.' Rosemary rose to throw the doors to her wardrobe open. Half turning towards him, she allowed the strap to fall provocatively from her shoulder. 'Now . . . what have I got to wear in black?'

Henry's mouth dried and he whispered, 'Your slip. I should spank you for teasing me.'

'I might allow that, but only if you go on your knees and beg. You could use that little silk whip.'

'You bitch.' He fell to his knees, folding his arms around her legs. Breathing through the curling tangle of hair hidden behind the silky material of her slip, he inhaled the smell of her rising musk and reared in response to it. 'Please, Rosie . . . please.'

* * *

It took a couple of weeks for Livia to be able to think coherently.

Beamish and Florence were to depart in two weeks, exactly a month after the funeral. She rang Mr Stone.

'Ah . . . Mrs Sangster. I was just about to contact you. The board has decided not to replace Mr Beamish, since your late husband employed him. And Mrs Beamish will be leaving with him, of course. Considering the circumstances, it would be best for Foxglove House to be left in the hands of a skeleton staff until the matter of Richard Sangster's will and the custody of the coming Sinclair heir is resolved. Mrs Anstruther and Mathew Bugg will be asked to stay on. Letters are being prepared for the staff and I'd be obliged if you wouldn't mention this until they have received them.'

'What about the cook? She's been here a long time.'

'Mrs Starling is nearly of retirement age, so she'll be let go. We can't go to the expense of keeping a cook on staff when there is no Sinclair in residence.'

Connie would be upset, and Livia wondered if she had anywhere else to go. 'I see . . . and myself?'

'You still have the use of Nutting Cottage.' He cleared his throat. 'There's another complication. The Scottish kin, Alexander Sinclair, has signed away any right to the legacy, should he become eligible to inherit.'

'Oh . . . why is that a complication? Richard said he didn't want the legacy. And do you know something, Mr Stone, I really don't want my child to have it either. It's too much of a responsibility.'

'I think you're forgetting that the legacy is supporting your brother during his educational years. Besides, it will be up to the coming child to decide whether the Sinclair estate is of value to it, when it comes of age.'

'Yes of course. I'm sorry if I sound ungrateful. I'm tired and I can't think straight. I don't know if I'm up to a court battle over somebody else's money.'

'If I may say so, none of us know what the future holds. By the time the child has come of age, the Sinclair funds may have deteriorated, because the estate around the house hasn't been worked since Margaret Sangster's father died. Basically, it's a farm, and a farm needs to be kept productive. Now . . . enough of what you already know. What's more important in the short term is that you retain your husband's estate. That issue must be resolved first.'

'It's all so complicated, Mr Stone . . . why must it?'

'So you'll have the means to bring the child up. The major will then have to prove you're a bad mother.'

'How can he do that, when I've never experienced being a mother? I intend to be the best mother in the world, in fact.'

'Exactly. Cheer up, Mrs Sangster, we have some strong irons in the fire.'

He'd used the word 'we', and Livia was relieved that he'd aligned himself with her.

She was tempted to contact Denton and tell him what was going on, but decided against it. He had his professional training to complete, and although Richard had been his lifelong friend and she knew she'd be able to depend on him, she couldn't quite bring herself to burden Denton with her problem.

A week later Connie Starling received a letter of termination, along with a year's wages by way of compensation. Although Livia could see the sense of the arrangement, she felt guilty when she saw how put out the cook was.

'I'll be moving back into the cottage again,' Livia told her. 'You can move in with me if you've got nowhere to go.'

Connie sniffed at that, and her bottled-up resentment was given an airing now she had nothing left to lose. 'The Sangsters can keep their charity if this is all I get for my years of loyal service. I've been working here since I was a girl. I've saved nearly every penny of my wage for retirement. I can afford to rent my own house.'

'But you would have retired next year anyway, and you haven't lost any wages in the time you'd have been working.'

'That's not the point . . .' and she went on to tell Livia what the point was. 'If anyone deserved to be awarded Nutting Cottage, it's me. It would have suited me in retirement. It shows a lack of respect, so there! But don't you worry about me. You always did think you were a cut above. You can keep your cottage, Mrs Richard Sangster. The major and that tart he married will soon have it off you, you mark my words.

And don't come running to me when you and that young brother and sister of yours are out on the street begging for food.'

Livia burst into tears at the thought of sending the children back to the orphanage. She'd worked hard to gain their trust and affection, and if the major succeeded in his quest, the lives she'd created for them would be shattered.

'None of this is my fault, Connie.'

'Aye, so you say. You turned out to be as bad as the other one, working behind everyone's back to attract the interest of the master of the house,' Connie sniffed, beginning to run out of steam. 'What's more, I'm going to pack my bags and leave now. You can do your own cooking.'

'But where will you go? At least wait until you've had time to arrange some accommodation.'

Connie thought for a minute or two. 'Aye, that makes sense, and I daresay Mr Beamish and Florence will put me up until I sort myself out.' That settled in her mind, she stomped off, then turned, glaring, to fire her last shot. 'We can't all be favoured with rent-free cottages, but it's you who will get her comeuppance and be thrown out on the street in the end, you mark my words.'

Florence, deciding to take Connie's side, walked around with her nose in the air and barely spoke to Livia for the next few days.

Beamish seemed to be the only one sympathetic to her plight. 'Don't you worry, Mrs Sangster. I'll sort the pair of them out. I reckon I can buy a right nice house with the money the captain has left me. Me, Florence and my dad can live in that, and Connie can rent the rooms over the shop if she wants.'

'Thank you, Mr Beamish. That's taken one worry from my mind.'

'Oh, I daresay Connie will calm down. She won't want to part on bad terms. You settle in that nice little cottage and prepare for the arrival of the baby. I'll come and visit the next time I'm passing through if you don't mind, and if you need me I'll be at the end of the telephone.'

She hoped she'd never have to take advantage of this kind man. And he was right about Connie. She made a teary apology for her outburst and they hugged each other tight. 'Now, you let us know whether you have a boy or a girl, since Florence and I have got a wager on it,' she said, trying to cover her embarrassment at the need to part on good terms and the necessity to back down to achieve it.

'I will.'

Livia drove them to the station along with their luggage, and the three of them left together. She felt lonely when the train disappeared into the morning mist.

The house she returned to was suddenly an empty husk, except for silent echoes of a past Livia didn't feel part of. She stood in the hall, listening to snatches of Richard's laughter, of his childhood feet pattering on the stairs, and of time ticking her life away on the same grandfather clock that had ticked his life away. The hands had moved on, and now she must do the same.

She was given the incentive to move when Mrs Anstruther began to shroud the furniture in dustsheets. She now felt like a small nut in the big shell of what had been her home when Richard was alive.

'Come on, Esmé. We'd better pack our things into the car. It will take us a few trips.'

'Don't you do too much, Mrs Sangster, not in your condition,' Mrs Anstruther said. 'Tell me what you want to take, and Matthew will carry it down. We'll help you at the other end, too. We've got time on our hands now. And you'll need the cradle and the cot from the attic, and the bedding for it from the linen cupboard. I'll make sure it's all in order and clean, and if Matthew may borrow the car, he can deliver it.'

'He may borrow the car at any time he wishes for estate business. He need only telephone me.'

'That's kind of you, Mrs Sangster. Then perhaps he could drive me to the market tomorrow like he usually does. I need to go to the butcher. You could come with us; you really do need to get out a bit. We could look at baby clothing, and buy some napkins. And you'll need a perambulator. It's likely we'll find one for sale second hand.'

'What about our six chickens?' Esmé cried out in sudden alarm. 'We can't leave them behind else they'll be lonely.'

'You tell Matthew which six are yours, and he'll catch them and bring them over. We'd better pack some feed for them, and some straw.'

'Oh, Matthew knows which ones are ours; he helped me name them. They are Lavinia, Susannah, Alice, Joan, Maisie and Mistress Cluck, and they'll come running when he calls their names.'

The next day the hens arrived at Nutting Cottage, in a rather undignified manner, tied in a sack. Matthew had made sure the garden was in order, and after a few ruffled feathers and disapproving clucks at being uprooted again, the birds settled happily in the henhouse Richard had designed, and which Beamish and Chad had built.

It was a rather grand affair, with painted windows and an arch for a front door with a portico. The opening was large enough for the hens to enter and leave with ease. Each hen had its own coop. The construction looked rather like a manor house, with a red roof on brass hinges that lifted up, allowing for ease of egg collection and cleaning.

There was a name painted over the door: 'Cluckington Hall.'

'That will keep the foxes at bay. I should have designed chicken coops instead of wasting my time becoming a lawyer,' Richard had said, and had smiled proudly at it. 'Well done you two.' She remembered that Chad had beamed with pride at being praised.

Whiskers found that his former patch of afternoon sunlight on the windowsill was still there, and he settled on it and set about cleaning behind his ears.

'It means it's going to rain – at least, that's what Florence said,' Esmé told her.

Bertie investigated the hedge round the garden, renewing his boundaries and trying to flush out a few mice he could dispose of.

The sewing machine also went back into its original position. She would need that shortly.

It had been as though Livia had never left, except for the burden she carried. She smoothed her palm over her stomach, trying to eradicate the persistent niggle of resentment that this pregnancy had been forced on her. Feeling the new life inside her respond with a strong surge, she told herself once again that the child was innocent of any wrong. If only her nature was as generous and forgiving as Richard's had been.

She sighed, and supposed she should start getting a layette ready for the child. After all, there was only four weeks to go, and she prayed it would arrive late rather than early.

Tomorrow she'd purchase a pattern book and some wool and needles, and hoped she could remember how to knit.

The day after Livia left, Rosemary Sangster arrived at Foxglove House. There was no answer to the doorbell.

She still had a key to the place, and she let herself in. She was, after all, a Sangster now, and had a legitimate excuse to be in the family home. Henry had turned out to be a bore. He was weak, too, and lived a life far beyond his means.

She'd had no idea that he was so broke. And neither did he have a living now. All he was good for was keeping her satisfied.

The furniture was shrouded in dustsheets. Only the housekeeper's quarters looked as though they were occupied. That upstart, Livia, must have moved back to the cottage.

Rosemary went upstairs and collected the few items she'd left behind, then quickly made her way to the room where Mrs Sangster had died.

The safe was hidden behind a carved panel in a cupboard, the key kept in a secret compartment inside a drawer. She pushed the concealing panel of wood aside, took the key and applied it to the lock.

Inside the strongbox was Margaret Sangster's jewellery box. Opening it, she gazed at the glittering contents, a smile on her face. There was nothing else worth having in the safe. She locked it, then put the key back in its place and tucked the box under her arm.

She was just about to go downstairs when she heard a noise from the hall. Her heart quickened as she listened, but she heard nothing else except the tick of the clock.

There were letters on the mat. She picked them up. One was an account, the other was addressed to someone called Mrs Anstruther. She must be the new housekeeper.

The letters reminded her that she'd seen an address book in the housekeeper's room. Throwing the letters on the hallstand she went to the housekeeper's quarters and flicked the book open. Under Beamish, Joseph and Florence, she found an address and phone number. Beamish & Son Ironmongery, Ashley Road, Parkstone.

Considering what she'd been up to, she'd best not show her face at the cottage, or in the village, she thought. She didn't want anyone to know she'd been here, including Henry. Besides, this might be her way out.

Within minutes she was on her way.

The ironmongery was in a busy part of town, and people went in and out.

After a while she saw Beamish come out and stroll towards the bank. She crossed the road to the shop. There was an old man inside.

'Is Florence in? she asked.

'She's in the back room. Florrie, someone here to see you,' he called out.

She came out from behind a curtain, her smile fading. 'Oh, it's you. Can I get you something – a pound of tin-tacks to eat for dinner, perhaps?'

'Don't be like that, Florence. I was in the district and thought I'd look you up and take you out for afternoon tea. There's a café across the road.'

Florence looked gratified and began to remove her apron. 'Can you manage for half-an-hour or so, Dad?'

'I reckon so, since I managed by myself before you came here and took over, with your bossy ways. Aren't you going to introduce me?'

'You are a nosy one, aren't you? It's Mrs Rosemary Sangster.'

'How do, Mrs Sangster. I was sorry to hear about your husband.'

Florence gave an exasperated sigh. 'It's not that Mrs Sangster . . . that were Livia Sangster. This here is the older Mrs Sangster; the one who married the major.'

Insulting cow, Rosemary thought.

'The one having the baby?' He gazed her up and down, like

most men did. Only this one was too old to be any use to anyone. 'I thought you were a bit on the slim side to be in the family way, Missus.'

Rosemary forced a smile to her face. How dare this common little man be so personal?

'Get off with you then, Florrie. Don't be long, else Joseph will wonder where you are.'

'Let him wonder. He's gone off to look at a house for sale, so he'll be ages, I expect. Mr Richard left him one thousand pounds in his will,' she said, sounding self-important. 'That will set us up nicely.'

They went into the café a little way up the road and Rosemary ordered tea and cakes.

'So, Livia is having a baby, is she? Such a shame when she's lost her husband.'

Florence selected a lemon curd tart. 'She knew he was dying when she married him. As for the baby . . .' She looked around her and lowered her voice. 'I reckon she's further gone than she's letting on . . . but we'll see.'

'Never.'

'It was a quick wedding with a special license . . . though if you ask me, Richard Sangster didn't look as though he could find the energy to father a child, poor bugger.'

With a bit of prodding, Florence told Rosemary all she wanted to hear. That most of it was supposition didn't bother her.

'I don't suppose you'd put that in writing, would you?'

'In writing?' Florence looked dubious. 'I can't read and write very well. It would take me a month of Sundays. Besides, I gave a statement to that lawyer fellow.'

Rosemary seized on that. 'He needs another one. Look . . . I'll write it for you and read it back to you. Then you can sign it. You do know how to sign your name, don't you?'

'Course I do . . . the doctor taught me. And talking of doctors, we thought it was young Doctor Elliot Livia were after. He looked ever so disappointed when he came home and found she'd married the captain. And at Richard's party the pair of them stood behind the potted plant. Very close they were, and whispering together . . . like lovers.'

Like most gossips, Florence didn't know when to stop.

'It was observant of you to see that, Florence dear. Why don't you eat that last cake while I'm doing this? Oh, by the way, I'll pay you five pounds for your trouble.'

Florence's eyes began to gleam as Rosemary took out a notebook and pen and began to write.

Sixteen

Chad arrived home from school flushed with the success of his second term of exams. A pity he didn't have Richard to share it with, Livia thought. It fell on herself and Doctor Elliot to lavish praise on him after he proudly showed off his report.

Denton telephoned to congratulate him one evening, and they had a short, mostly one-sided conversation, with Chad chattering about school, cricket teams and other manly pursuits. Their parents would have been proud of him . . . but then, Chad couldn't remember a time when he had parents, and now the male influence of Richard had gone it looked as though Denton would be the one to bear the brunt of his youthful exuberance.

'When are you coming home, Doctor Denton?' Chad said at last, and his glance turned her way. 'Yes, Livia is here. Did you want to speak to her?'

Indeed she was there, hovering by the telephone and impatient to hear his voice.

He sounded far away, and rather remote when he said, 'Livia, how are you keeping?'

'Apart from feeling rather fat, I'm well. You?'

A low chuckle reached her ear. 'Well, but rushed off my feet . . . in fact, I've only got a few minutes before I'm due to go to the theatre.'

'I won't keep you then. Thank you for remembering Chad. I appreciate it, and I know he does.'

'I'm proud of him and the progress he's making, and I'm sure Richard would have been. Chad is certainly proving his worth in our sponsorship of him. I'm surprised to hear that you moved back into the cottage, though. I thought you and Richard wanted the baby to be born in Foxglove House.'

So he hadn't heard about the challenge to Richard's will. She didn't want to burden him with her troubles. 'Richard wanted it more than I did. He said the Sinclair heir should be born there. Personally, I like living in Nutting Cottage, and so do the children. It feels more like home to us.'

'Whereas Richard always regarded Foxglove House as his home.'

'Yes . . . he did, and he was used to having space around him, and servants. Coming up from the ranks of those servants, I didn't feel all that comfortable being elevated to mistress.'

'You wouldn't have known it.' There was a short pause, then he lowered his voice and said, 'Honestly now . . . are you looking after yourself, my love.'

'I'm doing my best to get used to being . . . alone.'

'I wish I could be there for you.'

There was a woman's voice in the background. It sounded like Bernice. 'What are you doing, Denton? Do hurry up.'

'I'm talking to Mrs Sangster and her brother.'

'Oh that's too bad of you when we're already late, darling. Give Livia my best wishes, and don't let her keep you too long, else we'll be late for curtain up and the opening act.'

Livia had assumed he'd meant the hospital theatre. She felt sick at heart, even though she knew she had no right to be, 'I have to take Bertie for a walk while it's still light. I hope you enjoy the play, Denton.'

'Don't go, my sweet, it's so lovely to talk to you and a few minutes more won't make any difference.'

They would. They would lull her into thinking he'd be as forgiving and generous about the baby's parentage as Richard had been. Even if she could lie well enough to fool Denton, and even if the birth of her child fell within a credible range, she didn't want to deceive him. He'd never forgive her if he found out, and once this baby was born it wouldn't take him long to realize that all was not as she'd have him believe. And she wouldn't have Richard to defend the lie.

'I must go Denton . . . and so must you. Will you hang the receiver up first, or shall I?'

'I will.'

There was silence and she whispered into it, 'Denton, are you still there?'

He laughed. 'I'm always here for you my pheasant-feathered friend. I just wanted to listen to you breathe. Now I *am* going to hang up.'

A giggle escaped from her just before a definite click told her he'd gone.

Bernice sighed as Denton hung up. 'It was unforgivable to keep the Harrisons waiting.'

He pulled on his gloves. 'Don't be silly, Bernie. Some things take precedence.'

'Especially good-looking young widows called Livia Sangster. Good grief, where's your sense of decency? Her husband is barely cold in his grave, and she's expecting a baby at any minute.'

'Hardly. The child is two months away.'

Bernice snorted. 'Earlier, I'd say. She was showing signs at the end of June.'

'I didn't notice.'

'You're a man, you wouldn't have.'

'My father said the baby is due around the end of November or early December. Livia has only been married since March,' he pointed out. 'She's had a rough time of it lately. Richard was my best friend. He'd expect me to take care of her.'

Bernice snorted. 'But not in the way you want to take care of her.'

He sighed. 'Are you going to be disagreeable all evening?'

'What do you expect? A woman likes her escort to pay her attention, not spend the evening wearing his heart on his sleeve for another woman.'

He didn't bother to deny it. 'Yes, I suppose she does. May I point out that we only exchanged a few words on the telephone.'

'Oh, don't sound so stuffy. You and I have an understanding, and I'll hold you to that.'

'An understanding?'

'Why else would we be going out together for all this time?

My parents want to know when I'm getting married, or at least engaged.'

He supposed he might have given her the impression that they had an understanding, and he'd certainly taken advantage of what she'd freely made available. But she'd known her way about a man, and hadn't been an innocent. He couldn't remember indicating that they might marry. He'd never even met her parents. He'd started going out with her when he'd learned that Richard and Livia had married.

He thought about that now, remembering his shock at hearing the news of the marriage, and the sense of betrayal he'd experienced. That had quickly become anger. He hadn't expected his best friend to steal Livia from under his nose.

The marriage had happened fast. Too fast. Not even the staff had known a wedding was going to take place until it happened. The event was out of place with Richard's character, because he'd always loved being the centre of attention. At first Denton had wondered if Richard's money had attracted Livia, but he'd dismissed that as an unworthy thought. Seeing them together, there was no doubt in his mind that Richard and Livia had adored each other.

She'd provided Richard with an heir for the Sinclair legacy. That had surprised him. He remembered Richard's injuries. The chance of his friend fathering a child had been very slim, yet he had managed it!

Worse had been the conviction that Livia had cared for him, then the discovery that she didn't. His eyes narrowed. Damn it, she *did* care for him. He knew it.

Bernice slid an arm through his and kissed his cheek. 'You're gathering wool, darling. Come on, slow coach. I'm sorry I was cross. We needn't go to the theatre if you don't want to.' Her voice was placating, but the impatience not very far from the surface.

'Of course I want to go.' The alternative was to spend the evening in Bernice's exclusive company, which wasn't very appealing when she was in a fractious mood.

The same could not be said for Livia. He'd crawl a hundred miles to spend an evening in solitude with her, whatever her mood. But it was much too soon to make an approach. She wouldn't be over Richard's death yet, and had the birth of her baby to adjust to.

He'd need to straighten Bernice out about their relationship, and conceded that she had a right to know where she stood. But she didn't have the right to take marriage for granted. It was something he didn't want to think about now. He wanted to relive in his mind the short conversation he'd had with Livia.

'Denton, are you still there?' she'd said, as cautious as a mouse emerging from its hole. And she'd given a delightful giggle when he'd answered. He smiled.

Bernice broke into his thoughts like an abrasive shriek of chalk on a blackboard. 'Well, are we damned well going or not? Really, Denton, you're so annoying at times. You're standing there like a wooden donkey nailed to the floor.'

Ah . . . love. The fool it made of a man, he thought.

When he patted her hand and he-hawed in reply, Bernice laughed, like he knew she would. 'Come on, let's go. We still have time to get there before curtain up, if we hurry.'

Chad went back to school and autumn came with its riot of glorious colours and flying leaves. The climate was mild and Livia mostly sat in the sitting room, looking out over the garden and making clothes for the baby.

Her layette had grown, and it seemed impossible that a child could be so small as to fit into the miniature garments.

Mrs Anstruther looked in on her every other day, and Matthew Bugg did the same on alternate days.

While the world turned its efforts towards winter production, Matthew Bugg did wonderful things in the garden. The shoots of winter vegetables began to spear through the earth, while the boughs of apple, pear and plum trees were weighed down. The fruit was taken away and reappeared as bottled preserves. They filled the pantry shelves in orderly coloured rows, wearing labels and frilly hats. If she ran out of money she and Esmé would still be able to eat.

Livia's stomach ballooned and she became lethargic. She missed her clinic appointment and Dr Elliot came to check on her.

'I forgot about it.'

He checked her over and listened to the baby's heartbeat through a cold metal horn placed on her stomach. 'The baby's head has engaged and it could put in an appearance at any time over the next six weeks. I'll tell the midwife to expect the baby sooner rather than later. It's not a big baby, so you shouldn't have any trouble giving birth.'

She didn't bother looking for an excuse, just said, 'Thank you, Doctor Elliot. Whatever you think is best.'

'Have you got everything ready for the birthing?'

She smiled at him. 'Yes . . . the midwife gave me a list.'

He took her hands in his. 'You've been through a great deal lately, Livia. Are you able to cope, do you think?'

Tears pricked her eyes. 'I feel sad, I think. It's as if the world has revolved too fast and my happiness has spun off into the sky like Fairy Floss.'

'It sounds as though you need some company.'

'I have Esmé. And Mrs Anstruther visits me every other day.'

'Esmé is a dear girl, and Mrs Anstruther is a very nice woman. The child will bring some joy back into your life, I promise.'

She doubted it, and felt guilty at being so negative. 'Would you like some tea?'

'I haven't time for one. A cool drink would be welcomed.'

'I have some lemon barley water in the larder. Mrs Anstruther made it. Richard used to like lemon barley. He told me it would be good for the baby if I drank a glass a day.'

'He was right. You mustn't dwell on Richard, m'dear. It won't bring him back.'

'I know, and I mustn't bother you with my troubles either, you're busy enough as it is.' She managed a strained smile as they went into the kitchen together. 'Have you heard from Denton lately?'

'Yesterday. He sent his best wishes, and hopes to get down for a weekend before too long. I imagine he'll bring Bernice with him. She seems to have become a permanent fixture in his life. We've never known him to attach himself to one woman for such a long time. Helen thinks they might be engaged by Christmas.'

Livia's heart turned to ice at such a prospect.

The birth date grew nearer, and the baby filled her with roundness, so she waddled rather than walked.

The last of the golden harvest had all been gathered in and the fields were as stubbled as an old man's chin. Then the stubble was tilled into brown ridges of earth, and early morning spread them with frost.

At the beginning of October her heart warmed again when Bertie did his usual dance at the front door and she opened it to find Beamish on the doorstep. Connie Starling was with him. She carried a suitcase.

Beamish had a box in his arms, and shuffled from one foot to the other. 'We . . . that is, Connie and I don't feel right leaving you here to cope all by yourself. We reckoned you might need somebody to look after you until you're over the birth, and Connie said it was going to be her.'

The cook was wearing a hat with a bluebird nesting on it. 'Just say if you want us to go away,' she said.

Livia began to weep; she couldn't help it.

Connie took charge. 'There, that's what I thought. I said so to Florence. She'll be moping all by herself, and her with no husband to turn to. Put that in the kitchen and go and fetch the other box of groceries, Beamish, while I mop up her tears.

'There, there,' Connie said, taking her in a hug. 'Don't you worry about anything. I'll look after you.'

Esmé was pleased to see the cook and gave her a hug, too. 'You can sleep in Chad's room for now if you like,' she offered.

'Just for the time being. You never know what you'll find lurking in boys' rooms, and he'll need it when he comes home. I thought I'd sort the junk room out. It's about time somebody did. You can help me if you like. The village usually has a bonfire on Guy Fawkes Night. If we put everything not worth saving out it will be picked up.'

Much to Livia's relief, Connie soon had them organized, and her company kept her mind from her own predicament.

The infant decided to help her in her quest to deceive, by conveniently arriving two weeks late.

She and Connie had spent the morning picking the last of

the blackberries from the bramble bush at the end of the garden. They were to make some jam to help see them through winter.

'Now you watch where you step. I don't want you to fall on your belly in the middle of the bramble patch, else I'll never get you up,' Connie had warned.

October had brought sudden flurries of chilly breath with it, which set the multicoloured leaves swirling into the sky. Spotted red toadstools grew amongst the damp mosses in the roots of trees, and the hawthorn was hung with flaming berries.

The babe had been quiet inside her for the past few days. The delay had taken it well past its proper birth date, which had been two weeks earlier. Livia had a niggling worry that it might not be alive. She telephoned the midwife.

'Quite normal,' the midwife said cheerfully. 'It's just having a rest. Usually it means that the birth is imminent . . . but you still have a while to go before it's due, don't you? Don't worry, Mrs Sangster, it's just being lazy . . . though the doctor thinks it's going to be an early birth.'

Connie made the jam and the cottage was filled with the smell of boiling blackberries.

Backache niggled at Livia all the next day, and she was glad to get to bed. She fell asleep immediately.

Pain woke her. It gathered force in her back and surged strongly into her stomach. She groaned.

A few minutes later, Connie appeared at her door. 'Started, has it?'

Livia nodded.

'I'll go and ring the midwife, then I'll dress and we'll get both you and the bed ready. First babies take ages . . . or so I've been told.'

Esmé appeared, her hair tousled. 'Why are all the lights on?'

'The baby's coming,' Livia told her.

'At two o'clock in the morning?' Esmé groaned, but the sleep in her eyes had been replaced by excitement at the news. 'Can I help? I won't be able to sleep.'

'You can make sure the dog and cat are kept out of the way, if you would, Es. I don't want anyone tripping over them.' She swung her legs out of bed and cautiously stood, cradling the bulk of the baby with her hands. Odd to think that in a few short hours this troublesome little creature would be born, and she'd be a mother.

Another pain wracked her and she doubled up, groaning. Her waters broke and she could feel the baby pushing. The next pain came almost on top and she felt herself stretch. This was nothing like the maternity clinic had described. There had been no gradual onset of contractions . . . no long drawn-out, agonizing labour. She remembered her backache of the previous day, and wondered.

Connie came back up. 'The midwife is out seeing to another birth. Her husband said he'll tell her when she returns. It's not urgent, seeing you have only just started.'

'It is urgent! I can feel myself stretching. Esmé, go and ring Doctor Elliot. Unlock the front door and turn the lights up so he can let himself in. Tell him the birth is imminent, and we can't get hold of the midwife. Connie, throw a sheet and some towels on the floor over that wet patch. It feels as though the baby is going to arrive at any moment and I'm going to soil the mattress if I get back in bed.'

Connie was wringing her hands by the time Esmé returned. 'I don't know what to do.'

Esmé calmly took over. 'I do. Don't sit there trying to hold it in, Livia. Get on the towels and I'll catch the baby when it comes out.'

Livia was shivering, but whether from cold or shock she couldn't say. She lowered herself to the floor and stayed on her hands and knees, it seemed more comfortable and natural that way. The next contraction made her shriek, but she couldn't stop herself from straining as the contractions pushed the baby's head through.

'Don't push now . . . the baby has to turn and I have to check that the cord's not wound around its neck. Oh, I haven't got time to look . . . there it goes.' That event was followed almost immediately by a gush of liquid as the body slithered out of her like a floppy octopus into Esmé's waiting hands.

There came a warbling screech of complaint from under her body, like an opera singer who'd sat on a drawing pin.

'Oh, my God, that was close!' The release of pressure was enormous, and Livia's laughter was almost hysterical.

Esmé was laughing, too. 'Wasn't that the most wonderful experience!'

Connie looked pale. 'It was lucky that she wasn't in the privy. Now . . . what should we do?'

'Wrap the baby up in this towel so it doesn't get cold,' Esmé said, and Livia marvelled at her sister's practicality. 'Move forward a bit, Livia. There's something coming out of you. The afterbirth, I expect. I remember reading about it in those leaflets you brought home. Ugh! It looks like liver.'

'I'm glad somebody read the leaflets.'

'They didn't say what a gory business giving birth actually is. The baby is attached to the afterbirth. I don't know how to cut the cord, so I'll wrap it up with the baby and the doctor can see to it.' Esmé giggled. 'Can you get on to your back now? You don't look very elegant in that position.'

They could already hear Dr Elliot's car bumping along the road at speed. When it screeched to a halt, with some relief, Connie said, 'I'll go and make some tea.'

'We'll need some water to clean Livia up with, and the baby as well. '

Connie stopped in the doorway and looked back at them. 'What was it, did anyone look?'

The three of them gazed sheepishly at each other, and Esmé grinned over the din the infant was making. 'I forgot.'

Connie laughed. 'I think its Scottish blood is coming out; it's got bagpipes for lungs.' She folded back the towel and took a look. 'You have a daughter. Good. Florence owes me half-a-crown.'

Esmé placed the baby in her arms. 'There you are, Livia. One daughter.'

Livia took one look at the infant and fell helplessly in love.

'It's a small baby, about six pounds,' Dr Elliot said a little later, after he'd shown Esmé how to cut the umbilical cord. 'You can't expect much fat on them when they arrive early. She'll soon put on weight when she starts feeding. A good clean birth and no stitches needed. Well done, Mother.'

Nice of him to lie, she thought, and kissed the sparse dark cap of hair on the baby's head. The child nuzzled against her breast, making little mewing noises, with the odd demanding yelp thrown in.

The midwife arrived, admonishing her for being inconveniently early, and taking over. The baby set up a clamour when her warm body was laid on a cold metal scale, like a plucked chicken at the butcher's shop. She was weighed, and measured for length and head size. Her fingers and toes were counted, her heart listened to. The midwife smiled. 'Everything is perfect, especially for a prem.'

Livia's newly discovered motherly instinct came to the fore. 'She's getting cold.'

The midwife wrapped the baby tightly in a flannel sheet and placed her back in Livia's arms with a smile. 'There you are, dear.'

The doctor aimed his smile at Esmé. 'I understand you were the heroine of the hour.'

'I'm going to be a nurse when I grow up. Then when Chad becomes a doctor I can work for him.'

'It's a jolly good idea to keep it in the family, Poppet. For one so young you seem to have an instinct for nursing, because you did everything right. Now . . . I'm going to have to fill out the paperwork, and at this time of the morning I do it best with a cup of tea, so I'll go down to the kitchen. Why don't you help your sister put the child to the breast while I do that? Babies need to learn to suckle as soon as possible. Does she have a name yet?'

It was a spur of the moment decision, because deep in her heart she'd never seriously considered that the child might be a girl. 'I might call her Margaret, after Richard's mother, and Eloise, after mine.'

'Margaret Eloise Sangster . . . a very pretty name.'

Margaret Eloise took to the breast like a duck to water and was soon making contented sucking noises.

Esmé put her arms round Livia's shoulders and kissed her cheek before gazing down at her niece. 'Did I feed like that from our mother?'

Esmé didn't often mention their mother, and her voice had

adopted a wistful tone. 'You did . . . only she had Chad to feed as well.'

'I wish I could remember it.'

'Babies don't remember such things, but somewhere inside you is a hidden memory of all the love she felt for you . . . because she did love you, Es. So did our father. To be loved gives any child a good start in life.'

'I love our baby already. She's so sweet and pretty, and she looks like you. She's going to have your dark hair and eyes.'

'You have the same hair and eyes, so she'll look like you, as well.'

Esmé gave a faint smile at that. 'It will be nice to be an auntie. Looking after her will help to take our minds off Richard. I miss him so much. I cried and so did Chad, though he told me not to tell anyone. He said a chap has to be brave when he loses a chum, like Doctor Denton is.'

She had not considered that Esmé and Chad might be grieving for Richard, or that the death of his friend would have been felt keenly by Denton. Thinking about it now, her sister and brother would feel the uncertainty that came with his loss more than anyone. Their lives had been unsettled since the day they'd been orphaned. And this little girl she'd brought into the world would also grow up without a father in her life.

'The baby looks a little bit like Richard, doesn't she?'

Because Major Henry had fathered both of them, and Richard was the infant's half-brother, she thought – a rather shocking thought now it was no longer an abstract one. Thank goodness the resemblance was slight. But there was no way she could charge the major with this crime against her, not even as a last resort. It would mean ruin for all of them.

The midwife said to Esmé, 'You'd better go back to bed, young lady, else you'll be asleep at your desk in the morning. And your sister needs to rest.'

'I'm too excited to sleep.'

'Believe me, you'll be begging for sleep once this little one gets you both trained to her way of doing things. You did a good job and kept your wits about you by all accounts, so well done. But even we nurses need to sleep.'

Livia was the recipient of a hug. Esmé kissed the infant. 'Goodnight, Meggie. Welcome to the family.'

So, it was to be Meggie, was it? Livia gave a faint smile as her sister left. She didn't mind. It was a pretty nickname for any child to have.

Seventeen

Livia soon got into a routine, as Meggie was easy to please. She'd received several gifts for the child, including a gold bangle from Denton with her name and birth date inscribed on it.

Esmé had made a friend her own age, Suzanne, who'd moved into the village with her parents. The pair spent a lot of time together, and Livia was pleased for her . . . especially since they both had a place reserved for them at the girls' grammar school in Parkstone.

Beamish appeared on the doorstep, a teddy bear tucked under his arm. She was surprised Florence wasn't with him.

'She wasn't feeling well,' he said, when she enquired after her.

'She was acting a bit funny before I left, sort of shifty. If I know Florence, I reckon she's got something on her conscience,' Connie told him. 'Have you got yourself a place yet?'

'Yes, we have. It's a house in Palmerston Road, on the other side of the park. It's semi-detached. We're doing it up before we move in, and I'm thinking of buying the attached property and renting it out to give us an income. The captain was a great believer in having property to fall back on. He said it always appreciates in value.'

Connie scoffed. 'That's all right for those who can afford it, I suppose. Getting ideas above your station, you are, Beamish, and I bet you've got Florrie on your back now you've wed her,' to which he offered a sheepish smile, and the comment, 'There's nothing wrong in bettering yourself.'

'I reckon I could do something like that too, but I don't feel the need to better myself, since I've got nobody to leave it to. So what's the point? How's your dad now? Looking after himself, is he?'

'Missing your cooking, Connie. He wants to know when you're coming home.'

Connie dimpled a smile. 'Tell him it will be when I'm good and ready.'

December brought gales and rain. It also brought a knock at the door, setting Bertie on a noisy alert.

Livia grabbed him by the collar. 'You don't have to bark every time somebody knocks at the door. You keep waking Meggie.' She kept a hold on his collar as she opened the door and gazed at her visitor, someone she'd not expected to see again. 'Bernice! I wasn't expecting you.'

Bernice growled at Bertie. Looking worried by the challenge, the dog skittered off towards the kitchen, his tail between his legs.

Livia laughed. 'I've never seen that done before. I'll have to try it.'

'I never thought to ring first. Sorry . . . is it inconvenient?'

'No . . . it's all right. Can you stay for lunch? We usually eat at twelve.'

Bernice consulted a marquisite wristwatch circling a slim wrist, to which was attached a white hand tipped with nails of flamboyant red.

'I'd like to.' Waving a hand at the car outside the gate, she called out, 'Return for me in an hour, Jerome.'

'Come in, Bernice, so I can shut the door and keep the heat in.'

'Brrrr . . . it's cold out there.' Taking off her outer garment, an olive green coat that revealed an unseasonal floating cream dress, Bernice went to stand by the fire. She placed a box on the table. 'It's an ivory teething ring and rattle combined. They chew on it when their teeth are coming through, the salesgirl said. I don't suppose the baby has got teeth yet, though.'

'No, not yet, but I can feel them in her gums. Meggie hasn't got a teething ring, so it will be useful. She's asleep at the moment.'

'Denton said the baby arrived a month early?'

Livia was wary. 'Yes, she did, and the birth was very easy, almost instant.'

'That must have been awkward, since you hadn't been married very long.'

'Oh . . . why should it be? She wouldn't be the first baby to come a month early. Meggie arrived before the midwife and doctor did. She was very small.'

'People tend to invent scenarios to suit these instances.'

'Yes . . . so I notice.'

'I suppose you're refering to me.' She shrugged. 'I don't give a damn about what other people get up to. I live my life as I see fit, and if people don't like it, they can go and take a long walk off a short pier.'

Livia felt a sneaking regard for the woman's attitude. But then, she was only responsible for herself, not several others.

At that moment Meggie gave a cry for attention. Livia smiled. 'I'll go upstairs and get her. I might have to give her a quick feed to top her up. It won't take long. Can you amuse yourself in the meantime? Connie is in the kitchen. She used to be the cook at Foxglove House. Tell her you're staying for lunch, if you would.'

When she appeared over Meggie's cot, the infant contemplated her through deep brown eyes for a moment. Then, as if realizing she'd conjured up the right person with her cry, her smile came and she blew a bubble.

'We have a visitor, so I hope you're going to behave yourself,' Livia said, and her daughter punched the air with delight at the sound of her voice.

Livia put her to the breast, experiencing deep contentment at the sensation. Afterwards, she changed her nappy before brushing her inch of dark hair into curls. Then she took her down.

'Goodness, she is tiny.'

'Meggie has gained a pound since she was born,' and Livia grinned as she caught herself using a proud mother voice. 'She has a loud voice to make up for her lack of weight. Would you like to hold her?'

Bernice raised an eyebrow. 'As long as it's not catching.'

'Don't you want children when you get married?' And to

her shame she sneaked a look at her guest's finger to see if she wore an engagement ring. She didn't.

'It's not always up to the woman, is it? Men seem to need to reproduce themselves at regular intervals, as though they're personally responsible for replenishing the human race. Then they go and start a war and kill their damned fool selves all over again. However, there are measures to prevent conception now, so at least women can have one or two children, then say enough, without forgoing the pleasure of copulation.'

Livia captured a stray thought from the air that wondered what it would be like to make love with a man like Denton, who was whole and complete, and who was healthy and full of vigour, no doubt. Her face warmed.

Bernice gingerly took the offered baby and gazed down at her. Meggie gazed back at her, then offered Bernice her best smile and managed a dovelike coo.

'She looks a lot like you.'

'Yes, she does. I was hoping she'd inherit Richard's blue eyes and fair hair.'

'She's pretty as she is, and her looks will keep people guessing.'

'About what?'

'About whom, you mean, don't you? You know perfectly well what I'm talking about.'

But Bernice didn't. She was fishing. With sudden surprise Livia realized that Bernice suspected Denton had fathered Meggie. How perfectly delicious it was. Well, two could play at that game.

'I'd heard you'd become engaged.'

Bernice became evasive. 'See what I mean about people making things up?'

She handed the baby back and Livia laid her in her pram, where she blew bubbles and kicked her legs until she fell asleep.

Livia engaged Bernice's eyes. 'Let's put our cards on the table, shall we. It will save choking on our food when we're trying to eat lunch.'

With a throaty laugh, Bernice said, 'If we must. Denton hasn't asked me to marry him, no matter how much I push. I think you know damned well that he hankers after you. I need to know your intentions towards him.'

'I have none besides friendship. And no, Denton didn't father Meggie. Our relationship has always been platonic, except for a brotherly kiss or two.'

'So the child really is a Sangster.'

'She really is.' Put like that it wasn't even a lie.

'Then you won't mind if I go after Denton?'

Livia would mind like hell. Bernice was wrong for Denton. She liked to be the centre of attention, and Denton needed someone he could come home to; somebody he could relax with, and who would adore him . . . herself in fact.

But that was out of the question, she reminded herself.

'Why should I mind? I have no claim on Denton, and he has a mind of his own – a damned fine one, I might add. It's not up to me to arrange people's lives for them. Can we now drop the subject and go and enjoy our lunch. Your escort will be back before long.'

'Jerome is my employer,' Bernice said, a little too quickly.

Livia didn't think Denton would bow to pressure from Bernice. He was a man who'd been through a war – a man who'd made a wonderful career for himself, despite that. There must have been other women before Bernice, and he was too sensible to be coerced into a marriage he didn't want.

Livia's next visitor was Simon Stone.

After admiring Meggie, the solicitor gazed at her and smiled. 'I don't think we need to question your fitness as a mother, do you? I have statements from Doctor Elliot, and the orphanage staff have given testimony of the way you supported your siblings over the years. The whole charge is ridiculous, including the reason for the marriage. All the staff, except one, vouch for your character.'

'May I know which one says differently?'

'It's Florence Beamish, and her testimony is scurrilous. In fact it's supposition, with nothing to back it up. But it's unsavoury to say the least. Given that it cannot be proved, it will cause a scandal nevertheless, I'm afraid.'

Her heart sank. 'Florence? I can't believe it. What did she say?'

'That you were in love with Doctor Denton Elliot, but you

married Richard Sangster for his fortune, knowing he was dying. The whole statement is libellous, and a direct attack on your character.'

There was a fair amount of truth in it, but she couldn't tell him that. And the fact that Florence had named Denton would put a question mark over him. 'All Doctor Denton Elliot is guilty of is being Richard's childhood friend.' Her heart gave a painful thud. 'Does Beamish know about this?'

'It seems not, but he'll have to be informed. If the statement isn't withdrawn, I shall have to attack her on the witness stand.'

'May I read the statement, please?'

He slid over a sheet of paper. 'My secretary has copied this exactly as it was written, only on a typewriter.' He passed over a piece of paper, and Livia's heart sank as she read it. 'This is just awful.'

The door was open and Connie appeared with a tray of tea. Her colour was high. 'I couldn't help overhearing. I thought there was something odd about Florence before I left. She seemed awkward and couldn't look me in the eyes.'

Livia wondered if Connie would ever grow out of the habit of eavesdropping.

'Can I read the statement please?' Connie asked.

She might as well, since she knew most of it already. Livia pushed it across to her, and a few minutes later was glad that she had.

Connie looked up. 'Florence didn't write this. To start with she can't spell. And neither can she read or write to this standard.'

'Her signature has been witnessed by Rosemary Sangster.'

'That may be so. But she didn't write those long words, and she wouldn't have known what they meant, even if she *could* write them. I expect she was having a good gossip, like she does from time to time. It doesn't take much to get her going, and she wouldn't have meant anything by it. This has been written for her and they got her to sign it. I bet Beamish doesn't know. I reckon it would have been that wife of the major's. She'd be behind all of this. She can't wait to get her greedy hands on that money.'

'Which money are you referring to?'

'The Sinclair legacy, of course. I've got it all worked out. If she can find a way to blacken Mrs Sangster's name and get custody of the child, then they also get control of the Sinclair legacy.'

Simon Stone and Livia exchanged a glance.

'Likely they'll be after the captain's estate as well, since one thing follows another when a name is being blackened. Everyone will believe the worst, of course. It's no wonder Florence didn't come down to see Mrs Sangster when she had the chance. She was too ashamed of herself to look her in the eye. I bet she can't even look at herself in the mirror.'

'You could be right, Mrs Starling.'

'The major was all right until he met Rosemary Mortimer,' Connie fumed. 'He always was easily led by a pretty face. Old Bugg said the major kept what was left of his brain between his legs. He was a man with an itch he could scratch but never satisfy, and was after women all the time.'

The lawyer spluttered over his tea, 'Dear oh dear,' and he didn't know where to look. 'This case is getting messier than I thought it would. They have a lawyer representing them who is known for his dirty tricks. His name is Philip Conrad, and he's suggested that perhaps we could reach a mutual settlement, to save your name being dragged through the courts.'

'A settlement?' Livia drew in a deep breath, one that only added fuel to her anger. 'The time for that is past . It would be tantamount to admitting there is some truth in these accusations. I'm not going to sit here and be attacked from left, right and centre. I'm going to call the major's bluff. Tell this Philip Conrad his client has seriously misjudged me if he thinks I'm going to allow the major to take what rightfully belongs to my child. If I'm to be dragged through the courts I'll drag his client's name behind me. Tell him I intend to sue him, and all his supporters, for libel. See if he likes that.'

Simon Stone nodded. 'You're taking the stance that the best defence is to go on the attack? You have a point, but it's risky.'

'What's risky about it? Unless they can prove the accusations, which they can't because they're not true, then I have nothing to lose. We should start with Florence. If we can get her to tell Beamish what she's done, he'll persuade her to withdraw the statement. It's better than us telling Beamish first.'

Connie nodded. 'She'll be afraid she'll get into trouble if

you or Mr Stone tackle her about it, and she'll dig her heels in. I'll be happy to ring her if you like. She usually listens to me.'

She did so then and there. 'Florence, I've just read a statement you were supposed to have made. What on earth came over you to talk to that horrible woman? You know what might happen now . . . they'll try and take Mrs Sangster's baby away, and the dear little soul will never see her mother again. Then Esmé will have nowhere to go except back to the orphanage, and it will all be your fault.'

Livia heard a loud wail of distress, followed by garbled talking. Connie certainly knew how to apply pressure.

'I realize that, but Mrs Sangster was always good to you, and she doesn't deserve this. Isn't it enough that she's still grieving for her husband?'

There was a scramble of words from the receiver, then Connie looked at them and nodded, saying, 'Beamish doesn't know? Well, I didn't think he did, since he wouldn't have allowed that woman to creep around bothering innocent folks, would he? Your man is as honest as they come. Perhaps it would be best if you started setting things right again. He thought the world of the captain and his lady, and if he finds out what you've done from someone else, he'll be cross.'

Again came the scramble of words.

'Yes . . . I'll tell her. The baby . . . she's a sweet little thing. Her name is Margaret Eloise and she's named after her two grandmothers. We call her Meggie for short. She's the very image of Mrs Sangster.' There was a pause, then, 'You are?' A smile lit up Connie's face. 'No, I won't tell Beamish. Congratulations, my dear. That news should sweeten Beamish up when you tell him what you've been up to. What day did you say that woman visited you? A Monday, was it?' A few moments of small talk later and Connie hung up and turned to them. 'Rosemary Sangster wrote the statement, and she promised to read it back to Florence and pay her five pounds. She did neither. She made Florence sign the statement, then said she'd left her bag in the car and would fetch the money and bring it back. She didn't. She just got in and drove off.'

'So Mrs Beamish was offered a bribe, and she didn't know

what she'd signed.' Simon Stone smiled. 'Now we're getting somewhere.'

'Florence is expecting a baby in June. That should keep her out of mischief. And there's something else that's struck me as odd. Florence said Rosemary Sangster was wearing a diamond brooch in the shape of a swan, and the last time she'd seen it was on the dressing table at Foxglove House when the captain's mother died.'

'She couldn't have. It's in the safe at Foxglove House. I itemized all the jewellery and gave Mr Stone a list.'

'Have you checked on it lately?'

'I haven't been back there at all. Mrs Anstruther calls in, and so does Matthew Bugg. They tell me if they've had visitors, or needed to ask me if there's something they're not sure of.'

Mr Stone stood. 'Perhaps we should check on it while I'm here.'

Livia gazed at the pink carriage clock Richard had given her. 'I have an hour before Meggie needs feeding. If she wakes, would you mind keeping her occupied until I get back please, Connie?'

Mrs Anstruther opened the door to them with a smile.

'Mr Stone and I are going upstairs to check on something. We shouldn't be more than ten minutes, Mrs Anstruther.'

Foxglove House was an empty tomb shrouded in dustsheets. Livia could feel the sadness of abandonment in it. Their footsteps echoed across the hall.

Here was the room in which Margaret Sangster had died, and in which Richard had spent his last painful few months struggling for breath. She'd thought she'd be able to feel his presence, but she couldn't. It was just an unoccupied room, and she realized that she didn't think of Richard as much as she used to, or in the way she used to – with such an aching intensity of emotion.

She pulled the key from its compartment, fitted it into the lock and swung the door open. She couldn't believe what she saw. 'It's not here,' she spluttered. 'The jewellery box has gone.'

They questioned Mrs Anstruther. 'Has anyone been here . . . any workmen or the like?'

'No, Sir.'

'Not even family.'

'Not that I know of, Sir, except . . . there was something that struck me as odd.'

'What was that?'

'Matthew took me into the markets a little while ago. A Monday it was. You came with us, if you remember, Mrs Sangster. We bought some baby clothes and you fell asleep in the car on the way home.'

'I remember.'

'That was about two months ago. We used your car, though nearly came a cropper when we rounded the bend and almost collided with a woman driving towards us. It was her fault, but she honked the horn as though she owned the road, and you woke with a start. Anyway, when we arrived at the house the postman had been.'

'And?'

'Well . . . the letters were on the hallstand instead of on the floor. Matthew and I checked right through the house, and we saw nothing amiss. All the windows and doors were still locked. To be honest, I thought it was all a bit creepy. Then I thought the postman must have come earlier, and I must have been a bit absent-minded and picked the letters up and put them there myself.'

'Can you describe the car you nearly collided with?' Mr Stone asked her.

'One of those little ones with two seats, a Morris Oxford, I think, though I'm not much good with cars. It was green. Is something missing, Sir?'

'Some jewellery – it was in a jewellery case in the safe.'

'I didn't know there was a safe. I've never seen one. Have the thieves taken that as well?'

'No, but it's well hidden, and only a few people know where it is and how to open it.'

'Including me,' Livia said.

When they were outside, she asked, 'What would you suggest we do? Report the theft to the police?'

'We shall have to, I'm afraid. The jewellery was part of your husband's estate. I have an inventory of it that could be circulated.'

Livia sighed. 'I really don't want my life to get any messier than it is at the moment. We both know who's at the bottom of this, because Rosemary Sangster was wearing that brooch. What if the jewellery was returned, no questions asked?'

He turned his eyes on her and smiled. 'I could drop a suggestion into an ear or two and see what happens. We'll give it until the end of the week. If there's been no progress we'll have to report it, I'm afraid.'

The word in the major's ear came via Philip Conrad.

'Word is out that Foxglove House has been robbed. Someone with inside knowledge has removed your former wife's jewellery from the strongbox.'

'Good Lord,' Henry spluttered, his surprise unforced, for although he was sure Rosemary had taken the jewels, she had forgotten to tell him. 'Are you sure she hasn't mislaid them?'

'She?'

He seized the opportunity to wear Livia's reputation down. 'The maid my son was tricked into marriage with. Livia.'

'Livia Sangster is now a mother, and has gilt edge references as to her character. I might as well tell you now, you won't win a custody battle.'

'The baby is born then? A little early, wasn't it?' Henry felt uneasy. 'What did she have?'

'A daughter. You know, Henry, you really should drop this case. Simon Stone has all the cards. Blackening a young widow's name and dragging her through the courts to gain control of her child and inheritance has an unpleasant whiff to it. It's simply not gentlemanly to go after a defenceless young woman like this. It will be reported in the newspaper, I expect. The public will be on her side. The house being robbed without any sign of breaking and entering will just add fuel to the fire.'

'It won't go to court.'

'Then what the hell am I supposed to be representing? This sounds like a private vendetta against your daughter-in-law, not a legitimate challenge to a will.'

'You owe me a favour . . . several favours in fact, and I don't think your wife would appreciate hearing about them.'

'What do you know of my wife?' Philip turned hooded eyes

his way. 'You know, that sounded very much like a threat to me, Henry.'

'I'm merely reminding you. The fact that the jewellery is gone only proves one thing . . . that if somebody can walk into Foxglove House, sight unseen, and steal my former wife's jewellery case, then the security is non-existent.'

Philip picked up a paper knife and dug it into the blotting paper on his desk. His expression was one of distaste, as if he had a bad smell in his nostrils. 'Apparently, no questions will be asked if the jewellery is returned by the weekend. After that, the matter will be placed in the hands of the police.' Philip gazed up at him. 'Are you implicated in this, Henry?'

Of course he was implicated. It had been his idea. But Rosemary had conveniently forgotten to tell him she'd been successful, which made him uneasy. 'Why do you suspect me?'

'Apparently the robbery took place on the day your wife interviewed Florence Beamish. And by the way, Mrs Beamish has retracted that statement. She said your wife wrote it, and she didn't know what she was signing.'

'The hell she didn't. Rosemary said she read it.'

'She couldn't have done. Mrs Beamish is almost illiterate, apparently.'

The major shrugged. He felt tired and dispirited, and wished he hadn't started this. He shouldn't have listened to Rosemary in the first place. 'Didn't you offer them a settlement?'

'Forget that. You threatened to take Livia Sangster's child away, and she's going to fight you every inch of the way if you persist. If you or your wife has that jewellery, returning it is the only concession you'll get. I'd be happy to deliver it.'

'I daresay you would if I had it. But I don't.' The major rose, experiencing an urgent need to get back to London. Rosemary had been impatient, eager for him to leave, and his feeling of unease grew. 'Keep in touch, old boy. Let me know if anything develops.'

'By the way, my wife passed away two years ago, so you couldn't tell her anything. It was Spanish flu.'

'Oh . . . I see . . . bad luck.'

'Yes . . . for you. My resignation will be in the post tomorrow. Find yourself another legal representative. I thought you might have a legitimate claim against your son's estate after his wife and child, but I don't want the rest of it on my conscience. Besides, your case is collapsing like a pack of cards.'

'Just remember that anything I've said to you is confidential.'

'I know the meaning of the word. It's a pity you don't. Good-day, Henry. Off you go to that young wife of yours. I hope Rosemary proves to be worth it, but I doubt it.'

The blinkers fell from Henry's eyes when he discovered that Rosemary definitely wasn't worth it although he'd always suspected as much. When he arrived home it was only to confirm that she had gone. The drawers in her bedroom were empty, suitcases missing. There was a pawnshop receipt on the dressing table, dated the previous month, and brochures from a steamship company. India, America, Canada, Australia. It would be fairly easy to find out which ship she was on, but he saw no point. Rosemary planned things carefully, and it would have set sail.

Downstairs he found a letter of foreclosure from the bank. The apartment was to be resumed at the end of the week. The game was up. Now he had to put an end to it. He was ruined.

He took the picture of Richard down from the mantelpiece and gazed at it. The boy greatly resembled his mother. Now there was a son to be proud of, he thought. For once he'd done something right in his life. It was a pity Richard had died so young.

Going upstairs again, he dressed in his military uniform, his Sam Brown and his boots. The uniform made him feel important and useful. He fetched his army issue revolver from his desk and attached it to the lanyard. The Webley had never fired a shot, yet he still cleaned it regularly, and it didn't have a fleck of dust on it. He loaded one lethal dose of lead into it, the only bullet he had, then spun the chamber and held it at arm's length, awkwardly twisting his hand so the barrel pointed towards him. He closed his eyes and felt the sweat bead on his forehead.

He thought he heard a quiet chuckle and opened his eyes again.

Richard looked at him from his frame. Instantly, Henry felt

guilty. His son had loved that girl, and now there was a daughter from the marriage – one that neither of them would ever see if he carried this out. And he was curious to see the infant.

Richard wore a faint smile on his lips, as if amused by Henry's predicament.

Livia might allow you to be the child's grandfather.

'After the way I've treated her? She'd never allow it now.'

She's only human. She's got her back to the wall and has come out fighting, just like I thought she would. What were you thinking of, coming between a mother and her child? Put the proposition to her. Give her room to breathe and allow her to think about it. She's not unreasonable.

Henry shook his head. 'I'm too ashamed.'

So you should be. You might think what you intend to do is the easy way out, but you're a coward, and you're weak and you haven't got the guts to do it. Look how your hand is shaking. You've never seen a man with his head blown off, have you? Your brains will be splattered all over the room.

'I know what I am, Richard, but you're wrong about me not having any guts.'

Holding a conversation with a dead man struck Henry as bordering on madness. It was ridiculous! People would think he was insane.

Giving a high-pitched giggle, he pulled the trigger.

Eighteen

'Henry Sangster has abandoned his plans to challenge Richard's will,' Simon Stone said. 'That will make its passage through probate faster. I think we can arrange an advance if you need one.'

Relief washed over Livia. Her supply of money was rapidly dwindling and she had to be careful of what she spent. 'My funds are getting a little low. What about the jewellery; was it recovered?'

'Rosemary Sangster has pawned it and gone abroad. I thought you'd like it returned, since it was legated to you. Rather than have a scandal, I've redeemed it for the same price loaned on it. I pointed out to the broker he could be charged with receiving stolen goods, in which case he wouldn't get anything back. I'll make sure it's accounted for in the books, but if we ever see the thief again we can pursue her for reimbursement of the debt.'

'Where did she go? America, I suppose. She wanted to become a film star.'

'We believe she may have gone to Tangiers with a man who passes himself off as a minor Polish royal. He's an adventurer and wanted by the police for fraud. She'll be in good company until she runs out of money, and as soon as she steps back on British soil, she'll be arrested.'

Livia couldn't find it in herself to feel sorry for Rosemary. 'What about the major?'

'He's deeply depressed. He'll be kept in a mental institution until the doctors say he's completely recovered, and can be trusted not to try and kill himself again. They will probably give him electric shock therapy treatment. Attempting to commit suicide is a crime, as you know, so charges could have been brought against him.'

Livia shuddered. 'I'm surprised he missed, when it was almost point blank range.'

'He'd never fired a gun before. What he didn't know was that the Webley has quite a kick. It takes lots of practice to become a proficient shot with it, even using the accepted practice of handling it. Either his hand jerked upwards as he fired, and the bullet lodged in the ceiling, or he changed his mind at the last minute. The kickback broke his wrist and several bones in his hand. He's a broken man, who has nothing left. No wife, no home, no children, no friends and no money.'

Despite what had happened, now that Livia was over the anger and depression Richard's death had brought with it, she felt sorry for the major. He'd been brought down as low as a man could go, and though his downfall had been brought about by his own actions, it had been a long way to fall.

'Richard wouldn't have wanted his father to be left destitute,' she murmured. 'Perhaps I can help him when the time comes, though at the moment I never want to see him again. He can't live with me, because I'll never forgive him for threatening to take my daughter. I'll never be able to trust him with her, you see. Let me think about it, Mr Stone, and you do the same, since you know my legacy better than I do. We might be able to provide him with suitable accommodation of some sort, and an allowance.'

'You have a kind heart, my dear. It won't be for some time, so we needn't be in too much of a hurry. Think it through carefully. You know what they say, marry in haste and repent at leisure.'

'Only I wouldn't dream of marrying the major.' She only just managed to keep the bitterness from her laughter at the thought. 'Richard and I married in haste, you know, and I'll never regret it. He said life was too short for regrets, and for him it was true. He treated me as though I was precious to him. We laughed a lot, and I loved him dearly. I sincerely hope I made him happy.'

'Oh, you did, my dear. He told me so. 'Now, have you made any plans for Foxglove House?'

'Plans? None at all, but the fact that you ask leads me to believe you might have.'

'Land is meant to be worked, and your daughter's estate has been neglected for several decades now. It's unlikely that Meggie will grow up to become a farmer, so I do think we should try and find someone from the district to run the estate as it should be run. It will not make a profit for a year of two, of course, but it's better to try and make it a going concern now, than allow the land to lie fallow and the house go to rack and ruin.'

She said with a smile, 'I suppose you just happen to know a farmer looking for an estate to manage, too.'

'No . . . but it would be an ideal start for a younger man who'd grown up in the district. One who knows farming and wants to start out on his own.'

'May I make a suggestion, Mr Stone?'

'Of course you may, Mrs Sangster.'

'You might like to ask Matthew Bugg to take on the task.'

'Of course I might . . . I should have thought of him myself.'

Connie Starling was still living at the cottage after Christmas. Although she was a guest, she couldn't cast off her service habits, and she cooked and cleaned and generally took over the housekeeper's role.

Livia would miss her if she left, but sometimes she longed for solitude, so she could be alone with her thoughts and without the constant stream of advice coming her way.

Meggie thrived. She'd trained the household to revolve about her needs. Livia kept her comfortable. Esmé kept her amused. Chad was the recipient of her feminine wiles. Connie chatted to her and patted her bottom every time she walked past. Now and again Meggie rewarded her, and Connie would exclaim in a high-pitched voice, 'Has Connie's little darling done a naughty wee-wee then?'

So when a stranger with slightly familiar eyes peered over her cot, she first checked that one of her immediate family was present with a reassuring smile, before smiling back and cooing dribble at him.

'She's a dainty little creature,' Denton said, and gazed around the room, with its lavender-sprigged wallpaper, lace curtains and painted wardrobe. 'So this is where you sleep.'

'It's a big enough room to accommodate the cot, as well as the bed. Having a washbasin in here is a bonus.'

Denton offered a finger to Meggie, who tried to pull it into her mouth.

'Be careful, Meggie already has two teeth,' Livia said.

'A most remarkable child indeed.'

Livia laughed. 'Well, I think she's clever.'

'Of course she is. Look who she picked to be her mother. Meggie looks just like you.' Denton took her hands in his. 'And you're the loveliest woman I've yet to meet.'

'How lovely one looks in an apron at eight a.m. is debatable.' She detached her hands from his and pushed her hair back from her forehead. 'I was just about to wash and feed Meggie.'

'I'm sorry I'm so early. I thought I'd take Dad's dog out and use it as an excuse to drop in on you.'

How tall and graceful Denton was. All she'd ever felt for him came flooding relentlessly back, like a high tide. 'You don't need an excuse to visit me.'

'How are you, my love?'

His voice was so tender and beguiling that her heart became

a swirl of melting caramel. She didn't dare look at him, yet her eyes were drawn to the mossy green of his and her mouth was overwhelmed by an urge to be kissed.

He fulfilled that urge, lodging his thumb into the little notch under her chin and securing it with his forefinger on top. His lips tasted of cold January wind, and icicles that melted and sizzled against the heated surface of her mouth.

He gazed down at her afterwards through dark, quivering lashes, a tiny smile playing around his delicious mouth. 'I've been longing to do that.'

'You've only been here a few minutes.' Yet she now had a longing for him to do it again, and would crave another kiss like that forever more. 'You shouldn't have, Denton.'

'Of course I should have. Didn't you like it?'

'You know I did, which is why you shouldn't have.'

'I'm not going to have one of those cock-eyed explanations with a reverse conclusion from you, am I?' His nose twitched. 'Does your daughter always smell like that? If so, remind me to stand upwind when she's around.'

'Not always, but now and again.' Laughter bubbled from her, a reflection of the happiness she always felt when she was around this man.

Meggie grunted shamelessly, her red face indicating that she would shortly be due a comfort adjustment, as well as breakfast. Livia spread some towels on the bed and filled the basin with warm water. She laid the baby's clothes out and plucked Meggie from the cot. 'I must see to her before she starts kicking up a fuss.'

'She's more of a Sangster than a Sinclair.'

Livia didn't want to discuss the pros and cons of her baby's parentage. It was a road fraught with peril. 'Would you pass over the baby powder please? I've left it on the window sill.'

'You're busy. I'd better go.'

'Nonsense, you've only just got here, and I want to hear all about what you've been up to.' The smell of bacon wafted up the stairs. 'Can you stay for breakfast? The children have gone to the henhouse to collect the eggs; they'll be pleased to see you. Chad will want to show you his end-of-term report.'

'I'll see you shortly then.'

She heard the children come clattering in, exclaiming excitedly when they saw Denton. They were a far cry from the withdrawn, unhappy children she'd brought home from the orphanage. For a fleeting moment she wondered what had happened to Billy, who'd joined them on their eighth birthday, and Billy's younger brother, the one she'd hugged because he'd missed his mother. She couldn't remember his name.

She could have asked Chad, but he didn't like talking about the orphanage. His aim was to put it behind him and make something of himself, so he could support his sister. He was pathetically eager to succeed, and she hoped he wouldn't be disappointed. When he was home there was an air of you-and-us about him, as he unconsciously resumed responsibility for Esmé. The age difference that existed between the twins and herself encouraged such thinking, and she knew she was regarded as more of a foster mother than a sister to them.

Esmé was turning into a practical, sensible girl – and one with a mind of her own now she was separated from Chad for much of the year. She didn't possess Chad's flair in her school results, but nevertheless, she worked steadily towards her goal and showed a definite improvement. Livia was proud that she'd been designated a place at the girls' grammar school, and despite the fact that they were twins, she doubted if Esmé would allow Chad to run her life as they grew older.

Meggie was washed and fed, then taken downstairs and laid in the pram. Reassured by the familiar sounds of the cottage, she played with her feet, making contented little noises until she fell asleep again.

Denton thanked Connie for the breakfast before turning to Livia. 'Why don't you fetch your coat and walk with me for a while . . . I'm going along the cliff top. It's my favourite place. I like the wind up there, it blows the cobwebs away.'

'That's a long way to walk.'

'I have the car.'

She laughed. 'I thought you said you were out walking the dog.'

'I am. It's just that the walking bit hasn't started yet.'

'It will be a couple of hours before Meggie sleeps off her

breakfast, so I'll keep an eye on her,' Connie said. 'And before you children think you can use this as an excuse to get out of your chores, you can stay home and help me. You have your rooms to tidy while I put the baby napkins on to boil and rinse.'

The twins grinned at each other, exchanging a fleeting thought that Livia wasn't a party to. They could be disconcerting at times.

Livia had taken to wearing slacks around the cottage, mainly because they were warm and comfortable. Today she wore her favourite brown pair. Over them she wore a long-sleeved pink jumper in a lacy pattern, one that Connie had knitted for her. Pulling her coat over the top she was reaching for her scarf when Denton plucked it from her hands and arranged it around her neck.

His closeness was disconcerting, the small space between them a ferment of turbulence trying to absorb her into its pulse. How easy it would be to take that moment and make it hers, and in so doing, to close the space so they became one.

He was as instinctively aware of it as she was, the warm column of his body charged with the living energy of him. She sensed a moment when her heartbeat changed to match his – as if he'd captured it and made it his own, so they were marching in the same step.

'There, is that comfortable?'

She daren't look up at him . . . daren't absorb the woodland depths of his eyes and see the naked truth of what they held for her. Comfortable? There was nothing comfortable about Denton, though she hadn't realized it before. He was at one with the power of his maleness. He was playing the game to his own rules, and had been since they first met, and even while she was married to Richard. When she took a step back to widen the distance between them he gave a faint grin.

The drive took only a short time. They left the car on a bumpy road, climbed a stile and headed for the cliff.

Denton took her hand in his and refused to release it when she gave it a tug, lifting it to his mouth to drag his lips across her knuckles instead, then bearing it into his overcoat pocket to keep it warm. The dogs darted on ahead, following their own trails and scents and being brought back to heel with a whistle every time they wandered out of sight.

It was fifteen minutes before they reached the cliff top. A turbulent breeze whipped a salty smell into their nostrils and occasionally snatched the words from their mouths to carry them away across the sea – to whisper into the ears of sailors perhaps or to visit foreign lands.

'You look far away; what are you thinking about?' he asked.

'I was wondering where words stolen by the wind end up.'

'You have seriously unusual wonderings. Let me think about that.' Denton considered it, his face grave.

Livia waited, while beneath them the waves pounded at the cliff base in a furious attempt at demolition.

Seagulls floated in the currents of air. At this point, the incoming waves collided with those outgoing in a thrash of spray thrown high, then they dragged back to comb noisily through the shingles. Clouds feathered upwards from the horizon like the wings of angels.

'Well?' she said, dragging her mind from the excitement of the elemental power at their feet.

He bestowed on her a smile of great tenderness. 'I have no idea.'

'It took you all that time to come up with an answer like that?'

'Sorry' He gave a glimmer of a smile. 'I could tell you how to steal the words from someone's mouth in the first place, though.'

'How?'

She shouldn't have asked, she realized, when he kissed her for the second time that day. It was an earth-shattering experience that left her trembling, and longing for more, so her mouth absorbed the soft caress of his and her lips parted just a little, encouraging him to continue in this madness of feeling.

When his lips slid across her face and kissed her ear she felt reckless. She wanted him too much, not just his mouth against hers but a long saturation of loving, of his strong body against hers, his hands and mouth making her long for more and more pleasure. She stayed in his arms afterwards, her face burrowed in his neck, her nose inhaling the piquant fragrance of his shaving soap.

No . . . he mustn't be allowed to say he loved her. She mustn't allow herself to weaken. With the greatest of effort, she placed her hands against his chest and gently pushed. He stood firm, as though her resistance was a mere puff of wind against a dandelion clock. His hands closed over hers.

Tears prickled against her eyelids and rolled down her cheeks. Taking a folded handkerchief from his pocket he collected her spilled tears. 'Why are you crying, my love? Don't you like me?'

'Like' was too mild a word for the feelings churning inside her and she scorned, 'Of course I like you. Can't we just remain friends?'

He scrutinized her face then sighed. 'We can try. Would you give a friend a hug.'

She nodded and moved back into his arms again. Placing one hand against her back, the other behind her head, he cradled her against him. It was nice being held that way, her face pillowed on his shoulder, his breath warming her scalp and her mouth a heartbeat away from his chin, so she could kiss it, or nip it if she was of a mind to. She felt cherished, and her arms slipped round him. Denton was so dependable, so honest and so warm, and so . . . so . . . She felt the change in him and in herself. Lor, he was *dangerous*! She blushed and slipped from the circle of his arms, no longer feeling safe.

He smiled at her with great charm and the shrug he gave her was wry. 'I can't quite picture us as friends only, can you?'

Denton was more conventional than Richard had been. If he learned who'd fathered Meggie he probably wouldn't want her. Yet she couldn't deceive him, at least not for long. Neither could she tell him the truth – for Meggie's sake as well as her own. Already there was conjecture about the baby's birth date, and she'd die rather than hurt her sweet, innocent daughter in any way.

'I must get back, Denton.'

'What are you scared of?' he said. 'Every time we get close you push me away.'

'It's too soon to think about . . . anyone else.'

'You're hiding behind Richard. He wouldn't have wanted you to mourn for him indefinitely.'

'I know he wouldn't. You don't understand, Denton. There's talk, and I don't want to encourage it, especially since Richard is no longer here to defend himself.'

'There's always talk.' He gazed at her, his eyes giving an impression of knowing more than they offered when he took an unexpected and disconcerting stab at her. 'There's often speculation about a premature baby, especially when it arrives early in a marriage. Take no notice of it.'

She felt nothing but relief. At least Denton hadn't heard the rest of it.

Then he said, 'But if you're referring to our relationship, that's another matter all together.'

Her relief had been short-lived. 'What relationship? We've been friends, that's all.'

'You can hedge around it all you like, but what we feel towards each other is more than friendship. Friends don't look at each other the way we do, with such a need for intimacy. Richard knew there was more than friendship between us. He was aware that I loved you. He wasn't the type to muscle in on a serious relationship without good reason, but rather, he'd have kept you safe until the way was clear for me. Your marriage came as a great shock and I can only wonder why Richard took the action he did, and why you went along with it.'

Richard had married her to save her reputation, knowing she'd soon be widowed. But in the process something had happened that neither of them had predicted. Richard had fallen in love with her.

'I loved Richard. He was a caring and kind man and we enjoyed each other's company. I miss him, Denton. He was always there for me. Don't probe any further than that, please.'

'I thought you cared enough for me to wait. I thought we had an understanding.'

She'd wounded him more than she'd realized. She gazed into his dear face, absorbing the hurt in his eyes. In some ways he was even more vulnerable than Richard had been, for he'd loved her and he'd lost her to his best friend – a double betrayal.

But she'd also been betrayed. In the normal course of events, if the major hadn't attacked her and if Meggie hadn't been conceived from that attack, then Richard wouldn't have felt the need to wed her, and she would have waited for Denton.

She reached out and gently caressed his face. The world was full of regrets, and just at this moment she was experiencing every one of them. 'We did have an understanding. I'm sorry, I didn't deliberately set out to hurt you. It was all such a rush.'

'That was Richard all over. He made up his mind to something and you were just swept along. Were you happy with him?'

She smiled. 'Yes.'

'Good.' He took her hands in his again, his smile returning. 'Come on, I'll take you home. Did you receive an invitation to my parents' party? Yes . . . of course you would have.'

'I can only stay for a couple of hours, since I'll have to be back for Meggie. She's a bit of a dictator, I'm afraid.'

Gently, he kissed her forehead. 'I'll personally pick you up, and I'll deliver you back home. This isn't over yet, Livia. I don't give up easily.'

'No . . . I don't suppose you do,' and she wished she could tell him that everything would be all right for him. But she couldn't.

Nineteen

Livia dressed carefully in a waisted, ankle-length gown of midnight blue sprinkled with crystals. It was a gown Richard had insisted she buy. There was a silk jacket with a diamanté clasp in the shape of the moon. He'd bought her perfume to wear with it, *L' Heure Bleue,* which he'd said meant, The Blue Hour.

It was a perfume his mother had worn, and Livia had all but exhausted the small drop Margaret Sangster had left behind on her dressing table when Richard had bought her another bottle.

She went through the jewellery Simon Stone had returned to her. There was a pair of diamond earrings that were discreet. Clipping them to her earlobes, she slid her engagement ring on to her finger, then slipped the daisy ring on her other hand. She gazed at her wedding ring, wondering if she should remove it. She decided against it. It would remind people that she was the widowed Mrs Olivia Sangster.

Meggie settled down quickly. She was a child who responded well to routine, and Livia had arranged their daily lives around her comfort. Usually at this time Livia was helping with the washing up after dinner and looking forward to listening to the radio.

Tucking the covers round her daughter, Livia kissed the warm, rosy flush of her cheek and went downstairs. To Chad and Esmé, she said, 'Don't forget to go to bed on time.' She turned to Connie. 'I'll be back at ten o'clock. Call me if you need me before that. You know Doctor Elliot's number.'

'Goodness, will you stop fussing, Livia. You're only a mile away. There's Doctor Denton's car. Slip your coat on now, it's cold outside.'

'Now who's fussing?'

'I am. You don't want to catch a cold to pass on to Meggie, do you?'

A car horn honked.

Kissing Connie's cheek, she pulled on her coat and sped outside. It was a clear night and the moon reigned serenely over a cradle of stars. Frost rimed the blades of grass, turning them into spears. The trees clawed black skeletal fingers into the sky, as though trying to scratch the stars from their settings. Warmth was leached from her body with each vaporous breath.

Denton tucked a blanket around her legs. 'I like your perfume . . . it's so you . . . deep and mysterious, like the sky tonight.'

How close he'd come was an homage to the perfumer's art. 'That's exactly what it was created to be. It's called The Blue Hour.' She wouldn't dilute the compliment by telling him that Richard had chosen it for her.

'Obviously I have a good nose.'

She grinned. 'You have an excellent nose; like a bloodhound.'

He voiced a blood-curdling howl towards the moon.

They gazed at each other for a moment, laughing, then she said, 'Shouldn't we get going before you attract all the amorous farm dogs in the district? I only have two hours, and I don't want to spend it sitting outside the cottage listening to you howl.'

'I would quite happily sit here howling for two hours, as long as I had you to howl at. But if we must . . .' He gave her a smile and put the car in motion. 'I've been offered a job at Poole hospital.'

'Will you take it?'

'I haven't decided yet. Some time ago, just after I learned of your marriage to Richard, I applied for a position in an Australian hospital in Melbourne. They've also made me a tempting offer.'

Dismay yawned inside her as the realization that she might never see him again struck home. 'Australia is such a long way.'

'The contract would be for two years initially.'

In which time she'd probably get him out of her system . . . but no, she'd never be able to do that. Lord, how she'd miss him if he went away. 'What do your parents think?'

'I haven't discussed it with them yet.'

'Bernice?'

He slid her a quick look. 'What about her?'

'I thought you and she . . . Bernice loves you.'

'Bernice loves Bernice, and she's in love with being in love.' He gave a faint smile. 'How can you think such a thing? Didn't I make my intentions towards you perfectly clear in that letter I sent you? All right, so you didn't read it because it arrived on the eve of your wedding to Richard, but you must have read it since, and the sentiment is still the same.'

'I haven't opened it. I didn't like to while Richard was alive.'

'Why not?'

A little shyly, she said, 'I don't know if you'll be able to understand this, Denton. I never thought it possible that I could love two men at the same time, but I did. Richard was so good to me that I couldn't help loving him. I didn't want to feel as though I was being disloyal to him, even in my mind. So I hid your letter under the lining in a drawer in the cottage, and I tried to forget you, as I knew I must. But every time I saw you I knew I loved you with just as much intensity, if a little differently. The letter is still in its hiding place. Richard knew about my feelings for you.'

He gave her a quick smile as they turned into the driveway of his parents' house. 'Well, at least I know where I stand in your estimation now.'

She said, 'I know you doubt the truth of what Richard and I meant to each other, but it was very real and precious to me. I've brought this to show you. You'll need the flashlight.' She took a piece of paper from her beaded evening bag and handed it to him. 'Read it. I found it in Richard's diary.'

Denton's heart sank as he read the poem. The intimacy and heartfelt eloquence of it made him ashamed that he'd ever doubted either of them. He wished she hadn't shown it to him, and he wanted to tear it into little pieces and throw it to the wind. But she'd never forgive him if he did. This was something she could cling to, and reassure herself with.

There was a moment of silence in which he felt defeated by his own sense of inadequacy. But Richard was dead, and he wasn't, which gave him quite an advantage. 'I can't compete with Richard's way with words, but he's dead, and you're alive. Don't you think it's about time you read my letter?'

She reached up and touched his face. 'Yes . . . I suppose it is time, and I owe you that.'

The party was as Livia feared. The glances went from her to Denton, then back again, speculative.

Helen kissed her on the cheek. 'I'm glad you could make it, Livia. How pretty you look. How's Meggie?'

'Thriving. She's being christened after the service on Sunday. I do hope you'll stay for it. Mr Beamish and Mrs Starling will be her main godparents. And my sister and brother will also stand. They're a little young for the job, but the reverend has allowed it, since he's satisfied they know what's entailed.'

Someone nearby asked, 'Will the major be attending the christening? He's such a delightful man. We haven't seen him since . . . well, for quite a while. I would have thought he'd have been down to see his granddaughter.'

Livia cringed at the thought of seeing him again. 'The major is in hospital.'

'Is he? I hadn't heard. My, what a dark horse you are, Mrs Sangster. What's wrong with the major?'

Dr Elliot rescued her before she could tell the woman to mind her own business.

'Hello, my dear. You look absolutely glowing. Being a mother suits you.'

'Meggie's a good baby. She allows me to sleep for most of the night. She's got two teeth now.'

'I must drop in and visit her, so she can show me how clever she is.'

'What a scintillating contribution to the conversation that was,' she said, trying not to giggle. 'I'll be telling you how many eggs the hens laid this week.'

Andrew Elliot grinned at her. 'I'm sure that would be equally fascinating. Denton, my boy, take Livia's coat. Come into the drawing room where it's warm, my dear. Now, what can I get you to drink? We have some punch that packs a bit of a wallop. Helen made it and it's heavy on the gin.'

'I don't think that would suit Meggie, do you?'

'I'd forgotten you were nursing. Punch is out, then. I have a bottle of stout in the cupboard. It's nutritious, and just the thing for nursing mothers. I'll pour you one.'

'Thank you.'

The dark brown liquid with its topping of caramel froth looked somewhat unappetizing. She took a sip and only just prevented herself from grimacing. She looked round for Denton when Dr Elliot was approached by another guest, recognizing a few faces from church. They stood in little clumps, talking.

Denton came in. Smiling at her over the heads, he made his way across. He took out a handkerchief and dabbed at her upper lip, laughing. 'You have a frothy moustache. What's that you're drinking?'

'Your father told me it's stout, but I have my doubts.'

He took the glass from her hand and helped himself to a gulp. 'Yep, that's stout all right.'

On the other side of the room Bernice stood with two men. Dressed in striking maroon pants and a top with gold trim and a floating chiffon scarf, she looked vaguely oriental. It was not something Livia would have chosen for herself, but Bernice certainly carried it off.

Bernice's eyes narrowed in on Denton. Those same eyes

shifted to Livia. They were unhappy. She said something to the two men and the three of them sauntered across.

Bernice kissed Denton's cheek before latching on to his arm. 'Hello, darling.'

'You came then,' he said, but without much enthusiasm. 'I thought you were going partying with Jerome.'

'We are. We're here to persuade you to come with us.'

'I'm afraid not. I promised to take Livia home.'

Livia was looked up and down with some dislike. 'Goodness, her cottage is only up the road, can't she walk?'

'At night and in January, and when she has to get home to feed her baby? I think not, Bernice. Besides, it would be rude to walk out on my parents' party.'

Bernice persisted, her mouth shaping into a plum-coloured pout. 'Couldn't your father take her home?'

Livia intervened. 'Please stop trying to arrange my life, Bernice, and don't discuss me as though I'm not here. It's most annoying. And if you want to go somewhere else, please don't let me stop you, Denton. I'm sure I can manage by myself.'

'I don't want to be somewhere else.' Denton managed to detach his arm from Bernice's colour-coordinated talons, and turned to her, his smile easy, but his eyes slightly narrowed in irritation. 'Livia, have you met Jerome Scotter? And this tall chap is Bernice's brother, Nicholas. We studied together and lived in the same boarding house. May I introduce Livia Sangster.'

Nicholas flashed her a smile. 'Denton has mentioned you often, but he didn't tell me you were such a peach.'

Denton laughed. 'And I didn't tell her you were a wolf in sheep's clothing, despite your appearance.'

Nicholas resembled Bernice, but his clothes hung untidily on his frame, as if he'd lost weight since he'd last worn them. Jerome Scotter was shorter, but neat in an expensive-looking suit with velvet revers, and a gold brocade waistcoat under his jacket. His eyes were blue, and astute. 'Bernice tells me you're the daughter of Eloise Carr, the designer.'

'Yes, I am.'

'Your mother was very talented. She was an inspiration to me when I was studying art and design. She was a lovely woman, too, and you look a lot like her.'

'Thank you . . . did you design Bernice's outfit?'

Jerome flicked Bernice a look and gave a tiny shudder. 'Good Lord, no! She designed it herself.'

Bernice almost recoiled from the implied criticism, and Livia felt sorry for her. 'I like it.'

Bernice was not mollified in the least. 'You don't have to say the polite thing just to please me.'

Livia was tired of this woman's petulance. 'Pleasing you is the last thing on my mind, Bernice. I like the outfit. It's different, and it suits you. Take that as a compliment or not, whichever you please.'

An awkward silence followed.

Jerome gazed at his watch, then at his companions. 'Time to go, I think. It will take us a while to get to Bournemouth.'

'You should have telephoned me first, it would have saved you a trip,' Denton said easily.

Jerome shrugged. 'Yes, we should have, but we were down this way anyway. I have a maiden aunt who lives in Weymouth, and who needs to be buttered up now and again.'

'I'll show you out.'

When he returned he had lipstick on his mouth.

'Now it's your turn to have a moustache.' She took his handkerchief and wiped it off.

'There's mistletoe in the hall, I'm afraid.'

'You don't have to make excuses for her. Bernice put it there in an attempt to make me jealous.'

'She can be a bit obvious at times. Are you jealous? You needn't be, you know. As far as I'm concerned, it's over, and Bernice knows it.'

'You have a large ego, Denton Elliot.'

'Let's leave the complications of the id to followers of Freud. Psychiatry is too involved an art for a tradesman like me to grasp. I'm just a people plumber. Besides, my ego isn't large. I'm just . . . well, I suppose you could say I have confidence in myself.'

'If I *were* jealous, I wouldn't tell you. Or I'd tell you I wasn't jealous so you wouldn't be any the wiser. So no, I'm not jealous.'

The fact that she'd like to poke Bernice's eyes out had nothing to do with jealousy and everything to do with . . .

Well, all right. She couldn't think of a better explanation for her need to disable the woman, and she grinned.

So did he. 'It must be me who's jealous.'

'Of whom?'

'Richard . . . I think. He was such a hero.'

'Denton, you're fishing for a compliment. Stop being pathetic. You're so very different to Richard, but you're both tall poppies to me. Always have been.'

Someone put a record on and he took the glass of stout from her hand and placed it on the mantelpiece. Eyes sparkling, he gazed down at her. 'My dancing's just as pathetic, but will you dance with me?'

She couldn't get into much trouble dancing with him, she thought. 'I warn you, I'm not very good at it.'

'It's not something complicated, like a tango. All we need to do is shuffle around the floor with everyone else.'

She should have known that she'd fit into his arms like they were meant for each other. Because space was restricted they had to dance closer than was comfortable, which made them more aware of each other. There were interested eyes on them too, looking for little intimacies that might add fuel to the fires already burning around her.

When the clock struck ten Denton danced her out into the hall and arranged her coat around her shoulders. 'Here we are, Cinders, standing under the mistletoe. Are you going to turn me into a frog, or shall I turn you into a frog?'

His mouth felt nothing like that of a frog, but like that of a lover, and her heart set up such a clamour that the pulse of it beat inside her ears like a jungle drum. The instinct to run away from danger was thwarted by her muscles melting into fondant inside her skin, merely at the thought of loving him in a physical way.

She felt a comfortable rapport with Denton on the way home. She didn't want to part with him, and was tempted to ask him in for coffee. She didn't. 'I forgot to say goodnight to your parents, and thank them.'

'I'll do it for you.' His eyes looked into hers with an intensity that was scorching. 'Will you read my letter?'

'If I can find the courage.'

'We'll talk when you have. Call me when you're ready.'

And she would have to tell him no . . . that she wouldn't marry him. And that would break her heart as well as his.

Inside, she found that her sister and brother were sound asleep. Connie was in her dressing gown, her hands around a cup of cocoa.

Meggie was wide awake, and just beginning to become agitated as her stomach told her it was empty.

'She's been awake since eight-thirty, so she should be good and tired after she's had her supper.'

'She wasn't a nuisance, was she?'

Meggie let out an impatient warble at the sound of her mother's voice.

Above it, Connie said, 'Esmé kept her amused for an hour. She's just beginning to get fractious. Another tooth on the way, I think.'

'I won't be a minute, my love.'

Livia changed into her nightclothes, by which time Meggie was bellowing to be fed. Livia made her comfortable and put her to her breast. Her mouth nudged frantically back and forth, and the noise stopped abruptly as Meggie attached herself and began to suck strongly. A feeling of contentment and love stole through Livia.

'Did you have a good time?' Connie asked.

'Yes . . . most of the village was there. Denton danced my feet off, and I'll be glad to get to bed. You haven't got to wait up, Connie.'

'Can I get you anything? I've still got to fill our hot-water bottles, so it won't be any trouble, since I'll be going to the kitchen.'

'A cup of cocoa would be nice. It will help me sleep.'

'That Doctor Denton . . . he's a nice man. I always thought he'd taken a shine to you.'

Livia didn't answer, and after a moment the door closed behind Connie. She ran her fingertips through her daughter's dark wisps of hair. She could do nothing to jeopardize Meggie's future. She loved her too much. And she loved Denton too much to ruin his future, too. Better to let him go to Australia. He would meet someone else he could love there.

Later, she took the letter from its hiding place under the drawer lining and gazed at it. Denton's handwriting was strong, but it didn't give her any clues as to the contents. She didn't want to open it – didn't want to read what he'd written from his heart.

The clock chimed eleven. Time was getting on. Hands trembling, she slit the envelope along the top with the blade of the scissors and removed a single sheet of paper.

Livia.

I'm not a man who can write fine and persuasive words. But I do write this sincerely, and from the feelings I hold within my heart for you.

It seems appropriate for me to express my intention this way. I'd be honoured if you would agree to become my wife.

As you know, I'm expecting to further my professional standing, which will ensure a comfortable recompense into the foreseeable future. I will do my best to cherish and keep you, and to care for, and guide, Chad and Esmé until they reach adulthood.

You have given me reason to believe (or hope) that you hold me close in your affection. I am grateful for that small encouragement. I know I'll love you always, and will wait for you. Nothing can change that.

Truly yours,

Denton.

She closed her eyes and held the sheet of paper against her beating heart. Something could change it – the question mark hanging over Meggie's head.

Sooner or later Denton would hear the gossip, and begin to suspect that all was not as it seemed. He was not like Richard, who'd twisted things to suit the situation. He'd possessed the ability to laugh off any scandal with his devil-may-care attitude, and persuaded her to believe it didn't matter, too.

'Let people wonder,' he'd have said.

But then, the lie had involved his family's reputation, so he'd had reason to handle it, and hush it up in the way he had – the only way.

Richard had lied rather easily. In a social situation he'd sensed what people wanted to hear, and more often than not, agreed with them, whether he had his own opinion or not. That had made him popular.

She wondered now if he'd have married her without the incentive of a scandal hanging over their heads, and doubted if she could maintain the lie when faced with Denton's honesty.

She went to bed, her mind torn between doing what was right for Meggie and what was right for Denton, and not giving any thought as to what was right for herself.

Twenty

Major Henry had decided to escape from the prison camp he was in. He was going home. That morning, after his interrogators had gone, he'd put on his uniform.

Now he threw his greatcoat over his arm, pulled his cap down over his eyes and left the hospital, following a group of visitors.

The prison was short of staff and the male attendant gave him a cursory glance, smiled and tossed him a sloppy salute as he locked the door behind them. 'Enjoy the weekend, Sir.'

Henry smirked as he marched off, feeling rather pleased with himself.

There was a small amount of money in the coin pocket sewn into his overcoat lining. He took a bus to Waterloo Station, and spent some time in the café, eating buns and drinking coffee, until it was time to board the train. He was looking forward to seeing his wife and son again. Richard had married, he thought suddenly, and didn't he have a grandchild?

He shook his head. He kept getting confused about things. He must talk to Dr Elliot about it.

He boarded the train, taking a seat in the corner of a first-class apartment, next to the window, where he could watch the winter landscape speed by. It was quite a novelty after his time in the prison camp. There was a rather stout woman dressed in black on the opposite seat in their compartment. She smelled of mothballs and kept smiling at him.

He was no longer interested in women. They were full of deceit, and only wanted a chap for what they could get from him.

She leaned forward and tapped him on the knee, her smile smug. 'Surely you remember me, Major Henry?'

'Of course I remember you. Mrs . . . um . . .'

'Ada Rothwell.'

He remembered an Ada . . . a dancer from the Adelphi. It was not long after he and Margaret had married and he'd been in a bit of a bind. Richard had been on the way and Margaret wouldn't allow him any ease. The Ada he remembered had been a neat little thing in a frilly dress, and he'd had her in the dressing room while she'd sat astride his lap. Surely this stout creature wasn't her?

The door slid open, allowing a ticket inspector to intrude into the compartment on a cold draught. 'Tickets please.'

The major patted his pocket, feeling confused and distressed. 'A ticket? I don't think I've got one. I do have a warrant card somewhere. I think somebody has stolen it, though . . . my money as well.'

'I'm sorry, Sir. I must see the warrant card else you'll have to pay your fare. If you can do neither I'll have to escort you off the train at the next stop. '

When an embarrassed Henry began to go through his pockets, the woman leaned forward and pressed a pound into his hand. 'Allow me, Major. You can repay me when you're able.'

He handed the money to the inspector. 'Will that do, my man?'

He was issued with a ticket and the door slid shut. The inspector gave him a warning look as he moved on.

Mrs Rothwell simpered, 'I'd heard you were in hospital. Are you home for good, Major?'

So that was the tale they'd put around? The Sangsters wouldn't want anyone to know he'd been in a prison camp, of course. It just wasn't done in his family. One died rather than allowed oneself to be captured. He nodded.

'I'd heard you'd been ill.'

Had he? He couldn't remember being ill. His eyes narrowed in on her as he wondered if she was one of his tormentors at the prison camp. But he couldn't remember seeing her before.

As the train sped towards Dorset the woman began to prattle. Henry closed his eyes. He was tired and cold, and all he wanted to do was to get home, not make conversation with a woman who was a stranger to him.

Then he remembered what he'd forgotten, and his eyes shot open. 'Red garters!'

'I beg your pardon.' She gave a horrified gasp.

'You wore red silk garters.'

Shock appeared in her eyes. 'How dare you, Major! I don't know what the world's coming to if a decent woman can't travel on public transport without being accosted. I shall tell my husband. No doubt he'll have words with you about this.'

Henry remembered a grey little man, a browbeaten accountant who dropped food down his front and who wouldn't say boo to a goose. He got very little peace from his wife, Henry imagined.

All the same, it had been bad form on his part to give her garters a public airing, and all he could do was apologize and say something nice. 'Sorry, m'dear. You had shapely legs, so a bit of titillation for your husband wouldn't have gone amiss.'

A pair of plump feet withdrew under her skirt, like snails retreating into their shell. She sniffed, then gathered up her bag and left the compartment, her body tightly confined by a whalebone corset.

He was pleased she'd gone. Not that she was any temptation to him now. Smiling with relief, he closed his eyes again and listened to the wheels clackety-clack over the rails. After a while he went to sleep.

The major overshot Creekmore Halt. He got out at the next station and began to walk, grumbling a little because he was hungry and cold, and it had come on to rain.

He finally made it to Foxglove House. The lights were out, but smoke came from the chimney. He took the spare key from its hiding place in a crack between two bricks and let himself in.

'Margaret! Richard! I'm home,' he shouted.

There was no reply.

He went to the kitchen and found some bread and cheese. The decanter was on the dresser. He poured himself a brandy. It was a little rough, and he was tempted to go to the cellar and find something better.

His coat had begun to steam with the heat from the fire. 'God, I'm weary,' he said. He downed another brandy. It tasted better the second time round. It was strong, but warming. A third one would see him right. He staggered as he made his way upstairs, glass in hand.

He frowned. Everything was covered in dustsheets. It was typical of Margaret to make him feel unwelcome. Swigging back the brandy, he placed the glass carefully on the shrouded dressing table,

He dragged some blankets from the box at the foot of the bed, wrapped himself up and pulled the dustsheets back over. He chuckled. When Margaret and Richard came home he'd give them both a bloody fright, and serve them right.

The christening of Meggie took place after the Sunday service. The twins looked proud as they stood up with Connie and Mr Beamish as godparents, though the reverend had been a little dubious about allowing children to take on such an important role.

Livia told him, 'They spent several years in an orphanage, and this duty will help remind them that they're a part of a family. Our parents would have wanted that too. The alternative is to put the christening off for ten years, until the twins have grown up.'

The reverend gave in gracefully.

A few people stayed after the service to watch the ceremony, hoping to catch a glimpse of the baby. Mrs Anstruther was absent, having left that morning to spend some time with her daughter. Matthew Bugg brought old Bugg to the ceremony. He looked surprisingly spry with a drop of whisky inside him to ward off the cold.

Meggie behaved like an angel, quite happy to be the centre of attention, bestowing bountiful smiles on everyone and attracting comments. 'She's a dear little thing,' and depending on the eyes of the observer, 'so much like her grandmother-mother-sister-brother-father-grandfather.' Livia was glad that nobody thought to throw Denton's name into the ring.

And from those who thought they knew better, 'Not really like anyone in the Sangster family. She must have jumped a generation.' Significant pause. 'She has her own look . . . don't you, dear?'

Meggie's angelic frame of mind lasted until the reverend sprinkled cold water on her head, then she heaved in an indignant breath and let out a roar that made the rafters rattle and set the candle flames flickering.

'It's the holy water. It drives the devil out,' Florence told anyone who would listen.

A few people had been invited back to the cottage, including the Elliots, the Buggs, the midwife who'd attended Livia after the birth of Meggie, and the reverend. Connie had prepared a delicious buffet lunch, and after giving Meggie a feed to keep her happy, as well as fill her up, Livia helped Connie to carry the plates in.

Denton cornered her in the kitchen. 'Have you read my letter?'

'I have.'

'And?'

'It was a lovely letter, Denton; but this is not the time or place to talk.' It wasn't fair of her to keep him hanging on a thread much longer, and she must decide one way or another whether to cut him free. She kept telling herself that her deceit would never be found out, yet sometimes she felt as if the truth was tattooed all over her forehead.

'When then?'

'Can you make it tomorrow, in the afternoon? Connie has decided to go back with Beamish and Florence, to help them through the birth of the baby.' She grinned. 'Connie's experience here has made her an expert. The children will be attending Suzanne's birthday party.'

He touched her face, his eyes searching hers, as if looking for a clue. His mouth took on a wry twist and he said quietly, 'Bear in mind that I won't take no for an answer.'

* * *

Duly, Denton presented himself. He hadn't imagined Livia would put him through all this. He was a surgeon, a damned good one with a good future, and if he didn't love this difficult woman to death he would have walked away from such an indignity.

As it was he'd go on his knees and kiss her feet if that's what she wanted from him. But all the same, he felt uneasy. Nothing was going as he'd planned, and he wanted – and intended – to know the reason why. It was time to take the gloves off.

She landed her blow first, before he'd had time to put his case – one in the solar plexus that left him gasping like a stranded fish.

'I'm sorry, Denton. If I'd received the letter a month or two earlier I would have accepted your proposal.'

He hit back, and more savagely than he'd intended. 'Before Meggie made her presence known to you, do you mean?'

He hated himself when she flinched. The hurt he'd dealt her lingered on in her eyes, and he wondered if it was as agonizing as the hurt he felt.

'No . . . I meant before . . . Richard.'

'I'm a living, breathing man, and you're a living, breathing woman. I can stand playing second fiddle to Richard's shining star, but you've beatified him in your mind beyond reason. He's so perfect I can't compete with his bloody ghost. It's beyond my capabilities.'

When tears sprang to her eyes, he hated himself once more.

'You're not in competition with anyone, and you'll never be second fiddle to him. You never have been. I just can't marry you.'

'Why, for God's sake?'

Her eyes pleaded with him. 'Don't ask me why.'

'That's not good enough, Livia. All this time you've led me to believe you cared for me.'

'I do care for you, more than you'll ever know. I just can't marry you.'

He gazed at her, frustrated beyond measure.

The telephone rang.

She gazed at it for a moment then lifted the receiver to her ear. Her face fell and she dropped the instrument on to the table and sank into the chair, ashen-faced.

He grabbed it up, wondering what the hell had induced that reaction in her. 'This is Denton Elliot. I'm a doctor. Mrs Sangster can't answer your call at the moment. Can I be of help?'

'It's Simon Stone. I've just received word that Major Henry has walked out of the hospital. He's not considered dangerous, but he's been without his medication for some time and could be confused or agitated. He could be heading for Foxglove House.'

The major was in a mental institution? It was the first he'd heard of it. 'Does my father know? The major is his patient.'

'Ah . . . I'm not sure. I imagine the institution would have been in touch with him. It's not something the family would have wanted to get round, you understand.'

The major's family being Livia and Meggie, and that was a tenuous link at best. He gave Livia a glance, but she was gazing down at her hands, twisting her wedding ring around.

He had in his pocket an engagement ring he'd bought for her nearly two years ago. He'd never been given the chance of putting it on her finger.

He frowned. The news shouldn't have had such an effect on her. 'Leave this with me, Mr Stone. I'll find Matthew Bugg and search the place, then call you back if we find anything. In the meantime my father can ring the institution and find out what medication he's on. It's probably a phenobarbital. If need be, I'll arrange for him to be driven back to the institution.'

Denton rang his father and they discussed the matter. He turned to Livia afterwards. 'My father has reminded me that we'll need your permission to enter Foxglove House. The major could be there.'

'I have a key to the house. It's hanging on a hook on the kitchen dresser. Matthew stayed with his grandfather last night, so should be safe. I'll ring him and tell him to meet you there.'

Nobody answered the phone. 'They must be out visiting, but I don't think Matthew will mind you going in and looking.'

'Will you come with us?'

'No. I can't leave Meggie here by herself, and she'll need to be fed when she wakes.'

He nodded.

'Take care, Denton, especially if the major has been drinking, because when he's drunk he's strong, and he can't control himself.'

Denton had never known the major to be aggressive, and he found the statement slightly odd.

'Is that why he ended up in an institution?'

'I understand that he tried to shoot himself in the head after his wife left him. The neighbour heard the shot and called the police to investigate. He'd broken his wrist in the attempt.'

'Why didn't you tell me?'

She shrugged. 'Richard told me his father didn't visit him when he was in hospital. Major Henry was shamed by the thought of mental illness in the family, and that Richard might have been considered cowardly in the execution of his duty towards his country. I didn't think the major would have liked me to tell anyone.'

Exasperated, Denton said, 'It was mental and physical fatigue in Richard's case. If he'd got help earlier it would probably have been less severe. If you saw what the soldiers went through in France, you'd understand.'

'I don't need to have seen it, Denton. Richard talked in his sleep, and that was traumatic in itself.' She placed her hand on his wrist when his father's car skidded to a stop. 'I don't know if there are any guns and ammunition at Foxglove House, and I couldn't bear it if you were hurt. Don't leave me worrying about you.'

In a wry twist of imagination, he pictured his own funeral with Richard's widow weeping copious tears all over his coffin. Now that would add flames to the fire of scandal. He grinned at her and snatched a kiss before she had time to stop him.

'I'll be back, I promise,' he said.

To keep herself busy, Livia collected the eggs from the henhouse. Bertie followed her, dropping a stick at her feet.

'So you want a game, do you?' She placed the basket of eggs down and threw the stick as far as she could, laughing when he raced after it in short leaps. Sidetracked by a smell, he went off into the undergrowth and Livia made her way to the house. He would scratch when he wanted to come in.

The door was swinging open. She wasn't usually so careless, because the cottage soon lost heat. She closed it and set about making some tea. She cut a slice of Connie's gingerbread cake and set it on the tray. It was nice not to be bossed around in her own kitchen, but she'd appreciated Connie's help, though.

Meggie was making gurgling noises in her pram, which was kept in the sitting room. About to place the basket of eggs in the larder, she heard the major's voice.

'Has naughty Mummy left you all alone? I suppose she's gone off on that stupid horse of hers. Come and sit on Daddy's knee and he'll tell you a nice story.'

Livia's heart fell into the pit of her stomach and her mouth went dry. Dropping the eggs she snatched up a knife and edged towards the sitting room.

The major had Meggie on his lap, and she was gazing up at him, not knowing whether to laugh or cry.

The major looked up when Livia went in, and smiled. 'It's about time you came back, Margaret. Where were you? Richard needs feeding.'

'Fetching the eggs,' she whispered, her mouth so dry with fear that she could barely get the words out.

'You don't look pleased to see me.'

She swallowed. His mind was wandering, but she must try to make him understand. 'I am pleased, but I'm not Margaret. I'm Livia. The baby is your granddaughter. Pass her over to me, please, Major Henry. I'll take her upstairs and change her napkin.'

'I've been kept in a prison camp,' he told her. 'They keep torturing me. But I won't tell them anything.'

Denton had forgotten the key to Foxglove House. Because his shoes were muddy, he took them off and left them on the back doorstep. Livia would be feeding Meggie by now. He opened the door and stepped inside, on to something sticky. Broken eggs! The mess oozed through his socks and up between his toes. A tea tray was on the table. He took a bite of the gingerbread.

Then he heard voices and froze.

'Henry, I want you to hand my baby to me.' Livia sounded calm, but she was breathless, and there was an underlying fear.

'It's my baby, too. It's Richard. I want to hold him.'

'It isn't Richard. Richard is dead. Don't you remember, you attended his funeral. It's Meggie you're holding. She's your granddaughter. You can hold her again after she's had her feed.'

Meggie gave a cry, reminding her mother she had rights.

'See . . . you're making her upset.'

'I know my own child when I see him. You're lying to make me confused, Margaret. You're going to leave the child and go to Tangiers. Then they'll take me away to that prison camp.'

'I still have to feed the baby. Give her to me, Major. Please.'

Denton could hear the strain in her voice, and gazed through the crack of the door. The major was on the settee with Meggie on his lap. Livia was stood just a few inches from where he was, her back against the door. The arms at her side were balled into tight fists, and she had a kitchen knife in one of them, hidden against her skirt. She was nearly at breaking point.

He didn't want to frighten Livia any further, so he whispered, 'It's Denton. Move to the right so I can open the door.'

He heard her breath expel, and she moved quickly. As the door swung open he took two strides forward and plucked Meggie from the major's lap.

Within seconds Livia had snatched the baby from him and was gone, her feet scurrying up the stairs. The bedroom door closed and a key was turned in the lock.

He heard the window open and she called out from up above, 'Doctor Elliot, the major is here, with Denton. The back door is open.'

Denton tried to placate the confused Henry, who said, 'I wouldn't have hurt my child.'

'I know you wouldn't. You're not well, Major. You ran away from the hospital.'

'All I wanted was to come home to my family, but I can't find them.'

His father came in, a smile on his face. 'Hello, Major.'

'Andrew Elliot . . . glad to see you again.'

'You're in a spot of trouble, I believe. I'll give you your medicine, then we can talk.'

'I don't want to go back to that place.'

'I'm afraid you must, Henry. Expose his arm while I prepare the medication, would you please, Denton.'

'I thought I saw Margaret with Richard, but they've gone now,' Henry told him.

'I expect your mind was wandering a bit, old chap. The pair of them are no longer with us. Margaret never recovered from that accident on the horse, you know. Richard went to school with Denton, they grew up together, if you recall.'

'Yes . . . I suppose they did.'

'Your son died a hero.'

'Richard served his country well,' the major said. 'But who was that I saw?'

'It's Richard's widow. Her name is Livia.'

'She's a pretty little thing. Nice hips.'

The needle slid in with barely a prick. 'Livia and Richard had a daughter together. That's who you saw, Livia Sangster and your baby granddaughter. Her name is Meggie.'

'Ah yes, Meggie, is it? I thought the baby was mine. Richard's child, you say? She was my granddaughter then. I get confused.' Henry's eyes began to droop. 'I must do something for the child.'

'Poor sod,' Denton said. 'I'll take him back to London, if you like.'

'It would be best if we allow the police to do that. They'll send a Black Maria and he'll be secure.'

Denton went upstairs and said against the panel to Livia's room, 'The major is medicated, so it's all right to come down. He'll be picked up and conveyed back to London. My father will be with him all the time.'

'I'm not coming down until he's gone. I never want to see that man again.'

'Livia, it's perfectly all right.'

'I'm feeding Meggie now.' There was an audible sniff. 'Thank you for coming, Denton. I was terrified . . . and thank Doctor Elliot.'

'We still need to talk,' he whispered.

'No, not today – not ever. There's no future in it for you. You must accept that.'

'Is that your last word?'

'Yes.'

'Good. I'm not going to accept it. Whether you like it or not, I'm going to get to the bottom of this.'

The major was sitting in an armchair with the cat on his lap when Denton went downstairs.

'What on earth is going on between you?' his father asked.

'Livia Sangster is the most infuriating woman I've ever met.'

Andrew Elliot grinned.

Twenty-One

The shop smelled like most ironmongers; of metal, grease and rubber. Mr Beamish came through from the back room, wiping his hands on a greasy rag. He eyed his visitor warily. 'Oh, it's you, Doctor Elliot. What can I do for you?'

'You can tell me about Meggie if you would, Mr Beamish.'

Beamish's eyes became flat and impenetrable. 'Let's not waste breath. Specifically, what are you after knowing, Doctor?'

'Who fathered the child?'

Beamish gave a snort of disgust. 'You've been listening to gossip. The father's name is on Meggie's birth certificate. It's Richard Sinclair Sangster.'

'I was the doctor on duty when you brought Richard into the field hospital in France. I treated his injuries. The chances of him being able to father a child were slim to non-existent.'

'He beat the odds then. The captain always was a lucky sod, and his equipment was still intact, and obviously still in working order.' Beamish gave a faint smile and his eyes glinted. 'Livia Sangster made the captain very happy in the last few months of his life. She's a lovely young woman altogether. What business is it of yours, anyway?'

'You know what it is. I love Livia, and I know she loves me. She said as much. Yet she refuses to marry me. I think she's hiding something.'

'And if she is?'

'I need to know what it is.'

'So you're going to try and rake up some muck, whatever the effect it might have on her. Hasn't she been through enough?'

Anger flared through him. Was Beamish deliberately being obtuse? 'I know what she's been through,' and he did. First it was the loss of her parents, then being parted from her siblings. Now Richard had died, and even though she'd known he wouldn't survive long, that had been a tragedy. She'd told him she'd loved Richard, and he believed her. Still, the hasty marriage had a whiff of convenience about it.

'If you think I'd do anything to hurt Livia, you're insane. Whatever it is she's hiding, I think she's doing it to protect me.'

'So you've been listening to gossip.' He shrugged. 'Let me ask you something. Have you heard the rumour that you fathered Meggie on Richard's behalf, so there would be an heir for the Sinclair inheritance?'

Denton started. 'No . . . I hadn't heard that.'

'Is it true?'

'Good Lord, no. It's complete and utter fabrication.'

'Some people believe it is true, so there you are then. Why should I believe you? The thing is, half the district thinks they know something, and the other half are convinced they know something else.'

'And the truth is disregarded as being too obvious.'

'I'll tell you this for nothing. Livia Sangster and the captain were as cosy as doves. It's about time you accepted that you just might have been wrong in your diagnosis.' He threw a handful of nails on the scales, then tipped them into a brown paper bag and threw them on the counter. 'Here, take these with you. You might need them.'

'What for?'

'To hammer down the lid of Mrs Sangster's coffin after you've ruined the little bit of true happiness she's had in her life. She loves that child, so I advise you to tread very carefully, and let sleeping dogs lie, Mister. It sounds to me as if she doesn't trust you, and why should she, when you go sneaking about behind her back asking questions?'

Beamish was right. Even so, the man had given enough

away to suggest to Denton that Richard may not have fathered Meggie. But who was the sleeping dog he'd referred to, and was Meggie Richard's child? If not, had Richard known the child wasn't his?

'I only have Livia's welfare at heart, so I won't need the nails.'

'In that case I'll give you a tip you might be able to use. Livia Sangster can be as stubborn as a mule, but she reacts when she's angry.'

As he left the shop, Denton didn't like the way his thoughts were going; yet he couldn't imagine Richard allowing himself to be deceived, or manipulated into a marriage he didn't want.

Perhaps he was better off being left in ignorance. But then it would always nag at him. The truth would be better coming from her. He chuckled at the thought of people thinking he'd fathered Meggie. He wished he had.

He started thinking about the things he needed answers for.

Livia usually attended the morning service, but with Connie Starling absent, her sister and brother went alone, Esmé riding on the crossbar of Chad's bicycle.

They'd only been gone five minutes when a knock came at the door.

She knew who it was. She combed her hair then went to answer it. The urge to throw herself into his arms was nearly overwhelming. 'Denton. Come in. I was just going to make some tea. Will you have one?'

'Don't use tricks to throw me off course. It won't work. I'm here to finish a conversation we nearly had a few days ago.'

'I can't marry you – and stop being so disagreeable.'

When she tried to shut the door in his face he stuck his foot in the gap. 'I understood that bit. What I didn't get was why you feel you can't trust me.'

She turned and walked away. He followed after her, closing the door behind them. She had to be firm. 'I don't love you.'

'You're a bad liar.'

When he picked up her hand and kissed the palm, she jerked it away. 'Play fair.'

'It's not a game, Livia. I'm determined.'

'So am I.'

'No you're not. You're just being stubborn. There's a reason why you refuse to marry me, and it's not because you don't love me. I think I've figured it out, though.'

'I doubt it. Leave it be, Denton. Leave me be. You're right. I do love you, and because I do, I can't marry you. If the truth came out it would ruin you.'

'Now we're getting somewhere.'

'We're not getting anywhere. There is more than your future to think of. I cannot marry you. How many times must I say it?'

'Until the not at the end of cannot wears out.'

'You're infuriating.'

'Let me put this to you. You and Richard . . . and I can't imagine how, because he . . . Damn it, Livia, you know what I'm getting at. Your marriage couldn't have worked as normal in a physical sense long term, but Richard managed a lucky shot. Meggie was the result. When you told him, he married you and you passed the child off as premature. I can't see how that would ruin me.'

He was so far off the mark she wanted to laugh. In fact, she did laugh, throwing it in his face. 'Hah!'

His eyes darkened. 'No? Then let me put this to you. Someone else fathered Meggie, and you managed to convince Richard it was his. And why not, when Richard's estate, as well as the Sinclair fortune was going begging. The fact that there's a rumour about me being the father lends credence to this. No wonder the major was about to challenge the will.'

Anger began to build up in her. 'How many men do you think I've been to bed with Denton?'

'Oh, I don't know. You tell me. But first tell me who fathered that child.'

'Stop saying such horrible things to me. Go away. Go to Australia and hop around with the kangaroos. I don't want to see you any more. Better still, go to hell and stick your pitchfork in someone else!'

'Livia, you don't mean that.'

'Yes I do.' She could feel the tears running down her face.

'You have no idea how much I love you, Denton. This inquisition is tearing me apart. Leave me. Just go. It was nothing like you imagine, and Richard was not the fool you paint him to be.'

'Livia,' he said softly. 'Don't you trust me? Tell me who fathered Meggie.'

The soft reproach did more to unsettle her resolve than anything else, and she didn't answer.

'I suppose I might as well take that job in Australia then. I can't see any future in staying here and facing the agony of seeing you day after day.' He turned and walked away, and in that instant she knew she'd never see him again, and wondered if she'd be able to stand it.

This was it – the moment she'd been dreading. Either she had to tell him the truth, or let him go.

'Major Henry,' she said quietly

He stopped and turned, the expression on his face one of stunned bewilderment. 'What of him?'

'He attacked me when he was drunk, and he violated me. Chad nearly walked in on him. So did Beamish but it was too late. I didn't know what to do when I discovered I might be pregnant, so I told Richard.'

'Good God! No wonder you looked so terrified when he had Meggie on his lap. So Richard married you so there wouldn't be a scandal.'

'And he pretended to be Meggie's father so she could inherit the Sinclair estate. He said the baby was his heir; if it were illegitimate it wouldn't be able to inherit.'

'I'm so sorry I doubted you, and Richard.'

'As for our relationship, Richard and I did have one of sorts, but we only tried to make love on a couple of occasions, and to this day I don't know if we succeeded. I felt that I owed him that, to try. His breathing was affected so badly that I thought he'd die. He said it made him feel as though he was truly the coming baby's father, rather than its brother. The marriage gave me respectability, and also protected Meggie with a name she was entitled to have by right of blood. Without Richard she'd have been an outcast all her life. And she can never know who really fathered her. Richard was a generous, wonderful man, one who I'll always remember with love.'

'I don't know what to say. I think I've made an utter twit of myself.'

'Yes, you have, and you don't have to say anything. You can see now why I couldn't bring myself to tell you, and why I can't marry you. If it gets out, you'll be involved in a scandal. I thought I'd lose you if I told you, so I couldn't tell you in case you scorned me. Most of all, I cared for Meggie's sake.

'You should take that position in Australia, Denton. You'll probably meet a nice girl and get married.'

'Too late. I've accepted the job in Poole. Despite everything, I couldn't bear the thought of being so far away from you.' He came to where she stood and brushed the tears from her eyes. 'I've already met a nice girl I'm going to marry, and the fact that she has a family is a bonus.'

Her heart shot fireworks into an imaginary sky. 'Denton, do you know what you're saying?'

'I'm saying I love you, and nothing is going to keep us apart. You know what's going to happen when we marry, don't you? Those who think I fathered Meggie will be convinced that I did.'

He patted his pocket and came out with a ring box. The remains of a pheasant feather fluttered to the floor.

He stooped to pick it up and laughed. 'I knew you were going to be my woman from the moment you gave me this.'

'You stole it.'

'So I did. It's a bit short now; the dog ate the other half.' He flipped open the box lid. 'I've been carrying this around since I first sent you that letter. I hope you like it.'

It was a gold band with a bridge of diamonds and rubies. 'I love it, and I love you.'

He hesitated, then slid Richard's wedding ring from her finger and replaced it with the engagement ring.

He gazed at the inscription in the wedding ring and gave a faint smile before slipping it into her hand. It bore the words, Olivia and Richard, with the date of their marriage. 'You don't mind not wearing it, do you?'

'No, I've been hiding behind it. Now I'll put it away for Meggie to have when she's older.'

'Come here, my love,' he said, and she moved into his arms.

He kissed her, a long and tender caress that set her heart racing and the nerves tingling through her body.

On the mantelpiece, the photograph of Richard smiled down at them.